Praise for *So We Mee*

"Some books just feel like an old friend, their first pages embracing you with an instant familiarity and warmth you can't help but sink into. Suzanne Park's *So We Meet Again* is that kind of book. . . . A cinematic, charming heart-squeeze of a book that has found its way to my 'ultimate comfort reads' shelf."

—Emily Henry, *New York Times* bestselling author of *Beach Read*

"A funny, lovely mother-daughter story. And then there's Daniel—yummy Daniel—and great food. Settle in and enjoy!"

—Susan Elizabeth Phillips, *New York Times* bestselling author

"A laugh-out-loud comedy with a warm heart. Jess's journey of finding her way amid the noise of the world's expectations will make you smile and sigh and want to chase your dreams."

—Sonali Dev, award-winning author of *Recipe for Persuasion*

"*So We Meet Again* is a hilarious read. What can go wrong when, after a quarter-life crisis, you move back in with your hypercompetitive parents? This comeback story will charm you from beginning to end."

—Madeleine Henry, author of *The Love Proof* and *Breathe In, Cash Out*

Praise for *Loathe at First Sight*

"*Loathe at First Sight* bursts with humor, heart, and great energy. I loved it! Park is a hilarious new voice in women's fiction."

—Helen Hoang, author of *The Kiss Quotient*

"Hilarious and poignant, Park's debut sparkles as a great addition to the new voices of the rom-com renaissance."

—Roselle Lim, author of *Natalie Tan's Book of Luck and Fortune*

"Park gives us the story that only she could create. It's hilarious, smart, and the rom-com we need!"

—Alexa Martin, ALA Award–winning author of *Intercepted*

"Park has created a wholly original, smart, fierce heroine (with a hilarious inner voice) who takes on an industry hell-bent on underestimating her. . . . Just like the 'entertaining, fresh, snarky' video game she conjures in her novel, Suzanne Park has written a fast and fun debut, putting females in the lead."

—Amy Poeppel, author of *Musical Chairs* and *Small Admissions*

"A genuinely funny and charismatic heroine shines in *Loathe at First Sight*, the delightful and eye-opening debut adult novel by Suzanne Park. Park—a former stand-up comedian—negotiates her energized plot masterfully. . . . A multilayered happy-ever-after."

—NPR

"A smart, funny workplace romance set in the world of video game design."

—PopSugar

"[A] punchy adult debut set in the world of video game design. Park makes tough topics go down easy by couching them in wry humor and lighthearted romance, and her fierce, snarky heroine is irresistible. This smart rom-com is a winner."

—*Publishers Weekly* (starred review)

"Park's first book for adults is a funny and feminist geek novel. . . . Readers into both gaming and women's fiction will scramble for this fast-paced charmer."

—*Booklist*

"Melody's characterization and voice shine throughout. Smart, punchy, and memorable."

—*Library Journal*

So We
Meet
Again

Also by Suzanne Park

Loathe at First Sight

YOUNG ADULT NOVELS

Sunny Song Will Never Be Famous

The Perfect Escape

a novel

SUZANNE PARK

AVON
An Imprint of HarperCollins*Publishers*

This is a work of fiction. Names, characters, places, and incidents are products of the author's imagination or are used fictitiously and are not to be construed as real. Any resemblance to actual events, locales, organizations, or persons, living or dead, is entirely coincidental.

P.S.™ is a trademark of HarperCollins Publishers.

HarperCollins books may be purchased for educational, business, or sales promotional use. For information, please email the Special Markets Department at SPsales@harpercollins.com.

FIRST EDITION

Designed by Diahann Sturge

Title page and chapter opener art © SpicyTruffel / Shutterstock, Inc.

Library of Congress Cataloging-in-Publication Data has been applied for.

ISBN 978-0-06-299071-6

21 22 23 24 25 LSC 10 9 8 7 6 5 4 3 2 1

To everyone fighting the good fight

Chapter One

Jessie! My office. NOW!" Gordon Strauss had a German Shepherd–like bite to his bark. Referring to me as "Jess" or "Jessie" was his way of showing he was enraged, but not necessarily at me. When I did something wrong, he would yell my first and last name, akin to a parent yelling at his or her child. *JESSICA KIM, get in here!*

But this tirade wasn't about me. Thank God.

I slammed my laptop closed. The company policy was strict: anyone leaving their laptops unattended without locking their screens would be terminated. Too many leaks to the press about companies' bankruptcies, mergers, and acquisitions over the years made our higher-ups tighten security. I grabbed a legal pad and pen along with my computer and scurried to his office.

He motioned for me to come inside. "Jess, have you seen Wyatt Jenkins this morning? I've been trying to get a hold of him and he's not answering his phone. Is it acceptable to not answer an MD's call during work hours?" Gordon liked to ask rhetorical, nonhypothetical questions as his way of "teaching."

I shook my head.

"Exactly, Jess. It's unacceptable."

Good, he was furious with Wyatt, the senior associate. He'd been at the bank six months longer than me, and thanks to the good ol' boy tenure that relied more on seniority than merit, I reported to Wyatt, even though I knew more about raising money, selling distressed businesses, and cashing out than he did. He was the kind of boss who harangued his junior analysts and associates about deadlines and then claimed ownership of the work.

Deadweight Wyatt. Worthless Wyatt. Wanker Wyatt. That's what all the junior bankers called him.

I cleared my throat. "It's Friday, and lately he's been, um, taking half days for self-care."

"Half days? For . . . self . . . care?" His right eyebrow rose so high I thought it might lift off his face.

"Yes." I gulped. "Self-care."

He frowned. "I see. Well, I'll have to discuss this bullshit with him at a later time. Is the Beauchamp pitch document ready?"

My stomach lurched. What pitch document? "But I—I'm not staffed on the Beauchamp deal."

"I need the model updates sent to me by end of day. Plus

a color printout so I can look over them while on my Peloton tomorrow morning. Thanks." He grabbed his wireless headset and slap-motioned his hand, signaling for me to shut the door.

Did he not hear me? Or did he have me confused with someone else, like maybe the other Asian female, who was an analyst in our group? People here always mixed us up, even though we weren't anything alike. She was tall, svelte, and put-together, and I was . . . not. Beauchamp wasn't my account though. It was Wyatt's. He was supposed to work on the pitch document, not me. Where the hell *was* he?

Wyatt strolled in around lunchtime, sunglasses still on, even though he was indoors. A sunlit glow on his face suggested he'd successfully practiced his on-the-clock self-care. I didn't want to ask about where he'd been. Whatever came out of his mouth would infuriate me.

"Gordon's been looking for you all morning." I glanced at my wristwatch. "He says the Beauchamp pitch is due this afternoon. And, well, it's afternoon."

"I was celebrating." He leaned back in his chair, stretched, then laced his fingers behind his head.

Should I ask? He was baiting me, clearly. But I was curious.

I growled, "Celebrating what?" My computer screen froze, my cursor blinking inside a cell of a complicated Excel macro. It took all my willpower to not throw my laptop across our open workspace. *Please autosave, please, please, please.*

He jumped forward, nearly springing off his Aeron chair. “Wait, you don’t know? Do you have a meeting on your calendar for this afternoon?”

“Nope.” I’d cleared my entire afternoon in case I needed to work on Wyatt’s stupid deal. There was definitely no new mystery meeting on my calendar.

He grinned. “I heard that Hamilton and Cooper was having layoffs this year, and a friend in HR confirmed it last month.” After all the years he’d worked here, he still called the company by the wrong name. It was just Hamilton Cooper. No “and.” No ampersand.

Wyatt continued. “Pink slips go out this afternoon. I’ve been informational interviewing the last few weeks and I think I might have something lined up at my dad’s friend’s hedge fund. Or I might go out on my own since I’ve made so many connections here. The best part is—we get severance packages!” He tapped down his sunglasses so he could peer at me. “Well, if you didn’t get the invite, then looks like you’ll be staying, and maybe you’ll get my job. Or Sammy’s—he left last week. Oooh, a big promotion opportunity for Jessie when Wise ol’ Wyatt gets the boot.”

Deadweight Wyatt, actually.

He checked his watch. “Oh, my meeting starts at one thirty and I’ll need a coffee and a good seat. Good luck with the Beauchamp deal. See ya around Wall Street, kid!”

Kid. I rolled my eyes as he swaggered down the hall to the executive conference room, joining the stream of ten or so other people, all of them more senior than me. Presumably all deadweights too. But Deadweight Wyatt was right: when people left the firm or groups restructured, that left opportunities for moving up. And without a doubt, I could do Wyatt's job. Even without half days of self-care. I'd expected a promotion with my last review two months ago, but maybe they knew this time was coming. Maybe now, when the company trimmed its fat, I'd be brought in to lead my group. My stomach turned flips thinking about the promotion bonus.

Ding!

A new meeting request popped up in my calendar for 1:30 P.M. A Zoom link sent by HR accompanied the email along with the meeting description "The Future of Hamilton Cooper, Founded 1984. Virtual Attendance Required." Not the type of meeting I'd hoped to see. While I looked in Wyatt's shared drive to find the Beauchamp spreadsheets, which were a mess of hard-coded numbers, I put in my earbuds and clicked on the Zoom link, expecting a companywide all-hands meeting. The company had transitioned to more online meetings for company events, mainly so they wouldn't have to pay for a venue, or for catering. So many cost conservation initiatives at this bulge-bracket bank known for big deals and fat bonuses. Ridiculous.

On the call was a smallish group of maybe a dozen junior-level analysts and associates, all probably expecting to mute their audio and video and multitask while some executive talking head shared his screen to pontificate about the state of the industry and the vision for our company using a boring PowerPoint deck. Blah blah blah who cares, we had a ton of work to do. There was a small chance that this could be a group promotion call, with the layoffs happening in the other conference room—what better way to have people step up to take on more work than with a pep talk and maybe some public promotions in an intimate, albeit online, setting?

Come to think of it, something was amiss.

The head of HR appeared on the screen, one of many in the sea of faces in the video conference, unnerving me with her stern demeanor. Why wasn't she in the other executive room, laying off Wyatt and the other do-nothings?

She began. "Hamilton Cooper hires the best and the brightest from all over the world, and we compete with esteemed employers such as JPMorgan, Goldman Sachs, Morgan Stanley, and companies outside of banking like McKinsey and Google. We appreciate you. After all, you were the top recruits from your entering class, and the hard work and dedication you've put in over the years has had significant impact on our firm. You make Hamilton Cooper who we are—the world's best diversified financial services company engaged in investment banking and capital markets, asset management, and direct investing."

She should have been smiling with the spouting of this brochure jargon and praise. Alarm bells rang in my head as she continued her rehearsed speech. "After extensive work with our third-party organizational consulting firm Rowling and Associates, with the preceding two years of flat growth, we regret to inform you that the company will be rolling out a reorganization plan for the deal, equity, debt, and high-yield groups. As a result, your positions have all been eliminated. No additional head count will be added and we will be offering generous severance packages based on tenure and performance." She added robotically, "You are, however, welcome to apply for any openings, but do note that all of the open positions are entry-level."

My sushi lunch traveled up and I had to swallow hard to push it back down. Was this for real? It didn't seem like some kind of elaborate joke. Was this actually happening? Was I getting laid off on a goddamn Zoom call?

She continued speaking while hands shot up. We were all muted by the presenter and she was not yielding the floor. "This was not an easy decision to make, as you can imagine. Although we're still profitable, our firm is cutting back on hiring this year and reducing head count, but also reallocating budgets to IT spending and overseas virtual support. We've just emailed you all details about the severance packages and will remain on the call to answer any questions you might have. The remainder of the afternoon, you can pack your things and stop by HR to pick up hard copies of your exit packets. We'll unmute you now so you can ask questions."

An angry chorus of analysts and associates talked on top of one another. I managed to squeeze in a question uninterrupted: "But how did performance reviews factor in this decision?" Up to this point, mine were all positive. Glowing, in fact. With good reviews came nice bonuses, which I received. None of this made sense. Our midpoint quarterly perf review check-ins were due soon and I didn't expect anything other than high marks.

Jodi of HR cleared her throat and mass muted everyone again. "Those who were chosen for termination fell into three categories. One, performance. A number of you on this call have been on probation for months and unfortunately, the time has come to part ways." Many of the meeting participants wagged their fingers at their screens, shook their heads, or silently screamed, then blacked out their videos and logged out. The rectangles of remaining people shuffled on the screen to form a more intimate group of eight people.

"The second cause of termination was due to incriminating behavior or egregious spending under review by Human Resources. All of these cases were deemed negligent and warranted termination. Consider the severance a gift." Six employees rolled their eyes and although I was no lip-reader, most of their rebuttals were profanities. They blacked out their screens and left the meeting, just as the poor performers did.

This left me, alone with stone-cold Jodi of HR.

She looked straight at her webcam like she was peering

into my workaholic soul. "And you, Jessica Kim, are the other bucket."

I gulped as she pulled out a single paper from a red folder and placed it in front of her on the table.

"According to our records, you had a good run here. Great work on the Perkins Media and Dixon Communications deals. Those were well-earned bonuses." Those were my career-making, big-fish-big-pond deals.

She adjusted her glasses before speaking. "But this year, we almost lost Montgomery, one of our biggest clients." *Yes, Ryan Montgomery, the adulterer twice my age who belittled me in a meeting in front of my peers and got too handsy at an after-work function with another junior banker. I knew #MeToo Montgomery. All the women at Hamilton Cooper did.* "Your reviews over the years have been consistent. You're very analytical and don't make many mistakes. MDs and VPs love having you on their teams because you're heads down and get your job done. But you're at a turning point now. We needed to decide how promotable you were."

Were? She allowed me to unmute myself. "But those are mostly positive things. I had big wins. I don't understand."

She laced her fingers together and rested her hands on the paper. "In order to move up from associate to VP, we need to see leadership potential. Someone who can drum up new deals. Wine and dine clients. You're a great follower." A long pause. "But you're not a leader."

YOU'RE not a leader.

You're NOT a leader.

You're not A LEADER.

The world went silent. Those four words were sledgehammer hits to the knees, crippling me into anguish and silence. Had I even gotten any leadership opportunities with the grunt work avalanche I'd been buried in the last few years? After all of my eighty-plus-hour weeks, all the secrets I kept—from marital affairs to botched financials I had to fix—and all the sick-to-my-stomach things I witnessed, they were letting me go.

Me.

I had to look strong in front of Jodi on the Zoom call. Because that's what a leader would do.

But you're not a leader, Jessica Kim. If you were a leader, you would still have a job.

A faint buzz from Jodi's desk distracted her. She glanced down at her phone, her jowls resting on her neck as she furrowed her brow with a look of concern, showing more emotion toward her iPhone than she had with me in the last few minutes. "I have to run to a meeting, but feel free to speak with your team lead, Wyatt, if you have questions this afternoon. He and other managers are in a session now, being notified of these personnel shifts and how to cope with team change, and he'll help transition your work back to the remaining team. Your severance package is also awaiting your electronic signature. Good luck in your future endeavors."

"But—" My voice finally came back just as her screen turned dark and then disappeared. I was the only one left in the meeting. My sad face took up the entire screen. "What about my MBA program?" I whispered to no one.

I had been accepted into NYU Stern's part-time business school program earlier that week and was slated to start classes in the fall. My managing director knew that completing an advanced business degree was one of my career goals and was supposed to work something out with HR where I could transition to a business management role at the firm when school started. With Hamilton Cooper's Employee Assistance Program, my MBA tuition would have been subsidized. But not anymore.

Ding! A new member joined the video call. Cam Simmons, the guy who was hired because his dad was one of our clients. The dude who passed out under his desk after the company holiday party and woke up covered in a rainbow of Post-it notes, courtesy of his pranking peers. The associate who did half the work but took more than his share of credit.

He squinted into the camera and said, "Sorry I'm late. Long lunch. What'd I miss, Jess?"

I left the meeting. *You missed everything. And you can figure it out on your own, Cameron.*

I threw some personal items from my desk into my laptop bag and left my workspace in a hurry. My cheeks burned with embarrassment and I knew I had to hightail it out of there, or I'd burst into tears. I didn't have much time.

Mashing the button multiple times didn't make the elevator come any faster, but I found myself feeling so suffocated and desperate that I tried it anyway.

Three executives I'd worked with directly on recent deals walked down the hallway and stopped around the corner to chat. With everyone tied up in meetings, or being laid off, there wasn't the typical typing, arguing, or yelling surround sound to drown out their conversation. My ears perked when I heard my name.

"Jessica Kim was one of them. A damn shame, she was one of those Asian worker-bee types. Always here past midnight. I heard she worked on Christmas. A real numbers whiz."

"True, but she wasn't the best fit for client services. At her level, she needed to be a thinker, not a doer. I know this sounds crass, but her clothes never fit. They were a little too baggy for my taste."

"Maybe you should have paid her more so she could hire a tailor."

Laughter.

"Wasn't she already being overpaid anyway, especially for a female associate?"

My stomach lurched. I'd heard enough. My sadness vortexed into pure rage as I stomped over to them.

"I gave blood, sweat, and tears for this company." I growled and pointed at Robert, my former group director. "You begged me to cover for you if your wife called when you were wining and dining that female client last year."

Robert's face reddened. "But you didn't. I'm going through a divorce now."

I went down the line to the next asshole. "Shaun, you tried to expense your escapade at a strip club by saying it was my birthday dinner and HR thought I was in on the scam. And Dan, you transposed all those numbers on the deal sheet and I caught them just before they were sent out, remember? You could have been fired for that, especially for showing up to work high. I went above and beyond for you. I saved your ass."

Their jaws dropped. No, they weren't going to schmooze their way out of this one.

"I know what you're thinking. How dare she say these things to us? She's just bitter because she was let go. Well, it's partly true. I'm bitter because I've wasted seven years of my life at this company that turned around and stabbed me in the back. If I wasn't leadership material, why didn't a female mentor coach me? Oh right, because there aren't any female execs here. But thank you, sincerely, for the wake-up call. Now I can take my bonuses and severance and do something better with my time rather than covering for you and making you all richer."

The only good luck I had that day was that the elevator doors opened immediately, and no one was inside. Heaving my bag strap onto my shoulder again, I hit the lobby button and the doors closed on my past.

On the way down to the ground floor, it started to sink in.

The elevator dinged. I had no job as of today.

The doors opened. No career at Hamilton Cooper.

Through the lavish lobby with the crystal chandeliers and the white-and-gray swirled marble floors, I pushed through the revolving door and walked straight into an unyielding NYC spring thunderstorm.

With nowhere to be, I pulled out the travel-size umbrella from my bag and walked thirty blocks home to clear my head. I had no idea what to do the rest of the day. Even more tragically, I had absolutely no idea what to do with the rest of my life.

Chapter Two

Chuck-chuck-chuck.

Chuck-chuck-chuck.

Chuck-chuck-ch—bzzzzzzzzzz!

Mr. Fowler, my parents' seventy-year-old neighbor, had revved up the hedge trimmer. I could handle the lawnmowing whirs through the single-pane glass, the trills of cricket chirps all night to the wee morning, even the woodpeckers drilling the utility poles near my window throughout the day, all thanks to my former Lower East Side studio apartment located practically underneath the Williamsburg Bridge. I'd become accustomed to all sorts of noise and I could sleep through everything.

But Mr. Fowler's erratic hedge trimmer pull-cord technique, plus him yelling "GODDAMN IT!" with every few failed attempts, ripped through my concentration like an audial tornado.

There was nowhere else in this house to hide from the racket: opening my creaky door would signal to my mom that I was awake, and it was too early to deal with the onslaught of interrogation. She was rightfully curious about my sudden arrival home a few nights ago after I'd revealed my abrupt departure from my Wall Street job and canceled the lease to the fancy new apartment on the Upper West Side I'd signed only days before my layoff. The one with the doorman and the sizable, nonrefundable down payment. But I wasn't ready to talk about it. Any of it. The fact that I'd crash-slept for eighteen hours that first night alone probably raised a few dozen questions and red flags in her mind. She'd been nice to let me sleep and rest. And most momlike of all, she left me a fridge full of Korean food, a mix of homemade and store-bought favorites. This almost made up for when she greeted me at the airport with "Waaaa, you look terrible. You need to sleep because your face . . ." and then trailed off. I was doing exactly as she'd said. I got sleep. Because . . . my face.

And now, two days later, at 8:54 A.M. Nashville time, my face was well-rested but I needed coffee.

I opened my grocery delivery app and requested priority delivery of milk, sugar, and a twenty-four-ounce plastic bottle of Starbucks coffee, plus some nonperishables. Not my favorite choice for morning caffeine, but better than nothing. Tap, tap, tap, and . . . tap. Delivery in thirty minutes.

Through the air-conditioning vents, Mom hooted with

laughter. She was watching Korean dramas, apparently a comedy. Mom was an OG K-drama fan, renting DVDs from the local Asian market every weekend before streaming them was in vogue. She remembered everything too, a walking Wikipedia of K-drama trivia.

Buzz! Notification that Flora B. was shopping my order.

Buzz! Notification that Flora B. had replaced my 2 percent fat milk with a 1 percent one.

Buzz! My delivery was now en route.

While awaiting my groceries, I pulled my laptop off my nightstand and opened up the spreadsheet I'd worked on during my awake time: a robust color-coded Excel sheet with separate worksheet tabs reflecting all aspects of my life: job prospects, savings and budget, business books to read, people to contact, hobbies to try, places to live, side hustle ideas, and recipes to try while unemployed. This spreadsheet had already crashed my computer a few times because it was a huge file, more like a mood board than a data sorting or calculating tool, where I'd dumped inspirational pictures and copy-and-pasted articles on every sheet. It was my way of blending my artistic side with my analytical one. I'd tried to use one of those bullet journals, with their tedious hand lettering and fancy brush pens, but it wasn't very me. It was too delicate and pretty. It didn't feel results-oriented.

I wanted results. Immediately.

There was a problem though. The only blank page on the

spreadsheet was "job/business prospects," and that was the most important one to me. So important, in fact, that I dragged that page tab so it was listed first in the Excel workbook. I'd had a job since I was old enough to drive and took pride in being a hard worker: I had summer employment and internships all throughout high school and college when my friends took it easy. I was an absolute nobody without a job. And this absolute nobody had zero clue as to what she wanted to do about her career. Finance and banking were all I knew, and I'd been at Hamilton Cooper since college graduation. And as for my business school dreams, a requirement of starting the part-time MBA program was to be employed at the start of the fall semester, so if I moved back to New York and entered the program, I would need a new job—stat. There was no way in hell I was going back to Wall Street anytime soon, but what else was I qualified to do?

There was one other potential problem too: my savings. I had enough to hold me over awhile living rent-free with my parents, but not enough to live unemployed in a pricey one-bedroom apartment in Manhattan and carry out my year-long lease agreement. And certainly not enough to also cover B-school tuition costs. Living at home left me with the ability to seek employment on my own terms or to start a new venture, with some or all of my savings put toward capital. But this still led me back to the same question: What was I qualified to do?

My phone rang. "Hi, this is Flora. I'm outside and a little

confused by your delivery instructions. It says here that you want me to throw the bottle of coffee, the milk carton, and the box of sugar into your second-story window and leave the rest of the grocery items on your doorstep."

Mom's guffaws echoed through the vent. She was wide awake downstairs and the last thing I needed that morning was a wide-awake lecture from her.

I opened the window and waved. "Yep, that's right. I'm up here."

"Oh, oh yes I see you. Hi! I'll be honest, I usually just leave all of the groceries on the porch, or behind the potted plants or something. I've never been asked to—honestly, I'm scared."

"The window's pretty wide and not that high. You can get it up here. And you can leave the rest of the stuff on the porch."

She laughed. "I'm not worried about my throw. I'm worried about your catch." Flora walked up to my house and stood underneath me. "Are we seriously doing this?"

I put my phone down and shouted out the window. "Ready when you are!"

She put the bags by her feet and dug into the brown sack, pulling out the coffee. "Okay, I'm a little rusty. If I hit anything or cause damage, this isn't my fault." She pulled her elbow back and lobbed the bottle of Starbucks coffee straight at me. I caught it. Or, rather, blocked it from hitting my face and caught it on the downswing swat.

"Thanks! Okay, throw the others, but not as hard."

She smirked. "I need the velocity to get it up there. Sorry." With zero hesitation, she threw the milk and sugar in rapid succession. I caught the sugar while the milk soared high over my head, hit the ceiling, then fell onto my bed. Luckily, other than the crumpled corner, no milk was harmed or spilled by her arm cannon.

Flora put the rest of the groceries on the porch and came back out under the window, holding her hand up to block the sun from her eyes. "Sorry about the milk. I guess I don't know my own strength. By the way, you have a ton of packages by your door."

I'd purchased every "go get yours" feminist business book in stock at Barnes & Noble, Amazon, and Parnassus, my favorite local indie bookstore in town. Sheryl Sandberg's *Lean In* and Lois Frankel's *Nice Girls Don't Get the Corner Office* had arrived already, which made no sense to me how that was possible given that I'd ordered the books at nine P.M. the previous night, twelve hours ago. The Amazon shipment defied all laws of physics and time. Nonetheless, I was happy my comfort rereads had arrived. I'd hastily given away my own copies to a local Goodwill in my spur-of-the-moment decision to move back home to Tennessee, but I needed them to get me out of my rut. Because the rut I was in was the size of the Grand Canyon.

I shouted, "Thanks, I'll get those later. I'm Jessie by the way. And I know you're Flora B. according to the app. Four point eight stars."

"Nice to meet you. I'm glad you asked me to do that, to be honest. It broke up the monotony of the morning. I'm trying to earn some extra cash this summer while school's not in session and this grocery delivery has been a real drag. I'm in grad school and there are zero internships or research opportunities, so it's mainly all I have now to supplement my stipend." She switched hands to block her eyes.

"It's better than moving in with your parents after being financially independent for seven years. Related to that, if you know any places where a Nashville newcomer can hang out to get away from her mom and dad, let me know."

She smiled. "Hold on." She pulled a pad from her back pocket and scribbled something. She tore the paper out and stuffed it in an Altoid case from her front pocket, then threw the tin hard. I leaned out the window a little to catch it. In the candy case, the paper read, "Flora Barrios, @FloraBEconomist."

Flora shouted, "Let me know when you're ready to meet up. My friends and I sometimes do trivia night on Mondays at Falling Off the Red Wagon—it's the best coffee shop in the neighborhood. I'm a barista there sometimes." She headed back to her Jetta and waved as she drove off.

On my unintentionally shabby chic desk, I scooted over a family portrait, a picture from my high school graduation of my friend Celeste and me, and a framed photo of Dolly Parton I'd gotten from a high school trip to Dollywood to make room for a mini–coffee station. Chugging from the bottle of coffee, I made room for milk and sugar and then screwed the cap back on to shake it. Café au lait. Voilà!

In the groceries app, I rated Flora five stars for service, selection, and friendliness. With my fresh coffee in hand, I fired up my laptop again and got back to planning my future.

Chapter Three

Sweat trickled down the sides of my face as I pulled into a parking spot. Living in NYC for so many years, I hadn't driven since college and was terrified I had lost all of my spatial intelligence. Worried about my depth perception and that my reflexes would be slow, I'd driven at exactly the speed limit, which angered a lot of locals as they whizzed around me. Taking a deep breath, I dropped the keys in my purse and checked my messages for my mom's grocery list before I opened the door and stepped out into the thick, damp air of the sweltering South. According to the meteorologist on the radio, it was going to be an unseasonably warm spring day. He never mentioned the humidity.

Approximately twenty texts came through from my mom, one item listed at a time. A new Asian market had opened where the old Pets-A-Million once was. When I was growing up, the Korean grocery shopping options were limited, and

Mom used to drive to Atlanta, leaving Nashville at four in the morning to get to H Mart when the store opened. This brand-new market on Charlotte Avenue had a food court attached to it, and the aromas of stir-fry and tempura wafted my way as soon as the automatic doors opened.

Mom had asked me to buy regular staples like salt and cooking oil, along with some meat and fish. For me, I wanted to buy ingredients to experiment with on my newly resurrected Korean Food Hacks for Busy People YouTube channel. It was a fun media project I'd started in college after getting sick of eating pasta every night, which was only marginally better than eating the disgusting dining hall food each day. After graduating, I'd aspirationally amassed a collection of Korean cookbooks, with dozens of pages of recipes I'd earmarked and highlighted but never made because of my ridiculous work hours.

My last cooking video upload had been a while back. Two years ago—okay, maybe more like five years ago. The content and header graphics needed a huge overhaul. Now I had time to update everything. Maybe renaming the channel to Food Hacks for Lollygaggers would be more accurate now.

Grocery shopping was therapeutic for me. I could spend hours looking through all the imported snacks, sauces, and condiments. Aisle by aisle, I pulled products from the shelves and examined the ingredients. What had high fructose corn syrup? GMOs? MSG? My goal for this trip was to buy enough for two or three Korean meals to prep on video, to keep me busy during the day. Sesame oil, gochujang paste, and rice wine vinegar were my must-haves; my mom probably had all these things but I didn't want to dip into her supply since she had her own set of beliefs on what "use by" dates meant.

As I headed to the checkout stands, Mom called.

"Hi, I'm almost done."

"Buy fifty-pound bag of rice. It on sale, Ms. Chang from church tell me promotion end today. Hurry!" *Why, hello to you too!*

"I'll look for it." Fifty pounds would probably throw out my back, but this was rent tax for my mom. Being her rice mule was temporary. Only until I could get back on my feet. "I got everything you asked for except for the mackerel, they ran out."

"Okay." *Click.*

The rice section was right next to the checkout lines. Not only were the largest sacks of rice half price, but it was also a "buy one get one free" promotion. I had to get the second bag, or my mom would be furious if she found out I'd missed out on the biggest rice inventory sale in Korean American history, and Ms. Chang would definitely rub it in. *You only got two bag? We buy four!* She was petty like that. I could maybe carry one bag, but two? Could I carry a hundred pounds of rice? It's not something I would have ever thought to try.

Most of the workers there were elderly, right around my mom's age. No way could they carry a fifty-pounder. The shoppers were mostly women with small children, and I couldn't bear to ask them for help. If anything, they were the ones who looked like they needed support by way of tantrum relief as their kids begged for snacks and candies.

I made a plan: to buy the groceries and make two trips. I'd let the checkout clerk add the two bags of rice to my tab, load the car with the groceries first, and come back for the rice in another load, maybe grabbing a food court lunch special on the way out.

My plan worked . . . sort of. Checking out was fast, but after pushing the cart through the length of the parking lot in the torturous humidity, it was clear that I should have parked closer. After the unloading was done, I brought the cart back through the automatic doors, and the mouth-watering smells of the food court slowed my step. My stomach groaned, protesting that I was coming back in to get a hundred pounds of uncooked short-grain white rice instead of sitting down and eating a delicious bulgogi bowl first. *Quiet down, I'll tend to you after I get the rice bounty.*

One of the food court customers with his back to me caught my eye, mainly because he was the only person who wasn't a harried mother with small children or a senior citizen. His strapping shoulders pulled his polo shirt taut across his back as he hunched over his food. In one hand, he held his phone while watching a baseball game on ESPN. With his other, he shoveled fried rice into his mouth with chopstick dexterity I'd never seen before. *Impressive.* When I tried to eat rice like that, it was barely one grain at a time.

Back inside the store, there was a crowd around the rice bags, as quantity had depleted significantly and there were only a few left. But everyone had the same problem I did. How the hell were you supposed to get these heavy bags out the door? They also had an additional problem: all these onlookers were geriatric, some weighing far less than one hundred pounds. I had a receipt of purchase for two of those bad boys and held it out to prove I had dibs. People gathered around as I squatted to deadlift one bag of rice from the floor, my knees cracking in the process. With all the strength I could muster, I put it in my shopping cart. I wiped my brow with the back of my hand as a tiny Korean halmoni reminded me, "You have to do again. Two time."

I nodded. "Ne, ne." *Yes, lady. Twice. Trust me. I know.* "Al-gesseumnida."

She watched intently as I repositioned the bag in the cart to make room for a second one.

Crack! My knees popped again as I squatted like a sumo wrestler, grabbing a second bag on a higher stack and pulling it toward me like I was hugging a large bear I'd won at a carnival.

The halmoni leaned over and whispered to her husband, "Waaaa!"

An audience formed, but there was no more show. Whatever

strength I had was fading fast. A clueless woman with a jet-black Darth Vader helmet–shaped bob grabbed my cart and walked away, leaving me standing there with my rice bag.

"No no no no! I need that!" I waddled after her, my second fifty-pound sack slipping by the second. She stopped suddenly, only because her phone rang. In an out-of-breath way, I dropped the rice bag in the cart and explained to her in broken Korean that she'd taken my belongings.

She shook her head. Rather than apologize, she said in Korean, "You shouldn't leave your cart out like that then," and huffed back to the shopping cart area.

The crowd dispersed. The rice bags were all gone. In the few seconds I'd stepped away, shoppers had wiped out the inventory. Probably the Korean ladies from my mom's church. After all, gossip spread like wildfire there. Especially about rice sales.

Showing my receipt to the security guard at the store exit, I was again drawn to the smell of sizzling, marinated meat. This time I yielded to my hunger. My grocery cart couldn't squeeze into the tight enclave where the restaurant kiosks were, so I had to leave my rice somewhere to pick up a to-go order. And seeing as how that woman in the store had nearly taken off with my rice already, I didn't dare trust these silver- or black-haired ajummas by leaving a cart with rice out in the open.

The guy with the nice back was still seated alone, with plenty of room for my cart at his four-person table. Athletic build. Decently dressed. Good chopstick technique. A perfect person to ask to help watch my rice bags. Plus, we were in the South, where people were more willing to help out a stranger, right? As I walked toward him, I thought back to the last time I asked a stranger for something. My last week at Hamilton Cooper, when the heel of my shoe broke off thanks to the cobblestone walkway in front of my building. I wobbled and fell on the sidewalk, ripping my sweaty silk blouse and twisting my ankle on the way down. Passersby stepped over me while talking on the phone with their Bluetooth earbuds. I reached out, crying, "Help me please," thinking a man wearing a Brooks Brothers suit and a Hamilton Cooper security badge on his lanyard was holding his hand out to pull me up. But he was actually dropping a five-dollar bill on me, thinking I was homeless and asking for money.

I walked up to my potential good Samaritan. "Excuse me? I was wondering if I could get your help with something." On the table, the guy had a plate of charbroiled kalbi bones, a small bowl of beansprouts, and a mostly eaten bowl of kimchi fried rice (with SPAM!). Some of my favorite foods. I inhaled the smell of the Korean savory dishes. "Would you mind watching my rice while I grab something to eat?"

He turned around in his chair to face me.

"Daniel?" My stomach dropped and my appetite disappeared in a snap. He looked like Daniel Choi, but also looked nothing like Daniel Choi, the former church pastor's son who had moved away many years ago. Middle school Danny had chipmunk cheeks, a perfectly circular bowl cut, and wore oversize Predators jerseys, hand-me-downs from his much-older brother. He was a head shorter than me back then. But this guy had the same mischievous eyes. Same pink, triangle lips. Same sardonic smile.

Was it really Daniel? Daniel, who was my junior high lab partner and told everyone I threw up into the frog when we dissected it?

Daniel, who stuck ice down the front of my shirt at a party and a boy I'd been crushing hard on thought I'd drooled?

Daniel, who, like me, was nominated for "Most Likely to Succeed" our last year in middle school, but then campaigned for the OTHER girl Brit, saying she wasn't *just* booksmart like me. She won, by the way. As did he.

Behold, Asshole Daniel Choi. It was definitely him, with his trademark smirk, like he was in on a secret I wasn't smart enough to figure out.

He quirked his eyebrow and struggled with words. "J-Jessie? Messy Jessie Kim?" His eyes roamed down to my feet and up again, but not in a lusty, sexy way. I looked down to see things from his perspective.

Oh, for Christ's sake. I didn't think I'd know anyone at the market, so I'd thrown on any old shirt, which happened to be an old band shirt. Not *A BAND* tour shirt, like for a cool music group that performed at The 5 Spot or The Listening Room. It was *BAND* band. Like woodwinds, percussion, and brass *band*. I was first chair oboe, mid-state orchestra in high school. And my shirt mentioned this fun fact just above the pocket. Embroidered in cursive and everything.

Daniel had moved to Texas the summer before high school and I'd only heard about him via my mom through the church community rumor mill, tidbits here and there. His dad had become a senior pastor at a Korean megachurch in Houston, a huge step up from the small Nashville community church. Rumor had it that Daniel had won some Silicon Valley Young Engineering Award his senior year of high school and supposedly $10,000 plus an engineering internship with Google.

Mom and Dad always compared me to him: with grades, standardized test scores, piano competitions, height, you name it, even after he moved away. Thank God he moved away though. He was a barometer of my childhood failures, a constant reminder that I would never be good enough by Korean parental standards.

If this was Daniel Choi, my childhood nemesis, I'd rather die of starvation, weak and smothering under a hundred pounds of rice, than get his help with anything.

"Never mind." I turned on my heel and walked away, briskly pushing my cart toward the doorway. Daniel Choi not only ruined my day, he also ruined my lunch. *Sorry, stomach.*

"Jessie, wait!" The sound of his plea made me move quicker.

The automatic doors opened, introducing me again to both the blinding hot sun and the blazing hot, humid weather, temporarily disorienting me. Where did I park again? One thing about New York City was never having to drive anywhere. Getting to my car in a large lot with the blistering, fiery sun beating down on me was my own version of hell. Adding a hundred pounds of rice and warmed-up kimchi in the car: that was Hades level.

Mom texted again, asking for radish kimchi. *Don't bother rice, kkakdugi sale is better. You buy two get two free!*

No. No more of this torture. "Sorry Mom, I'm already heading back."

"YAH! YAAAH!" My head snapped up to see an old man with sprigs of gray hair yelling at me and pointing aggressively toward the lot. What was he—

Shit, my cart!

The cart had gained speed, thanks to the slight gradient and the hundred pounds of rice. I ran after it but couldn't keep up, due to all those years of being couped up in an office with no time for physical activity. A woman shrieked as she closed her SUV door, keeping herself from harm's way. The cart could have slowed down because there were speedbumps ahead, but the wheels were slightly turned, causing the runaway vehicle to veer left, full ramming speed.

I turned my head and winced. The cart was heading straight for a new Mercedes E-class sedan.

But there was no crashing sound. Applause filled the air as I opened my eyes. Koreans of all ages and sizes cheered. There was Daniel Choi, one hand waving, the other hand gripping the shopping cart handle.

I ran over. "Thank you," I mumbled. "So glad it didn't smash this car."

He laughed. "I couldn't let it smash this car—I only bought it a few months ago. It's practically new."

Of course this was his shiny brand-new Mercedes.

He continued. "I saw the commotion and ran over to stop the cart. It was like it had a homing device and the car was the target."

All the silver-haired ajummas who had stood around to watch the shopping cart spectacle cheered and clapped. Daniel had saved the day, like a superhero stopping a high-speed train full of children heading for a cliff.

Bravo, Daniel. Bravo.

In hindsight, this could've easily turned into something worse, like reckless endangerment. Or me having to foot the entire bill for car damage since I didn't have any kind of real insurance, except for temporary COBRA health insurance. Maybe I needed some kind of liability insurance though: I'd been in Nashville only three days and was already wreaking havoc.

The sun rays shined on Daniel in just the perfect way that he was instantly photo-ready, no filter needed. In the food court, I'd caught a quick glimpse of him sitting down. But now I could really take in the full Daniel transformation. His mirrored aviators covered his eyes, but his thick, dark hair and smattering of chin stubble on his sharp jawline reminded me that young chubby-cheeked Daniel was in the distant past. This Daniel was tall, lean, and muscular. His perfectly fitted navy blue polo hugged every muscle in his upper arms and chest, like the shirt was custom-made for his body. My gaze traveled down to his left hand to check for a ring. I tried to deprogram myself from looking, but I couldn't help it. It was a compulsory habit I couldn't break, similar to me eating an entire sleeve of Thin Mint Girl Scout cookies without being able to stop. The last few years especially, it was data I collected to compare me to my peers. And I really disliked myself for doing it, but that wasn't enough to stop me.

No ring.

"No 'thanks Daniel for stopping the cart from mauling the elderly Koreans in the parking lot'? No appreciation for saving the rice? Your mom would kill you if that happened. When did Messy Jessie get so rude?" He cocked his head and crossed his arms.

My cheeks flushed. It was rude of me to not thank him. And . . . did he see me checking for a ring? "Okay, what's rude is that I clearly don't go by Messy Jessie so you can stop saying that. And . . . I'm sorry about almost hitting your car." *Sorry about not apologizing right away. Sorry about running out of the store without saying a proper hello. Really sorry about being distracted by your fit-like-a-glove clothing selection. Damn.* "You can call me Jess or Jessie. I still don't go by Jessica. I only get that when older people like my parents or my boss are yelling at me." *Oof. Former boss.*

He laughed and pushed the cart to me. "Good thing I came out to find you. You haven't changed at all by the way."

Well, that was mildly offensive. Surely I wasn't the same gangly, awkward girl with an ever-present set of forehead baby hairs. I couldn't respond to him with *well, you haven't changed a bit either* because he and I both knew that would be a blatant lie. Grown-up Daniel's physique now matched his younger self's personality. Confident. Cocky. Smug.

I couldn't respond with *well, you've changed a lot* because that would allude to his metamorphosis, and his current state of hotness would become a topic of discussion, and I couldn't bear to elaborate on that topic. Not with this band shirt on. With no bra.

Words came out, but not very good ones. "I've taken a shine to shopping cart Olympics since we last spoke." *Who talked like that? Taken a shine? Could a runaway cart please hit me and push me away from him, please?*

I cleared my throat and tried again. "I thought you were living in Texas."

His mirrored aviators hid part of his expression, but his upturned lips gave me instant "old Daniel" vibes. Prankster Daniel, who brought sulfur to school and opened the bottle during the eighth-grade pep rally. Who spelled the word "disappointment" as "D-A-N-I-E-L" at the regional spelling bee just to get a laugh from the crowd when he could have easily won. Who ran for student body president on the platform of "Food Truck Friday" and then won. And kept his promise.

He was *that* guy. The obnoxiously endearing one who eventually burrowed his way into your heart.

But not mine. My heart was surrounded by wooden spikes and a moat of lava. Because every single miserable day of middle school, my parents compared me to him. After all, we were at the same school and in the same grade, so that made it easy for them. I had only a few things going in my favor for me then: I was taller than Daniel—a proud, fleeting moment for my mom and dad—and had band. But he was naturally smarter—according to the TCAPs, the standardized Tennessee Comprehensive Assessment Program tests. Thinking back, maybe this was the start of my anxiety-ridden school days.

This flood of memories kicked my dormant competitiveness back into gear. I needed to know what had happened to him after all these years.

"But you're back now? You were at UT Austin, right? Then Silicon Valley? Engineering?"

His deep, boisterous laughter prevented him from answering my important questions. I waited patiently for him to stop. "I'm sorry, I wasn't expecting you to fire off so many questions, it's very Korean nosy ajumma of you. Do you want to know my yearly income too? Mrs. Chae asked me last Sunday at church how much lawyers make. And wouldn't leave my side until I told her. Then she asked if companies still gave signing bonuses."

I snorted. "If you told Mrs. Chae, she'll definitely tell Mrs. Ahn, and then you've basically made it go viral in the Nashville Korean church community. Our moms will compare us again." *Daniel Choi making big money. Go back to your old job, make big money too!*

"Shit, you're right. Everyone at church knows now. Anyway, to answer your nosy questions, I went to UT Austin and double majored in math and econ."

Of course he did. 2 x NERD. Wooo Longhorns.

"And minored in French."

Of course. Double majoring wasn't enough.

"Then I went to law school after undergrad, same place, UT. Went to Silicon Valley and passed the California bar, and hopped around as an M and A lawyer until a few months ago. I'm on leave right now, or sabbatical—depending on who you ask—visiting my parents, who moved back here to take the reins of the church again. What's your story? Did you stay here? I thought you hated living in Nashville."

My stomach sank. He hadn't seen me in fifteen years and he never thought to ask around about me or google me? Was I that forgettable? All this time, years after he moved, a small part of me always wanted to know he was doing great and I could use this rivalry as a way to keep pressure on myself. Apparently he didn't feel the same, and that said a lot.

I glanced over at his car. It had a custom Golden State Warriors California license plate, which I didn't notice when my shopping cart was barreling toward it. The gold letters spelling out "CHAMPIONS" glistened in the midday sun.

Time to part ways with Daniel, who didn't give a damn about me. "I need to talk and walk because my groceries in the car are melting and the cabbage kimchi air freshener is going to permanently infuse into the fabric seats of the Camry. Plus, I need your help to load the rice in my trunk."

Daniel gestured "after you" with his right hand, and I wheeled the cart away.

I slowed my step and tried to remember where I'd parked my car.

He read my mind. "Did you forget where you parked?"

"No." *Yes.*

"What color's your Camry?"

"It's my mom's, and it's beige." A perfect car to camouflage in a large parking lot.

He pointed to the next aisle over. "Is that it?"

Lifting my head and standing on tiptoes, squinting in the blinding sunlight, I could make out a brownish car. All of the aisles looked the same and now I was approaching it from a different direction. The car looked like mine . . . but this was also my first time driving it, and I didn't know much about makes and models of cars. I knew about E-class cars because Wanker Wyatt from work had one.

With the back of my hand, I wiped the perspiration trickling down to my temples. The random burst of cardio from chasing the cart through the parking lot had activated my sweat glands. How come Daniel wasn't a faucet like me? He was better than me at everything, even staying dry.

As we drew closer to the car, Daniel asked, "Is that your license plate?"

"I don't know, I don't pay attention to those things." Holding my key fob high in the air, I hit the unlock button. The car taillights flashed twice. With the confidence of a mansplainy dude in a roomful of equally qualified women, I said, "Bingo. That worked, it's mine!"

I unlocked the trunk. Slowly and steadily, it opened and made a louder-than-expected whoosh sound, like a spaceship turning on thrusters.

Daniel rolled up his sleeves as we pulled the cart over to the back of the car. "You want both of them in here?"

"Oh, I was thinking you could load one, and then I could do the other so you don't hurt your back or anything."

His eyebrow quirk suggested I should be institutionalized and evaluated by a medical professional. "Why? I can just do both."

I shrugged. *Suit yourself, bro.*

Grunting loudly, he lifted a bag from the cart and placed it into my trunk with one smooth movement. The kimchi smell drifted in our direction as he tossed in bag number two.

Bam! He slammed the trunk with both hands. Nope, no wedding ring.

"Thank you! See? I remembered my manners this time." I smiled.

He adjusted his shirt by pulling it down. "You're welcome. So what've you been up to all these years?"

I fanned my face. "We have a lot to cover and it's hot out here. Let's do this rapid fire, round robin. You first."

He laughed. "Okay, so you know I moved to Texas for high school and got a full ride at UT Austin for undergrad and law school. Your turn."

Okay, I didn't know about the full scholarships but thank you for that.

I barked, "Went to NYU. I got in other places but NYU offered me more money." *That was for the scholarship talk.*

"I went to UT because of money too. I'd gotten into Harvard off the waitlist, but you know how that goes." *No, actually, I don't know how that goes.* Leave it to Daniel to rub in the Harvardness even though he never went there.

"So you're Jessie . . . Kim still? Or did you get married and change your name? And where do you work?"

This would be a big reveal for me. A Korean woman in her upper-twenties, unmarried, and, for the first time ever, jobless. Not something I wanted to shout about on LinkedIn. Or to Daniel Choi. "Wow, a lot of questions. I worked on Wall Street a long time, recruited right out of college. But then—" My voice hitched. I couldn't say it. That I'd been let go because of my inability to lead. And that I'd been accepted into a top business school but whoops, those plans were botched too.

I wasn't ready. "But I've got kimchi to deliver and your time just ran out. Nice catching up, Daniel."

He held his arm out, stopping me from getting into my car. "Hey, so let's meet up again, if you're in town a couple of days? I'll be here."

I'll be here too, like maybe forever? "Uh, okay." He recited me his number and I put it in my phone contacts.

BEEP!

He pulled his phone from his pocket. "A new message. *Thanks, Dan the Macho Mercedes Man*. And there's a clapping hands emoji . . . which I'm assuming is a sarcastic use of an emoticon. I take it this is you, Jessie?" He passed me his phone and I grabbed it.

I couldn't help it, the two corners of my mouth twisted upward. He always had a wry sense of humor, and always kept a straight face, no matter what.

Handing it back, I nodded.

He glanced at my left hand in the phone exchange. Oooh was he searching for a wedding ring too?

"I think you need to wash your hands."

Looking down, I could see black streaks of God-knows-what, probably from carrying the rice.

To my horror, he motioned toward his chin and added, "It's

also on your face." He didn't say where on my face, so for all I knew I smeared the black grime above my upper lip when trying to wipe my sweat, giving me a mustached appearance. I wouldn't know until I got into my car and checked the mirror.

I brushed by him and opened my car door. The kimchi, ripening by the second, had filled the car with pungency. A smell that would fade over time . . . hopefully.

"So message me. Let's catch up," he said as I closed the door in his face. *Be nice, Jessie. He helped put a hundred pounds of rice into your car.*

I rolled down the window to say bye, and to provide some air circulation. "Okay, I'll message you later." What was the least date-y place we could do with an easy out? Lunch? Coffee? A group thing? That would be perfect, except I didn't have a group. Well, except for—

"Maybe we can go to this coffee shop I like called Falling Off the Red Wagon. My new BFF works there. They have trivia night." *Okay, so I lied and hadn't met even one friend yet, and Flora, the grocery delivery economist barista, and I weren't exactly friends—yet. That would need to change.* I put my car in reverse and checked my mirrors.

"Sounds like fun! But do you really want to relive *those* days of Seventh Grade Quiz Bowl or Academic Decathalon?" *Right, he always had all the answers then too. Damn it. Why couldn't I find an activity I could do well, like building complex merger models or pulling company financial statements from out of my ass? He probably wanted to see me again just so he could rub his greatness in my face some more.*

I pulled out of the spot and saw him waving at me as I exited the parking lot. With my bounty of a hundred pounds of rice and jugs of napa kimchi safe and sound in my mom's car, I glanced at my face in the rearview mirror. My all-natural, no makeup face was clean, except for a streak of thick black grease on my chin.

But no mustache. Thank God.

Daniel Choi had seen me at my absolute worst, unshowered, no makeup, with a weird band shirt and a temporary half-goatee face tattoo. There was no place to go but up, right?

Chapter Four

The kimchi from the Asian market came with a "PERISHABLE, REFRIGERATE IMMEDIATELY" warning on a round, neon orange label, so those jars from the trunk came into the house first. The dense stacks of cabbage inside the containers looked fine to me, and the jars were sweaty but still reasonably cool to the touch.

I plunked the two jars down on the counter and startled my mother, who was busy making a gigantic vat of japchae noodles, maybe twenty-five times the typical quantity, which meant she was making it for a church function or a potluck picnic.

"You scare me! You knock next time. Or announce, HI UMMA, I'm home."

"Sorry." I shuffled and stacked items in the fridge and put the kimchi on the top shelf. Then ran back to the car to bring in the other groceries. The bags of rice would need to wait. I didn't have a plan for extracting those and my mom hadn't told me where she'd store them.

When I closed the refrigerator door the final time, Mom gestured toward a full plate of spicy squid, freshly made japchae noodles, and a steaming pile of "healthy" rice my mom was eating these days. It was purple and had beans in it. It wasn't bad; it was just different from the white and brown rice I'd grown accustomed to. She'd read in a study in *The Korea Times* that white rice caused diabetes and favored the heartier japgokbap purple bean rice—well, except when the Asian market had a two-for-one sale on bags of short-grained white rice that weighed as much as two Korean grandmas.

"I saw Daniel Choi at the store today. Remember him from middle school—the pastor's son? I guess his family's back here now?" I don't know why I was phrasing all of these statements as questions, because I knew the answers. Maybe it had something to do with how I always felt six years old around my mom. Or maybe it was what Hamilton Cooper had referred to when flagging my "lack of leadership skills"—grrrrr—

Mom stopped mixing the noodles and raised her rubber-gloved hand to reach for the sesame oil. "Pastor Choi come back a month ago. He like Tennessee better than Texas. His son is back too? I hear some things."

"Oh?" What kind of things, Mom? Spill it. "Like what?"

"He suppose marry and then they not." She added some soy sauce and resumed mixing the noodles.

"He was engaged? Or a long-time girlfriend?"

"You need to eat." She pointed at the plate she had fixed me.

I dug in. "This is so good! Thanks for making lunch."

She grunted and added a little sprinkle of sugar from a nearby bowl. "Not too salty? All my friend at church say when you get old everyone adding too much salty taste."

"No, it's perfect." She didn't often press about the quality of her cooking, because we both knew she was the best cook among all of her friends. The only complaint I had about the food was why she didn't put more on my plate. But if I asked that, she'd lecture me about needing to eat healthier instead of snacking, then ask me to exercise more, and then it would spiral down, down, down into not having a boyfriend, not having a job, and not being able to cook like her.

Two of those were true. I didn't have a boyfriend and I didn't have a job. But I could cook pretty well for someone who didn't do it often.

But not the way my mom could. She was a true culinary artist. Her ability to balance complex flavors and various textures was unparalleled. She favored the large, upscale family dining type of cuisine, ideal for mass gatherings. My style was more like whipping up a meal based on limited ingredients, putting me more in the food-truck-with-very-limited-menu camp.

"Your appa is coming home from work trip soon. This might be his last time to Asia for long time." Dad was in the dying traditional telecom business and worked out of a satellite office in downtown Nashville. The main office was in Atlanta—ever since his company was acquired, he had to drive to Atlanta a lot and flew to Asia a few times a year. Between Mom and Dad, I didn't know who would be more disappointed in me for losing my job and moving back home temporarily. Mom flat-out avoided the subject now that I'd settled in, like if she didn't talk about it, it hadn't happened. And honestly, I didn't want to bring it up. Dad had said a few years ago I'd make my way to the top of Hamilton Cooper in no time and would be in charge of the company one day and bragged to all his friends that I would be running all of Wall Street, like that was even possible.

And here I was, jobless, running shopping errands, and free-loading off them for meals. Not what I expected out of my life at age twenty-eight, almost twenty-nine.

Pitiful.

Even more pitiful was the fact that I'd brought the conversation back to my childhood nemesis. I wanted dirt on him. His mysterious sabbatical, his failed relationship, anything. "So have you seen the Choi family? Is Daniel visiting awhile?"

Mom had moved on to making mass quantities of mandu. She laid out the pot sticker wrappers, the marinated ground pork meat, and the whipped raw egg in a metal bowl to seal the stuffed, folded pouches like magical edible wrapper glue. I put my empty plate in the sink and washed my hands. Pulling up a chair, I joined her at the other end of the table. Grabbing one of

Mom's ancient knives closest to me in the dish rack, I minced napa cabbage, onions, and scallions on an equally ancient cutting board I'd found under the kitchen island. To add a little more color to the vegetable mix, I took some baby carrots from the produce drawer in the fridge and very carefully sliced those too. They had a tendency to roll, and the knife Mom always used was so dull it was practically a butter knife, so I had to take my time.

After combining the veggies and sprinkling in salt, I quickly pan-fried them and combined everything with the seasoned pork. Next, Mom would need help with the stuffing and pressing. I knew the drill: we'd made thousands of fried mandu for church picnics over the years. It was something you never forgot. Like riding a bike, but with occasional blistering hot oil splatter.

She grabbed a few spoons so we wouldn't have to take turns scooping the meat and vegetables into the wrappers. Very efficient.

After stuffing one dumpling, she passed it to me so I could use it as my model example. "Be careful, this wrapper is new brand. More thin and weak. Don't tear."

I'd done this so many times from my tween and teen years that I still had muscle memory, but I knew not to argue with her. She wanted perfection because this food was for the Nashville Korean community, not just for consumption at home. At home, we would eat the rejects. The deep-fried ones with torn wrappers. The ones that were too puffy with filling. Or the dumplings that didn't have enough stuffing, and those were actually my favorite, the ones with a lot of crunch to them. A high crunch-to-chewy ratio, the same way I loved my baked goods.

With great care, I put together my first one and showed it to her.

She nodded and went back to stuffing and sealing her own. I'd gotten the silent Korean mom approval.

"Choi family come back because our pastor retire. We ask Pastor Choi to come back to congregation and he say okay. His oldest son, Sam, go to MIT and was working at engineering company, but now he is finishing medical school." There was a long pause and at first I thought she'd forgotten about mentioning Daniel. "And Daniel, he youngest son, I see him at church."

"Yeah?" I scraped the side of the bowl and scooped up some scattered pork and cabbage remnants. "Does he live here now or is he going back to California soon?" Was he really on sabbatical or was he here now, indefinitely, like me?

She made a tut-tut-tut sound with her tongue. "He graduate from law school. He had good job in California. He supposed to marry long time ago but Mrs. Chae say wedding is cancel. Maybe something wrong with him." Mom shook her head and rearranged the dumplings on the tray so they were set apart but still close, without sticking together.

"People break up for all kinds of reasons, it doesn't mean

something is wrong with him." I couldn't believe I was defending know-it-all, overachieving, smirky Daniel Choi, of all people. But in this case I had to, because there was one main thing he and I had in common: we both had hypercompetitive Korean parents who embraced opportunities to elevate themselves sometimes by putting others down. Parents who would probably brag on their tombstones, listing their children's biggest accomplishments and their SAT scores. Possibly even their last car's make and model if it was impressive enough.

"Daniel is nice-looking boy. He look like good mix of mom and dad."

I knew what she was talking about: when he was little it was like his features were somewhat too big for his body. His eyebrows were bushy, and his thick, floppy hair looked so heavy. Daniel's mom was on the stocky side and had soft, rounded features. His dad was thin and wiry, like a heron. Daniel was a perfect blend of the two of them now, with his medium build, chiseled face, and styled hair.

"Maybe Daniel is home and that is good thing. Maybe you can know Daniel and if he's nice and not problem, you can date. I can arrange it, like snapping finger."

Then she snapped her finger.

I rolled my eyes. Typical mom.

After pouring oil into the wok, she asked, "You see anyone else at market? Everybody there for big rice sale." She crouched and peered at the rice bag she kept in the base cabinet. "I have old rice bag, almost finish. We can use new ones soon." Rubbing her hands together, she said, "Fresh kimchi too! Today is good shopping day!"

It was, except for running into Daniel. And driving home in a car with various ripened, fragrant groceries. Did I remember to crack the window?

She plopped a test dumpling into the wok. A faint swoosh followed by faint gurgling signaled that the oil was nearly ready. "You be nice to Choi boy when you see him. He is pastor son."

Mom was more fixated on him than I expected.

"I wasn't planning to ever see him again actually."

"Mrs. Chae told Mrs. Baek that Mrs. Choi say he is here because he need vacation because he work too much. Like you, but he making more money and still have a job. Maybe you try dating one time, I can ask Mrs. Choi—"

My hands instinctively shot out to a "HALT!" position.

She asked, "Just one time?"

"Whoa there. Look, all I said was that I saw him at the store. We said hi, that's it. Oh, and he helped load the car with the rice."

Her eyebrow quirked up. "He strong?"

Oh God. "Long story, my cart got away from me in the parking lot and almost crashed into his car."

She added a few more mandu to the hot wok. They sizzled, hissed, and popped. I inhaled the aroma of fried savory dough as Mom flipped the first dumpling so it could brown on both sides. She muttered to herself, "Maybe temperature is too hot." After lowering the heat, she asked, "He have nice car?"

"Can you stop, please? There's no way, Mom. He's annoying and obnoxious and an overachiever who still brags about getting into Harvard off the waitlist."

Shit, I knew I shouldn't have mentioned Harvard. Just saying that word was verbal heroin for every Korean parent. Mental note: no more H bombs.

She used her trusty long, wooden cooking chopsticks to pull a dumpling out of the wok and placed it on a plate with paper towels on it to soak up the oil. "Maybe he have girlfriend anyway. He nice looking now." It was true, he probably had a girlfriend. Maybe more. I could see other women falling for his easygoing, charming, coy, smirky bullshit. The schmoozy guys at my old firm were always dating. Some were dating even though they were already married.

She walked to the fridge and pulled out more cabbage, then put it on the cutting board I'd used on the island. Then all I heard was drawers and cabinets slamming shut. And yelling.

"WHAT HAPPEN TO ALL KNIVES? I NEED MY KNIFE! WHERE EVERYTHING GO? WHAT IS THIS WÜSTHOF?" Hand shaking, she pointed accusingly to a wooden knife block next to the paper towel roll. Shiny new silver knives only inches away from her index finger.

Some of my belongings from my apartment had finally made it here, and one of the few things I didn't donate or throw out was my set of Wüsthof knives. First of all, they were too fancy to give away. Second, they were the nicest thing I owned and I couldn't bear to part with them, especially since they were so practical and had been used only a handful of times. Mom's knives were mix and match from various cutlery sets she'd collected and broken over the years. She'd never once sharpened them and the one I'd just used from the dish rack was as bad as all her other ones. Some were rusty. A few even had wobbly handles, which is always a pleasant life-or-death challenge when chopping and dicing. After so many years of watching my mom nearly cut her fingers off every time she'd spin the amputation roulette wheel with her dull, heavy knives, I thought this was the right way to solve the problem.

"I want them back!" Mom rummaged through the kitchen, opening all the cabinets and drawers.

"The new ones are better. They're sharper. And better quality. Can't you even try them?" She continued to search for her cutlery. You would have thought they were heirlooms.

"I don't want it. I like old knife. What is Wüsthof? What do Germany people know about knife?"

I didn't know much about knives either, but I did know that they were nicer than hers. But she wasn't going to listen to me. "Fine, I'll go to the garage and get the old ones. I put them all in a storage bin in case this happened—where I would give you a nice thing and you would complain and reject it just because you don't like change."

"I don't like you to spend money on knife. I have knife already."

Then it hit me. This was how Mom and Dad were about everything. They wouldn't replace something until it was irreparable. Like their winter coats they would patch and mend for years. And their cars, which each had nearly a hundred thousand miles. And apparently knives.

I tried different logic. "But my knife set was on sale. A big discount."

"Sale?" She stood still. "How big?"

"I think thirty percent off?" Watching her face, I knew I'd said the wrong thing. "Actually, it was like a fifty percent discount." Her head tilted and she pursed her lips. Those lips tentatively turned up into a smile.

She walked back to the knife block and pulled out each knife from its hole, examining the size, shape, and serration. She spent a longer time studying one of the larger ones. After a minute, she used it to shred the cabbage. *Fffft, fffft, fffft.* Like an industrial meat slicer. "Be okay," she said, as she cut the leaves into thin slivers, with full control over the sharpened stabbing and cutting tool.

"You're welcome." I took a bite of mandu, crunching the crispy outside shell. A delicious creation born from short-lived mom-daughter cooperation, and it was the best thing I'd eaten in years.

Chapter Five

My two best work friends were able to have a video call with plenty of advance notice. In the office, we used to chat on messenger and grab lunch together at least once every few weeks. With me living in a different city, I was now out of sight, and therefore out of mind. We'd canceled and rescheduled our video catch-up meeting countless times, and thanks to my former company's layoffs, they weren't able to socialize at all during the work week because they were staffed on multiple deals. But late on a Sunday afternoon, five P.M. NYC time, two weeks after I'd moved, we were able to schedule a quick hangout.

Alice, my favorite, foul-mouthed VP, and Charlie, my former peer and one of the nice bankers on our floor, were already complaining about work when I logged into the call a minute late.

"—like, can you believe the balls on that guy? To make

everyone work this weekend when he went to his house in the Hamptons? What a motherfucking asshole!"

I interrupted. "Let me guess. You're talking about Martin?"

Alice barked, "HA! I wish. Martin is a saint compared to Goldstein."

"Which Goldstein? There's two on our floor, the asshole brothers," Charlie asked, half paying attention.

"The one with the good body, but that . . . ugh face."

Alice talked shit about people at work all the time, but she also seemed to thrive in the Hamilton Cooper male-dominated, bro-y workplace. She talked about dudes like they were himbos, which was hilarious to me. A lot of these guys hit on her when she first arrived, calling her "sexy girl" and "hot," not realizing she was Alice Lin, ballbuster and mankiller. With every jerk that winked, made kissy noises, or commented on how nice she looked, she launched into a tirade about women's rights, Asian American discrimination, and the company's harassment policies, making them shrivel up and slink away.

I asked, "How's work, Charlie?" He was staring at the screen, mouth slightly agape, but not looking at the webcam. Probably fiddling with an Excel model in another window.

"Huh? Sorry, I have to look at one last thing before I send this to Martin. Then I can . . . I'll . . ."

His thoughts drifted as he tapped the space bar. The space bar made a different sound than the other keys, especially if your thumb is slamming it with anger. I knew this all too well. Charlie ignoring us didn't bother me. I knew the drill: he needed to get the files to his team, and then he could relax. Well, until his MD came back with feedback, which could be in a few seconds to minutes to days. You never knew. But you always had to be available, especially where he sat on the org chart: under Martin Morris, the managing director notorious for sending emails in the middle of the night, expecting answers first thing in the morning.

Alice rolled her eyes and muted Charlie. The rapid-fire clicking sound went away. Ahhh, much better.

She leaned into the camera. "So, how's it going with you? Are you enjoying your freedom?"

Was this freedom? It was all so unsettling to me, not having a steady paycheck and not having employer-paid insurance. COBRA was my healthcare service bridge for a few months, or until I found my next corporate job. Moving back home helped my severance check stretch a lot further, but I'd need to find a way to make money in the next year to avoid dipping into my 401k.

I glanced around my childhood bedroom. My gaze traveled from my IKEA bookshelf filled with angsty teenage novels over to my old band trophies on the floor to my dated brass bed.

Freedom? Hardly. Could freedom feel so constricting? After spending seven grueling years on Wall Street, it was like getting close to the last squares of a frustrating Chutes and Ladders game and sliding back down, down, down to where I started.

Maybe the toy store in my neighborhood where I worked in high school was still looking for cashiers. I googled it quickly—it was closed permanently and had been replaced by Rejuvenate Vegan Juicery. Was there even such a thing as a nonvegan juicery?

I responded to Alice truthfully. "It's better than getting yelled at by my MD at five thirty in the morning, if that's what you mean." I'd even been scolded on multiple occasions by someone senior to me who wasn't even my boss or on my team, just for being in the wrong place at the wrong time. Once, when Charlie was an analyst, he was reprimanded because he was standing in front of his VP's office while tying his laces, supposedly blocking the director from entering. When Alice was an analyst, she was screamed at because the lunch order she'd placed was delivered late: the lobby attendant sent the food to the wrong floor. But of course Alice shouted right back, because Alice didn't take shit from anyone. It was an epic scene, a verbal showdown between her and the asshole forty-year-old Hudson Woodard. Even though Alice was immediately removed from all his projects, we knew she was right to stand her ground. She was an idol of sorts and got a reputation for being the kind of person you didn't fuck with. Charlie and I were good friends with Alice, but also a little scared of her too.

In his video frame, Charlie held up a handwritten sign: CAN YOU UNMUTE ME PLEASE. I'M DONE WITH MY WORK. I wondered how long he'd been patiently holding up the paper.

Alice flipped her hair back and allowed him to speak with a simple click.

"Heyyyyy, I emailed the deck and can talk now. You've got my full attention. What'd I miss?"

I sighed. "Not much, just catching up. Any gossip on your end? That's one thing I miss. Office drama, but the kind that doesn't involve me. All that's going on here is my mom updating me about what's on sale at the Asian market and what Ivy League schools the Korean kids here are getting into these days. Riveting stuff."

Alice said, "Well, Samantha said that Goldstein—with the ugh face—patted her back a few times at the summer barbecue. Friendly at first, but after a few beers his hand traveled down to her ass. She didn't say anything, but I'm thinking of asking her to bring it to HR's attention."

Appalling, but not surprising. I huffed, "There's a stark difference between a *back* and an *ass* and it's something you should learn about when you're in preschool. Maybe replace the song 'Head, Shoulders, Knees, and Toes' with body parts that apparently confuse men as they get older. Start the kids early."

Charlie scoffed. "At the barbecue, Goldstein was at the open bar saying that if he wasn't married, he'd be into Samantha. Then he said, and I quote, 'I know she wants this.'"

Alice and I cough-gagged into the microphone. We knew Goldstein was the bullshitter here. No one wanted *that*.

"I know, I know," Charlie said. "Like ninety percent of the guys we work with are assholes." He paused. "Um, who Alice and I work with."

Right. They worked there. I didn't.

Alice took a sip of Evian. "Goldstein has a type."

I asked, "You mean young?" Of all the attributes a woman could have—intelligence, beauty, wit—he preferred what the bankers called "fresh meat." Their words, not mine. Fresh out of undergrad or B-school. So gross. "Wasn't he the one who said he wasn't getting married until he was forty-five? And that his wife-to-be was a future pledge at a sorority somewhere?"

She put her bottle down and rolled her eyes. "There's a stall in the women's bathroom where someone's keyed into the door the tally marks of all of Goldstein's transgressions. Mostly of the lewd, drunken variety. He's up to twelve now. I think that's on the low side."

Charlie asked, "Oh wow, you think it's just one person updating it or it's a group effort? And don't the people in HR use those bathrooms too? How are they not seeing that?"

Alice shrugged. "I think HR are the ones to request the doors be removed or painted every few months so they don't have to deal with the graffiti. It's like the tree falling in the forest question: If a Goldstein brother oversteps HR boundaries and no one reports it, did it happen?"

"It's not just women who get harassed. This place is like a never-ending fraternity hazing for guys." Charlie sighed and wiped his glasses. "I'm tired. I've been working since six this morning. Twelve hours, on a Sunday, and I just got a voicemail from Martin. Since the bake-off audience is a bunch of twenty-somethings—like the CEO and board members are practically babies—he's thinking we need to add memes and gifs to the presentation. And of course since he doesn't know anything about what that means, he pronounced it 'mimis' and 'jeffs.' He's staffing the youngest analyst on this deal so that guy can help make the presentation more interesting and quote-unquote 'speak their language.' Jessie, can you please start a company and hire me as employee number one? I can't take this torture anymore."

I let out a sarcastic laugh, one that rattled so loudly that the mic gave feedback.

"I'm serious! Out of everyone from our analyst class, I always thought you'd be the one smart enough to find a way to escape these golden handcuffs. It's probably a good thing you aren't here anymore. This is an intellectual wasteland, where rich, boring people go to wither and die."

I never thought of myself as an entrepreneurial type. It's not like my parents would have pushed me in that direction: Dad had been middle management in the engineering group at one company for more than twenty years and was of the "get a good salary and health insurance" mentality. Mom worked in the accounts payable group at the same corporation a few years too, before she retired early.

Being an entrepreneur required leadership, eagerness, and vision, and I had that whole "Jess is not a leader" problem.

Alice barked, "Hey! Some of us are doing this grind so we can retire early. I only have ten years left of this rat race. Then I swear I'm moving to Puerto Vallarta."

The thought of being at Hamilton Cooper for ten more years made me shudder. Maybe Charlie was right: that job was never right for me.

But that led to the obvious question: What *was* the right job for me then?

Charlie asked Alice, "How are you holding up? Now that they laid a ton of people off in my group, it's twice as much work for everyone. And by everyone, I mean our level and below."

She snapped, "I'm fine."

He paused. "Oh, okay. I guess that's good then."

When Alice said she was "fine," it was never a good thing. If she really was doing well, she'd answer "Great!" or "Okay, how about yourself?" For her, and pretty much for any woman I knew, maybe 99.4 percent of the time "fine" actually meant "not fine." In extreme cases, it could also mean "fuck off." This didn't strike me as one of those times.

I inhaled deeply and asked on the exhale, "What's up, Alice? Is it work or personal life that's got you down?"

She clicked her nails on her right hand on the water bottle. "Personal."

Charlie's jaw dropped. "Wait, you have time to date?"

"I said personal, and that doesn't have to mean dating. It can be family, friends, or other things. In this particular case it happens to be a problematic hamster I'm pet-sitting for the time being. Did you know they're nocturnal? My sister broke up with her boyfriend and has sole custody of the hamster. On top of that she doesn't have any housing leads so she's periodically living on my couch. There's a hamster cage in the living room, and a squeaky wheel. I'm so tired, you guys. And there's no way I can ask any dates to come over with my rodent zoo at home."

Charlie smirked. "So it *does* have to do with dating, actually." I'd never seen him look so happy. He'd actually won an argument with Alice.

Alice rolled her eyes. "Sure, okay, whatever. But if my sister was out of the house and that damned hamster wasn't there, I wouldn't be having any dating problems, aside from having to work every weeknight and most weekends." She shook her head. "There's barely enough time to even have one-night stands."

Charlie asked, "Is your dating life better now that you're out of banking, Jess?"

I snorted. "I only moved back home, like, two weeks ago. There hasn't even been much time to unpack everything. And

I mean luggage, not unpacking in the broader sense of my life having no direction and needing to reexamine all of my choices that led me to where I am now. I'm here, in my childhood bedroom filled with mementos from my glory years of middle school and high school, in a house with low-end, unreliable Wi-Fi. Not how I pictured my life in my late twenties."

Alice asked, "But the guys are hotter in Nashville, right? I've heard that."

Leave it to Alice to focus on the important takeaways. "Honestly, I haven't had much time to notice." The only guy I'd really interacted with here was Daniel. Nooo thank you.

Charlie hit the delete key a few times. "If it were me, and I had all that free time, I'd be out every night, trying to get laid."

Alice added, "Me too."

"Both of you have way more game than me. What am I supposed to do, go to a bar, sit down, and buy a drink for an attractive dude?"

Alice and Charlie both responded in unison. "YES."

Maybe it really was that simple? For years, I'd been trapped in a catch-22: I worked all the time, so I couldn't date. I wasn't dating, so I worked all the time. Both situations were undesirable.

Alice asked, "Are you going back to banking or trying something else? Whatever happened with the MBA?"

I sighed. "The deadline for admission to the part-time program is tomorrow. I just started my job search. There's no way anyone will hire me if I say, 'Oh by the way, I'm going to school part-time this fall so I'll need manageable hours. And is there an employee assistance benefit that subsidizes that MBA tuition by the way?'"

Alice nodded. "Yeah, you're right. Have you thought about deferring?"

"Deferring admission?" I chewed my bottom lip. Alice always had great ideas. "I'll ask. Maybe if I beg, they can hold a spot for me next year." Deferring admission would keep that option open and make me feel like I had some control of my life again. That maybe I wasn't as big a failure after all.

"Great! Can I come visit you soon? I have a client in Nashville and I've been avoiding going to see them, but now I have a reason!"

Charlie chimed in, "I want to go too. I haven't had a vacation in three years."

"THREE years? How is that even legal? Why?" I couldn't believe his manager didn't even notice he hadn't gotten any work breaks. Actually, I could. He was probably the main reason Charlie didn't go.

He shrugged. "My family lives in upstate New York and I see them on the weekends sometimes. But honestly, all my buddies have gotten married and we don't go on trips anymore. I don't have a travel buddy."

"Alice can be your travel buddy." The moment the words left my mouth I regretted them. Alice would be the worst person to travel with, she was so particular about everything. Especially who she traveled with.

I backpedaled. "Or not, if you prefer to travel alone."

Alice clapped her hands. "Okay, Charlie. Put in your vacation request, we're going to Nashvegas! I need to get the hell out of my apartment until my sister gets a new place. You should have a million AmEx miles by now so you can get a free flight. Oh, and don't check a bag because I don't want to wait in baggage claim forever."

While she turned around to yell at the hamster for running in the squeaky wheel, Charlie gave me a head tilt and a look. *I can't believe you're making me travel with her.*

I returned it with a shrug. *Look, I get it. But do this for me, please.*

Alice turned back around to face the computer. "So next week then! I hear Nashville is big on the bachelorette party scene, so I can't wait to play tourist! Bluebird Cafe, Nashville hot chicken, Grand Ole Opry here we come! And best of all, we can be wingmen for each other. Jessica, we get to witness the invention of the new you!"

Her excitement was palpable. It almost made me happy I'd been laid off, and it felt like this was one of those "Get it, girl!" moments in life. And maybe it was. When was the last time I tried to "meet people"? Maybe a year ago? Maybe longer? My last serious relationship was in college, but we split up the summer after graduation. He was headed to the West Coast for grad school and I'd chosen to stay in New York to start my banking career. After that, it was a series of right-swipe, wrong matches. Like the salesman guy who talked about himself for two straight hours and then wanted to go on another date with me because I was a good listener. Or the corporate lawyer who asked me how much money I made within the first ten minutes of conversation, and then proceeded to tell me his net worth. Or the countless number of flaky no-shows. If I could charge billable hours for wasted dating time, I'd have enough to pay a sizable down payment on a studio apartment in NYC.

I'd been stuck in that weird chicken-and-egg-like paradox for far too long. I'd thought it affected all bankers, but apparently Alice was sort of dating. Well, it didn't matter anymore, because I was ready to "get it" now. A new lease on life. New year, new me. Out with the old, in with the new. Gimme all the clichés.

Charlie offered a gritted-teeth smile. "I'll send an email to request vacation now. And I'll put a Post-it note in his chair. Maybe if he sees I was here this weekend he'll offer it without bitching about me taking time off when it's crunch time. It's been fucking crunch time for three years straight!"

We said our goodbyes and for the first time since I'd been let go at Hamilton Cooper, a sense of relief washed over me. My friends were coming to visit. This was a very good thing. And with a shinier outlook on my future, I had two big things I wanted to accomplish. One, to take the leap and discover an amazing nonbanking career and two, to make time for a relationship. Not necessarily in that order.

My phone buzzed. *You're going to the church potluck tonight? Please protect me from Mrs. Chae. She asked my mom if I can get her son an internship. She also asked how much I would put into his 401K! Help?*

Daniel Choi.

The temporary reprieve of relief vanished, replaced by utter dread. Going to a Korean function as a jobless, single woman standing next to Daniel Choi, Korean Boy Wonder, was a special circle of hell that Dante hadn't even dreamed of.

Way to burst my bubble.

I responded, *Sorry, you're on your own.*

He replied, *Haha that's not what your mom told mine. She said that you were bringing a special dish tonight. Looking forward to it!*

Special dish? What the—

I stamped down the stairs to find my mom. What the hell did she sign me up for?

Chapter Six

"Mandu. I said to Daniel mom that you coming to church and bring everybody mandu." She paused. "I freeze some from other day so we have big batch and it is not lying. I unfreeze, bake, and they are crispy again. We have enough."

"It'd be pretty wrong to lie to a pastor's wife, you know."

She pointed to the aluminum pans full of japchae noodles. "I make that fresh. Bring those to the car. Take mandu too." I delivered them to the Camry and came back into the kitchen.

I knew the answer to the question I was about to ask, but I inquired anyway. "Do I have to go to the church potluck?"

"Yes. Your appa is on trip still and I need help to carry everything. I already buy two meal ticket and don't want waste money. Also, they have good food and you need to eat, you need to look healthy."

She left the room and came back a few minutes later wearing a new striped shirt and fresh lipstick. I followed her to the garage and she unlocked the door and sat in the driver's seat. She motioned for me to get in and handed over two gallon Ziploc bags. "When everyone is done eating and take their turn, can you fill these with dduk? Your appa loves Daniel mom homemade dduk. It is so soft and chewy. He like the round one filled with red bean. Green, pink, white, doesn't matter. Get whatever kind."

As we drove, she let me choose the music and didn't complain, though she did mutter that the songs sounded like "monkeys hitting trash cans." With every crescendo, my mom winced, and I laughed at her exaggerated reaction.

Mom parked her car in between two other identical sedans. Nearly all of the cars in the row were Camrys or Accords. Well, except for that familiar, conspicuous Mercedes at the end of the row. To make matters worse, while I had my arms full with the large aluminum trays of Korean appetizers, my mom, who knew absolutely zero about cars, said, "Fancy car. Mercedes! Did you see that?"

How could I not see? All the car needed was a loudspeaker with someone screaming "Bourgeois!" on repeat. It was so glaringly Silicon Valley new money. So attention-seeking. So Daniel Choi.

Mom opened the door, held it open briefly for me, and continued ahead as it slammed shut in my face.

"Admiring my dent-free car?"

I didn't need to turn around to know who that was. Or to know that he was smirking at me.

His voice came closer. "You need me to get the door for you?"

"No. I'm fine." I tried to rearrange the heavy trays so they were semi-balancing on one of my arms. Using the wall for support, I opened the weighty door with my other hand.

"Well, if you won't let me get the door, can you give me a tray or two so you don't drop everything? Like, how are you going to get through the door if it snaps closed like it did before, when your mom slammed it in your face?" *Damn you, Daniel, with your logic.* "There's something leaking onto your shirt." Okay, he was wrong about that. There was something leaking onto my *sandal.* The aroma of sesame oil, scallions, and garlic wafted from my footwear.

He was right, of course, about the poorly executed tray-balancing and door-opening plan. You didn't need to be a physicist to know this was not going to work without assistance. And since Mom had left me behind, Mr. Mercedes was all I had.

Without my permission, he grabbed the trays, turning the one on top around so the whole jenga stack of aluminum containers were weighted more evenly. Then, opening the door wide, he stuck out his foot and propped it open. I walked by him. "Your legs are longer, that's why it worked."

"Yeah, right."

Once we were both indoors, I grabbed my trays and he let go of the door.

SLAM!

The force was so strong that Daniel's manmade air current whooshed my hair. And, of course, since I was facing away from the door, long strands of my mane blew forward at full force and I was unable to pull my hair from my eyes or mouth, thanks to both arms being fully occupied by my food trays.

I literally couldn't see.

"It's dripping on your foot."

From the distance, I heard Mom bellow, "Jessie! I looking for you! Why you walk so slow? Mrs. Park just join church and want to try your mandu!" She flapped her hands toward herself. "Come!"

Daniel pulled the trays from my hands and rather than take them back in protest, I immediately brushed my hair back with both palms. He continued walking to the community area, where the potluck had already started. Mom took one look at him as he swaggered by her with the aluminum pans and gave him the biggest grin I'd ever seen. Never before had I seen her smile like that. Not when I got into a good college. Not when I landed a job at a top-tier investment bank. Not when I paid off my student loans with three years of savings and bonuses.

No, what made her smile was Daniel Choi hauling in trays of food that he didn't even make himself. He placed the food on an empty table and peeled off the top. First, the japchae. Then the mandu. Everyone flocked to him with their half-empty plates. Even people without plates patted Daniel on the back.

"Waaaa!"

"Good job!"

"Smell is good!"

No one even noticed I was standing by the door. Not even my own mother, who was standing next to Daniel, as if he were her son and the maker of the mandu.

This same type of shit happened all the time at Hamilton Cooper. A few months ago, Wyatt and a Wyatt clone named Chad presented my work to the client and took full credit for it. Well, partial credit, meaning 50 percent credit for each of them. Three weekends in a row, I'd worked on the financials, coming up with conservative to highly aggressive models for our media and entertainment deal group to consider. A team player, I delivered rock-solid earnings projections, which happened to be the main contribution to getting the deal. And when I brought it up to my manager, he gave me a $10K merit bonus on the down low. What I didn't realize though was Wyatt the credit stealer would get a promotion to senior associate thanks to my hard work. The other guy left to go client-side at the media company he brokered a deal with. Wyatt not only got that promotion, he got to stay at Hamilton Cooper while I got canned.

In Wyatt's and Chad's world, there were two *I*'s in team.

Daniel watched as eager Korean elders scooped heaping mounds of noodles onto their paper plates. With clean chopsticks, they grabbed a few fried mandu too. To his credit, Daniel said in a loud, firm voice, "I'm just the delivery boy," admitting he wasn't the chef.

But then he stuffed a seaweed-rolled kimbap into his mouth without clarifying who it was. *Thanks, Daniel, as always, for your support.*

I piped up. "I'm the mandu chef."

Everyone's eyes fixated on me.

Mr. Choi said to my mom in Korean, "You're so lucky that she cooks, my Hannah doesn't even know how to boil water."

Mrs. Kim, who owned the teriyaki place, had a similar sentiment. "When I ask Susie, she burns everything. You're lucky."

Beaming, with all of the attention put on her for once, Mom said, "I am lucky. How many older kids come home to visit parents?"

A crowd formed around her, standing and eating.

With everyone distracted by the food, I reached into my bag and pulled out three small Pyrex containers and three small spoons. Before leaving for church, I'd managed to whip up three dipping sauces for the mandu: spicy chili pepper, sweet and sour, and soy-vinegar. I placed them on the table, along with placards with names, ingredients, and a "Don't double-dip!" warning.

As I rejoined the group, Teriyaki Mrs. Kim said to my mom in Korean, "Very lucky. Pastor Choi and his wife too, their Daniel is home." I looked over to where the Chois stood. They looked so different from the last time I'd seen them back in eighth grade. Older, of course, and grayer, but they were now roughly the same height as each other, both commencing the older Korean parent shrinkage phenomenon.

Pastor Choi said, "Daniel is home to help us with expanding the church and helping find a youth pastor. He is on sabbatical."

Everyone nodded, even though I'm sure not many knew what "sabbatical" meant. They probably thought it had something to do with the Sabbath.

Daniel's dad continued. "You come home for vacation?"

All eyes were back on me; the Korean elders stopped eating. Young adults stopped talking. Kids stopped playing. Silence greeted me as the crowd stood with bated breath, waiting for me to explain the heroic reason I had for coming back to Nashville. Were we back to comparing Daniel and me, with his homecoming trumping mine?

I looked nervously at my mom. There was no way I could admit the truth: that I'd been let go from my firm and was unemployed and living at home. Daniel made eye contact briefly but then looked down at his Chinet paper plate.

Luckily, Mom had no shame with telling her version of the truth. "She had a busy job, make her tired, and she come home." A few adults nodded, understanding the concept of job burnout.

It wasn't enough though. Silence still hung in the air, Korean pressure squeezing me till I gave an answer with more details. Deep down, I thought they wanted to know whether I'd "won" or "lost" to Daniel again.

My mouth opened but no words formed. I gulped instead.

Mrs. Jung said, "These mandu are very good." She held a half-eaten crescent of fried dough and saluted me. Curious, Daniel grabbed one from the tray with his bare hands, sniffed it, dunked it in the sweet and sour dipping sauce, and shoved the whole thing into his mouth.

"Mmmmm," he declared loudly while chewing.

"Jessie special mandu creation," Mom announced. She wasn't totally lying about that. I did the bulk of the work for the non–previously frozen mandu, sautéing the inner ingredients and stuffing them into the dumpling wrappers. Mom's white lies morphed into tall tales. "She is cooking more at home. Practicing. Trying new dishes." Other parents my mom's age looked at me and smiled.

Mom bounced a little on the balls of her feet. Was she feeling the same pressure I was? Her words had tumbled out faster, but at the same time, she seemed to enjoy all of this attention. I certainly didn't. My gaze shifted left and right, looking for an exit.

Then Mom told the biggest lie I'd ever heard at church, in

English so the young kids would understand. "Jessie going to build big business. Be her own boss. Make lot of money!"

"Waaaa," they all marveled in unison. Everyone went back to eating, talking, and playing. Mom had declared to the entire church congregation, including the pastor, that I was going to be a business mogul. If she said this in a church, and I played along, was that the same thing as taking an oath on a Bible? Did I solemnly swear to become a business mogul?

The crowd went back to filling up their plates with the potluck dishes. Daniel walked over and held up a mandu. "These are really good. I thought my mom's were the best, but now I don't know. I tried all three of your sauces too. I know I'm in a church, and I'm the pastor's kid and all, but I have to say—they were pretty fucking amazing."

Just as I was actually going to thank him, Ms. Jo grabbed his elbow and said, "You were so little the last time I saw you. Daniel, you're so tall and good-looking now. So different." Ms. Jo had the knack of giving out offensive compliments. She turned to me. "Jessica, you're same age as Daniel?"

"Ne," I answered. "Both twenty-eight."

"You still look same." She patted my hand and walked away.

I muttered, "Okay, what's the deal with people thinking I still look the same?" First Daniel, now her? I'd gone to college. Added reddish-brown highlights to my hair. I didn't have glasses anymore. My braces were gone. I had fewer whiteheads and blackheads, though due to a poor skincare routine they weren't completely gone. Was I just a bigger, older, loser version of my awkward middle school self? WTF Nashville Korean community?

Daniel grinned. "It's a compliment. You look youthful and radiant."

I snorted. "Doesn't feel like a positive thing. Especially if I'm back living at home with my mom and dad."

Another elderly couple, Dr. and Mrs. Han, came by to say hello. "Daniel, Jessie. Nice to see you back home again. Last time we see you—"

I cut in. "Daniel was shorter than me? And he's changed a lot, and I haven't?"

The Hans looked at each other. Dr. Han said, "Yes."

Daniel chuckled while I took a deep breath in and let it out with a sigh. "Seems to be the theme of the day."

Dr. and Mrs. Han smiled a lot, but I knew better than to let that fool me. They were well known at church as being nosy and competitive, and they had a son and daughter right around my age, which made them nosier and more competitive around me. We all grew up knowing one another's accomplishments and failures in a cutthroat environment, and Dr. and Ms. Han thrived in it. I knew to brace myself for the next line of questioning. It was like tick-tick-ticking up a roller-coaster hill, knowing the plunge was moments away.

Mrs. Han said, "Charles is at Wharton for MBA, Chloe

graduating from law school this semester. University of Chicago. Top of class. They both went to Stanford for undergrad."

I remember. You threw them each a party and invited the entire Korean community. I heard their congratulatory cakes had the parents' faces on them, not the kids'.

She looked at me, then Daniel. Then back at me. "Where did you go to undergrad again? I know Daniel went to school in Texas but it wasn't Rice, which is a good school in Texas."

Ouch. I looked over at Daniel, but he was still smiling politely at them. Maybe that was from practice being a pastor's kid. Or because he had a Mercedes trump card in the parking lot.

"I went to NYU. I got into Dartmouth but NYU gave me more money." I didn't bother mentioning the MBA situation.

"Oh."

I knew I'd get this reaction. They knew Dartmouth was an Ivy, but not enough kids around here had gotten into Dartmouth to form a solid opinion of the school.

Then it became a ping-pong volley of questions and answers.

"What was your major?"

Him: "I double majored in math and econ."

Me: "Just econ for me." Since when had I dismissively said *just* econ? I added, "I got departmental honors."

Daniel shot me a surprised look.

Yeah, I pulled out my Korean Draw 4 of Uno cards. Bam. Departmental honors.

He quirked his eyebrow. "Well, I was a Marshall Scholar."

Damn it, Daniel.

And to rub more in my face, he mentioned, "You know that recent news of the MediaMogul merger with BCS? I worked on that deal." It was twelve billion dollars. With his cheeks puffed with food, he still managed to shoot me a smug look.

Dr. and Mrs. Han looked at both of us and nodded. "Charles and Chloe graduate soon. We can tell them Daniel and Jessica can give them good career advisement." But then came the inevitable question from meddling Mrs. Han. "Your mom said you have big Wall Street job. You married too?" The last part was asked in a way that implied that they knew the answer.

Dr. and Mrs. Han had their measuring sticks of success ready to size me up, with jobs and marriage being the two major life markers for Korean Americans in their late twenties.

For a brief second, I considered correcting her about my Wall Street situation but knew better. It also crossed my mind to quickly pull Daniel into a sham of a fake dating relationship, just to get my mom's fellow church members off my back. But it would be too weird, not to mention vomit-inducing, to even think of fake dating Daniel. Dating under a microscope was like the Nashville Korean version of Prince Harry and Meghan Markle, and it would be worse than being single. I'd rather tell Dr. and Mrs. Han that I was unemployed and unhappily unmarried than pretend Daniel was more than just this bad luck charm who always seemed to be in the wrong place at the wrong time by showing up in my life over and over again.

Daniel was still grinning. Probably loving this elderly Korean roast since they were going after me and had forgotten about him. He was definitely my bad luck charm.

Surprisingly, Mom came to my rescue again. Maybe she was getting a lot of these "Why is your daughter here?" questions and was trying to be my crisis management officer.

"Jessie had a big important job on Wall Street," Mom explained in Korean, making a gesture with her hands above her head, implying that I had a high-level position—or that I was taller than everyone I worked with. "Now she is home to work on a big business idea."

"I see, I see," Mrs. Han said. "Time to try the dduk." She walked toward the table with the rice cakes and Dr. Han followed. I let out a huge sigh of relief as my mom turned to a new group of people.

Daniel cocked his head. "You know, it's still unclear to me why you're here. What kind of business are you doing? Are you funding it yourself or looking for VC money?"

Mom really painted me into a corner with this business story. "Oh, I have a bunch of ideas, I'm just figuring out which are the ones I want to start first." I thought back to my spreadsheet, where the only sections thoroughly filled out were my lists of self-help books and dating requirements.

"Well, let me know if you want to bounce any ideas off of me. As you know, I worked in Silicon Valley for a number of years."

Yes, yes, Daniel. I know. We all know, thanks to your Mercedes trophy in the parking lot.

"I have connections, especially in the media and entertainment space."

"Me too, I worked in that sector when I was a banker." *Was. I said was.* "I want to do my own thing, you know, a start-up."

His lips twitched. "Okay. You have my number if you need me for anything. I've got nothing but time. And a lot of insight and experience that you might not have."

No thanks. I had a lot of time too, but now I needed to use it to start a new business. Especially seeing as how my mom promised this to everyone in the house of God.

Daniel used a fork to put rice, bulgogi, spinach, bean sprouts, and my mom's japchae on his plate. He ate the noodles first. "Your mom's japchae is better than my mom's too. Don't tell anyone I said so. Softer noodles, but not clumpy." Japchae was one of my few go-to dishes for my multicultural Friendsgiving potlucks, but my mom's always turned out better. I'd watched her make it the other day and didn't see any ingredients that seemed unique or special. But maybe it was in the boiling of the noodles. Or the brand she bought. Or the length of time of stir-frying. Maybe it was as simple as . . . TLC?

He ate all of the japchae in only a few bites and picked at the rest of the food on his plate. He genuinely liked the noodles and mandu we'd brought. "Do you have any secret ingredients or something? How is this so good? And your mandu sauce—those were so good that there isn't any left!"

This got me thinking. If the church congregation and Daniel liked them, maybe other people would like my sauces too. Aside from staples you could find in any grocery store, such as soy sauce, ginger, sugar, and garlic, most Korean dishes had a base of the same key ingredients, like sesame oil and chili paste. Red chili flakes, rice vinegar, fish sauce, and toasted sesame seeds were also nice-to-haves. And most of the recipes Mom taught me didn't call for ninety-three steps. Her cooking style was so straightforward and simple that it was hard to believe modern fancy Korean cookbooks and online recipes called for so many ingredients and elaborate directions when it could be executed in a simpler way. My mom's kitchen was always a mess after cooking any big meal, but that was cleanup, not the actual cooking part. My sauces were easy to whip up too. Maybe creating some kind of business related to the craft of simple Korean cooking would be something worth looking at more closely. At least in the short term.

My brain neurons were firing so fast I couldn't keep up. I needed to get home so I could jot down all of my new ideas before they flitted away and dissipated into thin air.

As Daniel shoveled a few more spoonfuls of rice and meat into his mouth and threw out his paper plate, I blurted, "I need to go home to work on something."

He asked, while chewing, "What's your primary business idea? Don't think I don't notice you avoiding business questions every time it comes up."

It was true. I was dodging them because I didn't have answers. Because I didn't actually have any concrete ideas. Well, except for the Korean cooking one. Was I an entrepreneur? Is that what you called people who had a bunch of unfinished creative projects or side hustles?

"Top secret" is all I said, and went over to Mom to explain that I needed to run home. She'd just sat down with her group of close friends. My stomach sank when I saw her disappointed face. Riding here together meant she needed to come home too, or I'd need to go home and come all the way back to church to pick her up. The latter, in her mind, was "Bad. Waste gas." No one in the congregation lived close to us. This group here was a Franklin crowd, not an Antioch one.

Daniel's dad, the pastor, clapped his hands together. "Oh, Mrs. Kim, you should come home with us! We have a new coffee cake from Whole Foods. We buy this morning."

Getting an invitation to the pastor's house was an honor, not to be taken lightly by the Korean church congregation, but Mom did that thing that Koreans do where they say no first.

"It's too much of a bother," she said, tsk-tsking and shaking her head.

Daniel's mom insisted. "The cake is fresh. We can have tea that Daniel brought from London."

"No, no . . . are you sure?" Mom asked in Korean.

The pastor and his wife nodded vigorously. It was settled. I'd hightail it out of here and get to work. Mom would go to the pastor's home, and I'd pick her up later. We said goodbyes, and I took the Camry home.

***

Our neighbor Mr. Fowler had his hedge trimmer at eardrum-bursting decibels just a few feet away from my window. Mom and Dad didn't believe in double-paned windows out in the suburbs. They said I needed that kind of thing in NYC but not here. "Too expensive," they said. But they didn't take into account that Mr. Fowler would retire and take on yardwork and landscaping as his new full-time hobby.

The blank spreadsheet taunted me, with all those empty cells, intimidating me to the point of brain freeze. Why did I rush home for this? Looking for something else to distract me, my gaze swept across my desk. My nonfiction business and female empowerment books had piled up, with *Lean In* and *Nice Girls Don't Get the Corner Office* still in pristine, unread condition. A few library books were on the top of the stack, Jack Welch's *Winning* plus one by Warren Buffett. As a sort of joke, I also checked out Sun Tzu's *The Art of War*, as a reference to thumb through to help me think more strategically. Out of all the books there, this one, with the striking red cover, was the only one I felt inclined to examine more closely.

The pages were well worn; clearly readers before me hadn't just thumbed through it or checked it out as a sort-of joke. Someone had written microscopic notes on many of the pages, as if the book were their own and not owned by the library system of Antioch, Tennessee. The handwriting was neat, bold, somewhat old-fashioned. Someone with much more discipline than I had. Someone who really wanted to know the art of war. Or maybe more accurately, someone who wanted to know the art of victory.

There were only a few Sun Tzu quotes that warranted underlines and stars from the anonymous notetaker:

> *"In the midst of chaos, there is also opportunity."*
> *"To know your Enemy, you must become your Enemy."*
> *"Know yourself and you will win all battles."*

Sun Tzu was pretty impressive; he'd make a good TED Talk speaker. This was A+ motivational content.

There were other highlighted quotes, covering the section in a deteriorated yellow that could at best be described as "depressing marigold": *"Appear weak when you are strong, and strong when you are weak."*

Sun Tzu, my friend, you're way too complicated for me. How would I apply this to my life? Maybe this wasn't the most useful self-help book after all. Turns out it was a book about actually killing people.

I needed a break from this. Or another diversion. In the rhinestone-encrusted picture frame, Dolly Parton gave me a reassuring smile. *You can do it, Jessie.*

A hot pink envelope caught my eye in the middle of a pile of forwarded mail Mom had stacked on a nearby chair. Using a letter opener that one of Mom's friends got me for my high school graduation ten years ago, I opened the envelope.

A baby shower for my high school friend Celeste. A graduation photo of us sat on my desk—a daily reminder to get in touch with her again, but I still hadn't. She lived nearby and had mailed this to my apartment in NYC, probably not expecting a reply.

JOIN US FOR A DOUGHNUTS AND DIAPERS BABY SHOWER
TO CELEBRATE OUR FAVE NEIGHBOR AND MAMA-TO-BE.
YOU BRING THE DIAPERS AND WIPES, WE'LL BRING A
GENDER-REVEAL DOUGHNUT CAKE AND DECAF COFFEE
(CAFFEINATED AVAILABLE TOO, PLUS BOOZE).

I'd never seen a doughnut gender reveal and had no idea how to even comprehend how that could work. Would it be colored dough? Blue or pink cream on the inside? Little plastic babies baked inside? There had been so much discourse around gender the past few years, I didn't know revealing gender at a party was something people still did. Or maybe it was just that I'd worked in banking so long that all the women I knew didn't have kids and hadn't been to any baby showers.

But back to Celeste. We'd texted a few times since college, to wish each other happy birthdays. I hadn't actually spoken with her in more than five years. Celeste had gotten married to her high school sweetheart the summer after graduation. She'd never left Nashville. We used to be really good friends in high school and started to lose touch in college, but she was also one of those friends who knew you so well that even as years passed by, when you picked up the phone to call or text, you had a conversation like you'd never spent any time apart. She knew all about my parents' high bar of expectations and my struggling hard to high jump to it, let alone over it. After college, our lives split off into two completely different paths: I went to Wall Street for a big, flashy career and she studied for a master of fine arts but quit when she got pregnant. She was on baby number two now. Or maybe three. Sadly, I'd lost count.

And now I had to RSVP to someone named Keileigh-Leigh by today.

I was torn. Yes, I wanted to be a good friend to Celeste and go to her baby shower. I'd apparently missed her other ones.

But I wouldn't know anyone there.

I also needed to make friends here, in this city I'd left ten years ago.

But would I be able to handle that she'd moved on, gotten married, and created a family, and I was back home with nothing to show for myself?

Doughnuts.

I RSVP'd yes and ordered two large packs of diapers for two-hour delivery, newborn and 3–6 months. It reminded me that I hadn't visited the coffee shop yet and of Flora, the grocery delivery friend I'd made. I needed to do that soon. Besides Celeste, she was my only friend prospect.

Keileigh-Leigh replied right away. *YASSSS THANK YOU!!!!!!!!!! We can't wait to meet you!!!!!!!!!!* Ten exclamation points, each time. I'd already painted a picture in my head of this exuberant and gregarious hostess. I pictured Mr. Fowler's loud hedge trimmer, but in human form. Was it poor form to un-RSVP?

For the next hour I focused on my spreadsheet, jotting down Korean cooking and food-related business ideas, each with its own set of pros and cons.

In my previous role, I'd been trained to look at the overall state of the economy and then the strength of a specific industry before concentrating on potential company performance, using public data and purchased research to evaluate the value of a stock or any other type of security. But this was different, because where I'd worked we dealt only with large companies and had lots of financial data to analyze. Here, looking at business potential for a company or idea that hadn't been created yet, I had to pull all these numbers and projections out of my ass. Sure, at my old job, I had to do some guesswork, but this was a different level of made-up bullshit. It was hard to stomach for someone like me who was quant-y and loved numbers. Numbers were so specific. I liked specificity.

I'd gotten as far as writing out my jumble of ideas into a nice, sizable list when my phone buzzed. Mom was ready for a pickup. Or, in her words, "Where are you? I'm waiting."

Daniel's parents lived on the same cul-de-sac as they had back when I was in middle school, but they'd bought a smaller house a few doors down. Since both of their boys had moved out, it made sense.

Daniel greeted me at the door. He scooched aside to let me pass while pointing to his earbuds, the universal sign of "I'm on the phone." Because the architect was the same for all of these houses, entering the Chois' residence felt eerily familiar. Same windows, walls, and carpet. Even the same permeating smell of sesame oil and scallions. The first-floor layout was nearly identical too. It didn't help that they'd hung up all of Daniel's and his older brother's old class photos and awards in the main hallway. I was in a Choi boy time capsule.

The only new additions to the wall of accomplishments were their adult accolades. Neither of the boys played sports after high school, but his older brother's medical school acceptance to UCLA was custom-framed, as was Daniel's Marshall Scholar letter. Damn, I'd hoped he was lying about that one.

It really was more impressive than anything I'd ever accomplished. Even when I was at my peak working at Hamilton Cooper, I didn't have anything like "Marshall Scholar" to add to my résumé to make me stand out. And he would always be able to say he was a Marshall Scholar, even when he was, like, a hundred years old, whereas my banking glory days were as good as over at the ripe old age of twenty-eight. Was this what Sun Tzu was going on about, appearing strong when I was weak? Because right now, as I walked down my Korean wall of shame, I felt nothing but unshakable and overwhelming inadequacy.

Mom and Daniel's parents were seated around the kitchen table, each of them with a cup of tea and a small plate of Pepperidge Farm cookies. A half loaf of coffee cake encased in plastic wrap was placed in the middle, like a holiday centerpiece. Everyone stopped talking when I entered the room.

Pastor Choi said, "Would you like some cookie? Your umma was just telling us about your big Wall Street job." Funny, Mom had never showed interest in my work before, but now it was all she seemed to talk about. Maybe it was overcompensating for the fact that I'd been canned and she was coping by ignoring that fact completely and exaggerating my importance.

Daniel pulled his pods from his ears. "Want a quick tour of the house while they finish up?"

I nodded. Anything to avoid the inevitable question, "Where are you working now?"

I'd pretty much seen everything downstairs: the foyer, kitchen, and living room. The wood creaked under our weight as we walked up the beige carpeted stairs, to the point where the stress on the stairs made it feel like they might cave in. He turned and smiled. "You get used to the sound. Plus, there are spots on the staircase that don't squeak. Part of the fun is figuring out how to get downstairs and sneak out without making a sound."

To the right, a dim bedroom with a simple wooden twin bed. No wall decor other than a few bookshelves and a desk. He explained, "That's my room, for now. Luckily my brother's not coming home anytime soon so we don't have to share."

A few steps down to the left, the master bedroom. Off-white walls. Popcorn ceiling circa 1970. Shag carpet and an old ceiling fan. Daniel turned the knob on the wall to make the fan spin.

"I like how this is a tour highlight. Do the lights clap on and off?" I joked.

He chuckled. "I'll add that to my list of home projects."

I followed him down the hall. Straight ahead, a very beige bathroom. To my right, a room with the door closed.

"What's in there?"

"It's my parents' home office. And exercise room. And storage."

I turned the brass knob and peered in. The lights flicked on, revealing a square room painted light pink. A pastel zoo animal border lined the top of all four walls. Randomly scattered baby monkey and banana decals had faded with age.

"Wait, was this a nursery?" A close examination of the power outlets revealed plug covers and light switches decorated with cartoon zebras and elephants. But how did I miss the baby animal mobile where the ceiling fan should have been?

With the same type of switch that powered the fan in the master bedroom, this one turned on the rotating mobile in different speeds. It rotated above my head, playing "Old MacDonald Had a Farm" in an old-timey, music-box-tinkering tune. Very disturbing, yet soothing.

I laughed uncomfortably as Daniel shrugged. "I don't even notice how weird this room is anymore, especially for my parents. They haven't mentioned painting it or anything. My guess is it's all staying."

I refrained from making any "saving the room for future grandchildren" quips. Lord knows he probably hated those types of comments as much as I did.

We both stared at the mobile going around and around. "This is surprisingly calming, maybe I should switch bedrooms."

I barked out a laugh and he smiled. It was the friendliest we'd been, ever. No competing. No quips. Just us.

He stepped back to the wall and turned the dial to the right. "Watch this," he said. The mobile picked up speed, flinging the animals outward like the swing ride at Six Flags. It picked up enough wind to make his front hair blow into his eyes. Did guys have bangs? Because if they did, Daniel's bangs were flapping in the wind. He looked like a smiling Saint Bernard.

My gaze traveled from his face to his shoulders, chest, and belt. All this time I'd thought of Daniel as an obnoxious middle school kid. It didn't register until now that he'd grown into this strong, strapping guy with a wry sense of humor.

Then I saw his dollar sign belt buckle.

Revolting.

He commented, "You jealous of my belt? My friends bought it for me when I went on sabbatical. I'm embarrassed to say that it's heavy, like a door knocker."

My cheeks flushed. He'd just caught me hypnotically staring at his hideous belt buckle, which of course was just a couple inches above—

"TIME TO SAY GOODBYE, DANIEL!" Daniel's mom shouted up the stairs, rattling the mobile. The acoustics were good in this house. Or really bad, depending on how you looked at it, if sound traveled far like that.

He turned off the light and gestured. "After you." We were greeted at the bottom of the stairwell by the Choi parents and my mom, who was putting on her shoes.

Our parents bowed to one another as Daniel and I gave each other a small wave.

"Thanks for the tour. See you around," I said and looked away, my face still hot from getting caught staring at his nether regions.

I opened the door and in the dark, nearly tripped over a package on his top porch step. “You have a late-night delivery. A big, lawsuit box.”

Daniel groaned. “These delivery guys never make it to the door, they leave the packages by the mailbox, or on the bottom of the steps, or at the top. And someone could break their neck falling over them.”

He maneuvered around my mom and me to pick it up. “It’s a new meal kit I’m trying out. A keto one.”

Behind us, his dad chimed in, “Daniel’s company help this meal business sell to BIG company.” He opened his arms fully to show the immensity of the deal. It was, like, dollar-sign-belt-buckle big. “Billion-dollar deal.”

Daniel scoffed as he set the box down inside the doorway. “Stop exaggerating, Dad. It was only ninety million.”

Still.

The meal-kit company was MealMakr and they were known for simple ingredients and high customization. I’d bought a monthly subscription after clicking on an Instagram ad back when I was fooling myself in NYC, thinking I’d stop buying takeout if I had more easy-to-make meals in my fridge. I tried boxes of everything. Organic prechopped and presliced ones. Grab-and-bake meals from supermarket chains. Celebrity-endorsed dinner kits.

Two months and five hundred dollars later, I’d proved my theory incorrect. I made about two weeks of meals before getting sick of the options. Backlogged with meal-kit deliveries with large portion sizes, I suddenly had no fridge space. I immediately canceled the subscriptions, but during those weeks I amassed a ton of waste and lots of regret.

Mom turned to me. "Maybe you should try cook more at home."

"I do cook. A lot." Okay, maybe only once every other day, and that was just for the purposes of creating and testing recipes for potential content. Nothing dinner-worthy.

"Bowl of Cap'n Crunch and milk not count. Cook big meal like Daniel. Give me a rest." She and the Choi parents exchanged exasperated looks. *Can you believe these grown children?*

I looked at the side of the box, where enormous "Beef pot roast" and "Southwestern chicken" glossy stickers caught my eye. "Do you like these flavors?" They seemed kind of bland to me. But then again, the whole point of these meal kits was to appeal to the masses.

Daniel shrugged. "It's all the same stuff every week, not much variety. I end up switching between meal kits because I get bored."

Thinking back to my failed meal-kit days, that was part of the problem. I ate a week of it and got bored. I wanted a little more zing, zest, or heat.

An idea popped into my head, nearly knocking me over with excitement. I looked at Daniel and grinned.

"What?" he asked, sensing my immediate improvement in mood. "You actually look happy."

"I need to get home. I think I've got my business idea!"

He scratched his nose and whispered, "Is it a secret or can you tell me?"

I couldn't get the smile off my face. "Sure. But don't tell anyone, I don't want to jinx it. I have you to thank too."

He lifted an eyebrow and smiled.

"I'm going to do cooking videos about how to hack your meal kit." My voice grew louder with each word. I lowered it to a hush. "Not just this one, I'm going to take all the popular meal kits and come up with ideas on how to Koreanize them. Maybe even create some meal-kit supplements too, like mixes and sauces."

He nodded. "There's definitely a market for it. Me, for example. And pretty much anyone who is sick of the same old shit every week."

It was simple. Easy to get off the ground. And I had all the expertise I needed.

It was perfect. And I couldn't wait to get started.

Chapter Seven

My phone buzzed at the worst time, during my third attempt at parallel parking on a busy street.

Alice: *BISHHHHH! WE. ARE. HERE!!!*

Charlie and Alice weren't supposed to come until later that evening. If anything, I assumed they wouldn't even bother getting in touch with me until they'd settled into their fancy rooms for a few hours at the Union Station Hotel. It wasn't even lunchtime.

Me: *Wow! Welcome to Music City USA!*

Charlie: *We took an earlier flight. Already dropped off our stuff. Where can we meet you?*

I'd just arrived at Falling Off the Red Wagon on Edmondson Pike, the half bar, half coffee shop where Flora, the grocery delivery grad school economist, had said she sometimes worked as a barista. It had great reviews on Yelp. Most important, there were power outlets at every table, which made working while drinking coffee much easier. And they served sandwiches and pastries that weren't flaky, which was a ridiculous thing to point out, but I'd always suspected it was something café owners maybe did on purpose to punish people who were there to work for a long stretch. A keyboard covered in a layer of flaky crumbs was the last thing anyone needed while trying to work.

Added bonus: there was no lawn trimming or mowing action by an overzealous elderly neighbor who was hard of hearing.

The aroma of freshly brewed coffee and ground espresso beans greeted me as I walked through the door. The Red Wagon had a woody, earthy warmth that chain coffee shops I frequented in NYC lacked. The café had a neighborhood feel, with old-timey decor and some country music paraphernalia on the walls, like costumes from an old show called *Hee Haw*, old photos of a younger Earl Scruggs playing the banjo, and some postcards sent to the café owner by Garth Brooks, Lonestar, Taylor Swift, and my idol, Dolly Parton herself. I already knew the second I stepped foot inside that I'd be back again.

The hand-lettered chalkboard menu included nearly fifty types of coffee and espresso drinks. The barista, with electric blue hair tips and fierce black lipstick, smiled at me as I tried to decipher the hieroglyphic menu. She tried to help but ended up confusing me more. "As you can see, we have a wide range in FABA: flavor, aroma, body, and acidity. If you tell me your preferences, I can give you some recommendations."

"Uh, do you have regular iced coffee?"

She nodded. "Yes, we just made some this morning, but we have only one kind. As far as FABA goes, it's sort of middle-of-the-road with flavor, aroma, body, and acidity."

One kind of iced coffee? It sounded plain and perfect. I ordered my drink and selected a carrot ginger muffin from under a heavy glass dome on the counter. "That's the last of our best-sellers!"

While inserting my credit card into the payment device, I asked, "Is Flora going to be here today?"

She grinned. "J'adore Flor? I think she's got a shift today, not sure when though. Someone got sick, so everyone's schedules shuffled, including mine. Today was supposed to be my day off." Sliding the iced coffee over to me, she added, "You won't miss her if she comes in though. Trust me."

While I was waiting for my muffin, the bell on the door jangled. Flora stormed in, swearing like a sailor. "Shit, how many times do I have to tell those goddamned assholes on the corner to stop it with the stupid catcalling and whistles?" She turned around and shouted back outside, "Y'all are creeps and you're scaring away our clients. I'm calling the cops."

A group of four guys walked by the door, peering in. One of them yelled back, "You're missing out on THIS." He grabbed his crotch as the other guys laughed. What made guys do that? Was it in their minds . . . sexy? Funny, in a fart joke sort of way? It's not like women do anything remotely similar. We don't grab our boobs after making a lewd statement. At least not while sober.

He spit on the sidewalk and the other guys followed suit. Another thing I didn't understand about men: gratuitous spitting in shared-use areas. Even when baseball players did it on mounds, I'd assumed it was chewing tobacco related. Women would never do that either, publicly or privately. Polling any woman in the entire world, you'd be told spitting like that is disgusting and we'd never do it, except when we had a hair stuck in our mouth. Did guys have overacting salivary glands versus women? Or were some guys just plain nasty?

The guys continued to walk down the sidewalk, but only after they pretended to dry hump the café window.

Thank you, nasty gentlemen, for answering my question.

Flora pulled her black curly hair into a ponytail and pushed through the EMPLOYEES MUST WASH HANDS! door in the back before I had a chance to reintroduce myself. After settling down in an area near the restrooms, I messaged Alice and Charlie, explaining I was working at a coffee shop near my house, and then opened my spreadsheet, which had grown exponentially in file size. I'd stayed up until three A.M. running calculations of my meal-kit ideas that I'd nearly overanalyzed, almost to the point of being sick of the whole thing.

A chair at my table squeaked. Startled by the sudden noise, I looked up from my screen and was pleasantly surprised to see

Flora's smiling face. "Hey stranger. You must have the weirdest impression of me. Well, first from that day I threw groceries through your window and now, from yelling at those assholes. I don't even understand how they have time to sit around doing nothing except making trouble." She paused. "Shit, I sound like one of those old people who complain about 'kids these days,' but seriously . . . *Kids these days*." She rolled her eyes and fell back into the wooden chair with a thump.

I saved my spreadsheet and closed my laptop. "I'd been meaning to come by since we met. The coffee's good here by the way. And so was your entertainment." The group of young men were going by the door again from the other direction and I gestured toward them. The same guy thrust his pelvis at me as the other guys laughed again.

Flora's bronze eyes darkened and narrowed. "What's messed up is I know a little about them. They're not tough guys. A few of those kids go to this prep school a few blocks away. I bet their parents are professors or doctors at Vanderbilt. And they're acting up to impress one another. Annoying high school kids." She checked her watch. "Shit, I gotta work. Good seeing you again." She smiled and walked to the counter, where she recounted her full day to her blue-haired coworker.

One thing I liked about Flora was that she hadn't asked me about my job. Or my past. She genuinely didn't care. This was so refreshing and so different from my mom's church crowd and my former friends and acquaintances in NYC, where everyone wanted to know three things about you right off the bat: what job you had, where you went to school, and where you vacationed. The ultimate rat race at my firm was the "What are you going to do with your bonus?" comparison game.

Just as I'd finished balancing my budget, the bell above the door tinkled as Alice and Charlie burst in like a gust of heavy wind on a frigid winter day. They looked like aliens who had landed on an unfamiliar planet. Though Alice had an understated, expensive look that blended in at the office, with everything she wore being black and an array of grays (charcoal, heather, smoke), in this coffee shop she stood out like a sore black-and-gray thumb. Charlie was no better, with his Burberry button-down shirt, khakis, and Italian leather loafers.

Warmth flooded over me as I jumped to my feet and hugged them. Maybe banking wasn't all that bad if I ended up with friends like these.

Both of their phones buzzed at the same time, and they silenced them, apologizing for the nonstop notifications. Charlie said with a sigh, "You know how it is. All work and no play."

Alice plopped down in Flora's old seat. "I'm starving! I'm still not over my jetlag from London." Charlie and I got to do some travel for work, but Alice was the true jetsetter and road warrior in the group. No doubt she'd gotten the plane tickets and hotel with all of her AmEx points. Probably paid for Charlie's airfare and hotel too. Alice was extremely generous. Except when it came to compliments.

"Jess, didn't we agree to take the town by storm? How can you do that in that orange shorts jumpsuit? You look like you escaped from a prison ward and kept the outfit." She smirked and took a spontaneous photo of Charlie and me.

I teased back, "It's an on-trend romper, and I prefer it to your black-on-black grim reaper leisurewear, thank you very much."

Charlie left us to talk about their flight as he walked around the perimeter of the café. He reported back with his findings. "Did you see that there's something called a hustle wall in the back?"

Alice asked, "A what wall?"

"Hustle wall. It's like the opposite of a wall of shame. People post their side hustles and help one another by either finding other likeminded people or customers looking for services. It's pretty cool."

I joked, "Did you see any other ex-bankers side hustling? Someone who has no skills other than building Excel macros and financial models with little to no supervision?"

"No, but I did see this, which might be interesting." He handed me a small piece of paper that he'd torn off a flyer. "It's a local Asian American entrepreneur group. They're meeting here tonight. I mean, those are your people, right?"

"You mean Asians?" I asked sarcastically.

"Noooo, entrepreneurs." He rolled his eyes at me. "I guess it makes sense though, we're near Owen, Vanderbilt's business school. Probably a decent-size entrepreneurial-minded community here. I just never thought of Nashville as being an Asian American hotbed for business visionaries. Maybe Atlanta, but not here."

"Me either." The funny thing about all the entrepreneur talk was that everyone was associating me with that community, even me, and I didn't actually know if I had a burning desire deep within me to start a business. Didn't people know they wanted to have their own company someday, and desperately want to be their own boss? Was it in their DNA, this yearning, entrepreneurial grit? I'd been perfectly content with being a well-paid cog in the money wheel at Hamilton Cooper. Well, reasonably content. There were times I'd drift into a daydream in meetings, fantasizing about retiring early, about ripping up all the printed, collated PowerPoint slides and yelling, "Fuck this shit," and giving my notice. But nothing had propelled me into action.

I also didn't quit on my own terms. Could I be an entrepreneur, building a company from the ground up, without leadership ability? Coming up with an idea was one part of entrepreneurship, and so was getting that idea off the ground through operationalizing it. But without leadership to build and grow the business, it would go nowhere. Not even Sun Tzu could argue with that.

That virtual layoff had really shaken my self-confidence. It had been officially documented that I didn't have any leadership skills, and I'd never be able to work at Hamilton Cooper again.

Even though there was so much dead weight at that company, enough senior people had given input to get me ousted. They say business isn't personal, but in my case, it was.

I folded the slip of paper and stuck it in my pocket. My Asian entrepreneur brethren might be revisited another time, just not today. Maybe once I got a few new cooking videos under my belt and could figure out how to monetize my content as I gained followers. My YouTube channel had twelve thousand subscribers: most were acquired a long time ago when I posted cooking videos from my dorm kitchen. Apparently, a lot of college kids were interested in cheap meal ideas as an alternative to dining hall slop. My account had been neglected for a few years but my "I'm back" video I posted the prior week had gotten new followers and lots of engagement. I still had an audience, even though my channel had been dormant for so long. Before that, the latest content I'd posted was a million eons ago in YouTube years, and it was just a simple recording of me apologizing to my followers for not posting anything new and swearing I'd do better. I didn't keep that promise back then, but I would make amends now. Perhaps some of those local Asian American entrepreneurs could provide me with tips.

"So tell me about what you've done since you left New York. Are you eating better? Any new exercise regimens? Taking any classes?" Alice asked.

Welllll . . . no, no, and no. How could I explain to go-getter Alice that I'd been holed up in my bedroom alternating between working on my master spreadsheet and binge-watching old episodes of *Top Chef*, *Cake Wars*, and *Nailed It!*, while simultaneously binge-drinking Diet Dr Pepper and binge-eating Korean shrimp chips and mochi ice cream balls? That wasn't the type of thing Alice did or had ever thought of doing. She wouldn't understand.

Flora came by to bus my table and winked at me. "Your girl here has been so busy. Keeps me company here on my slow days. We have a group of friends who go out a lot and we're lucky when she joins us."

Alice cocked her head like a bird. "Really? I imagined her being a recluse type."

Flora looked at me and smiled. A "you tried your best" smile a kindergarten teacher gives one of their kids who always writes their *s*'s backward. Flora was trying her best to make me look less loser-like, and I appreciated it so much.

Alice wasn't buying it. "Where do you all go? Maybe we can hang out tonight and you can take us to your favorite place."

Of all people, Charlie came to my rescue. "I thought she was going to the Asian American entrepreneur thing this evening."

I cleared my throat. "Yes, I'm going to that. But maybe I can join you tomorrow night. Um, I'll think of somewhere we can go."

Flora chimed in, "Didn't you say you wanted to take them to that Dolly Parton–themed rooftop bar?"

I had no idea there was a Dolly Parton–themed rooftop bar.

"Yes!" Alice yelled. "That. Sounds. AMAZING!"

"Definitely!" Charlie agreed. "I read about it in *The Times*."

Flora motioned for me to come follow her to the counter. "You can google the address. Tell the person at the door you know me. He'll let you in; he lives down the hall from me and we hook up sometimes. And don't wear that tangerine outfit to the bar. Oh, one more thing."

I whispered, "You saved my ass in front of my friends. I owe you big! What do you need?"

She laughed. "I need you to tell me your name. I remember your face but forgot your name."

I held out my hand. "I'm Jess Kim. Your loyal, new best friend."

Chapter Eight

The Asian American entrepreneur meeting was a bunch of college-aged and freshly minted MBA dudes, and me.

Having worked on Wall Street for so long I was used to all-male environments, but what I wasn't expecting was that they'd all know one another intimately, making me an outsider. So much of an outsider that when I walked into the coffee shop for the second time that day, all of the conversation fell to silence as one of them asked me, "Are you sure you have the right place? This is a closed business meeting."

"Is this the Asian American entrepreneur gathering? Was I supposed to RSVP?" I'd taken Charlie's word for it and hadn't read the actual posted flyer myself. Maybe this was more exclusive than I'd thought.

At night, with minimal lighting overhead, the coffee shop looked considerably less warm and friendly. The music was off and the wall art and tall potted plants cast eerie shadows around the room.

"Haunted" was a more appropriate word. Visually, the shop's dimness was a huge contrast to the inviting, earthy coffee scent still permeating the air.

A tall, lanky guy came over to me and shook my hand. "Will You."

"Will I? Will I what?"

He laughed. "No, that's my name. Will. You. Honestly, it causes confusion one hundred percent of the time, I should just go by William or Bill."

I smiled. "I think Bill You would make people think they owed you money." He had a slight southern accent and stick-straight black hair that was fuzzy from not being gelled or moussed. I liked Will You. Very endearing and friendly.

Will brought me to the larger group, where most of them were chattering about sports. A lot of Predators, Lakers, and Yankees fans. And golf lovers. Not too different from my Wall Street world. I could navigate this.

He shrugged. "We usually chat about sports and families before the meeting officially starts. Then we get down to business. Literally." He snorted at his own nerdy joke, which made me laugh. Most of these guys looked around my age, maybe a little younger than me. More than half of them wore wedding rings.

I put my bag down on the chair next to me. "I just moved here from New York, although I was born and raised here. Happy to join you all and meet new people."

He pulled a chair from one of the nearby tables and placed it by my feet. "We don't have an official name, it's more an informal gathering with a loose agenda. About twenty of us were in the local chapter of SBA and thought we'd form our own accountability group." When I didn't respond right away, he added, "Small Business Association. S-B-A. It's a pretty big deal here."

A shorter, stockier, muscular guy who kind of looked like a younger version of my dad walked up to me to introduce himself. "Paul Kang," he said.

"Jess Kim." We shook, and it was the first time I'd met anyone who had a hand that could also be described as short and stocky.

"We just had another new member come last week too. We've gained more members thanks to Will. He's our marketing guy." He slapped Will's back, making him cough and flinch.

Paul said, "Thanks for coming. And if you'll excuse me, I need to call the meeting to order."

We all took seats. While the crowd settled, he put another chair next to me. "In case anyone shows up late."

Sure enough, the door jangled as it opened and closed. We

were all looking at Paul as he went over the ground rules of the group: to respect who is speaking by listening and providing feedback only if asked.

"Is this seat taken?" The chair beside me was pulled back.

"No," I said.

I looked up and saw Daniel Choi. "I mean yes."

"Wait, Jess? Seriously? Are you stalking me?" His eyes glinted with amusement as I rolled mine.

"I am certainly *not* stalking you. And I could ask the same thing. Why are you everywhere? This is like a bad nineties slapstick comedy, like *Groundhog Day*, but worse. Also, you need to listen and stop talking," I whisper-hissed.

Paul stopped speaking and looked at Daniel and me. Ooooh, Daniel was going to get in trouble.

"My man!" Paul came over and slapped my nemesis on the back. Daniel took the hit in stride and returned with a hearty handshake plus arm grab. "You made it! Everyone, we have our very own celebrity Silicon Valley VC guy here, Daniel Choi! You should subscribe to his gaming channels on YouTube, Discord, and Twitch, he's a real pro! He'll be in town awhile and will be offering advice to anyone who wants it." He gestured to the chair by my side. "I put out an extra seat, right next to Joanna."

"Jessie," I corrected.

"Yes. Jessie. I think you two would get along." He winked at Daniel.

What the hell was this, the dude version of Korean meddling ajummas? Was this even really a business accountability group, or some covert, creepy matchmaking service?

Still standing, Daniel shifted from leaning right to leaning left. He cleared his throat. "Looks like no one else is coming. Okay to sit here now?"

I waved at the wooden chair but kept my eyes fixed on Paul.

Daniel pulled off his crossbody messenger bag and put it between our chairs. "I'm surprised to see you here."

"It looks like you and Paul are good buddies," I muttered.

"Paul's an elder at my dad's church. A couple of other guys here too. They graduated from Vandy and stayed in Nashville to raise families. They might know your mom, actually."

My stomach sank. I had no idea what kind of impression my mom left on people other than what I'd witnessed at the potluck. If it was anything like that, it didn't look good. I pictured Mom putting flyers under windshield wipers on all the cars in the church parking lot, advertising that I was available to date and suitable for marriage. I could also imagine Dad being the lookout.

Will stood up as Paul took his seat up front. "If anyone would like to share what you've been working on, we can add it to our spreadsheet."

The lights dimmed and the projector clicked on. On the white wall to the left of Will, a spreadsheet appeared, with color-coded cells and lots of worksheet tabs. Okay, maybe these were my people after all.

Will looked at me and nodded. "Everyone, we have a new visitor, Jess Kim. She moved here from New York. For her benefit and as a refresher for everyone, I'll just go over this accountability chart so you know what it is." He toggled between worksheets. "We have our broader group broken out into three categories—start-ups in tech, e-commerce, and brick and mortar. When we split up into small groups in a few minutes, we'll meet with our respective peers and discuss what the highlights and lowlights have been this week. We solicit advice from others in the group if that's what you're seeking. Not trying to put you on the spot, but it's perfectly fine to just listen in the first week, so you don't have to participate if you don't want to, okay?"

Before I knew it, after a lively discussion about funding and work-life balance, thirty minutes had flown by and it was time to circle up with the small groups. For my meal-kit business, I didn't know which faction to join: Did it count as "tech" because of the cooking videos, or "e-commerce" because I would maybe want to sell products someday too? I asked Paul which one I should choose if my business idea wasn't fully formed but straddled two categories. I was purposefully vague about specifics, because at Hamilton Cooper, people would take ideas and offer them as their own to win deals and get promoted. This group seemed genuinely helpful though, and they didn't look like the kind of crowd who'd be interested in hacking meal kits anyway. One, because it wasn't an easily scalable idea, and two, this bunch of dudes looked like grilling guys, not Iron Chef–types. Hell, it was hard to believe I'd be into meal-kit hacks, if you'd ever looked in my fridge anytime during the last seven years.

Paul shrugged. "I'd say go with either what you think will be the core moneymaking component of your business or what will result in faster growth, depending on what your goals are. It's only my opinion though. As you can see"—he waved his hands across the room—"there are lots of people here who might think otherwise."

Daniel stood from his chair and pointed his body in the direction of the e-commerce group. Because of that, I pivoted on my heel and walked the opposite way, joining the tech group instead, and was greeted by a small group of guys who were mostly former Silicon Valley and Silicon Beach transplants. Paul had a few different graphic design app ideas he was thinking through and wanted to share his progress with everyone. An older guy wanted to make plug-ins for videoconferencing tools and had personal connections at all the big tech companies. The guy next to me had an idea that would use Google Maps technology: an app for foodies that incorporated Zagat, Michelin Guide, and NYT food critic restaurant recommendations and offered suggestions based on your culinary preferences and geographical location. Appropriately, the app was called Foodsnob, and it was an idea I wish I'd thought of first because I loved it so much.

Being the newest attendee in the group, I was asked to give a quick rundown of my bio. They sat up attentively while I talked about my background in finance. After vaguely explaining my shift from banking to entrepreneurship, I paused to take questions.

One guy said, "Wow, I had a buddy who was rejected from Hamilton Cooper, that's a great company. I heard it's tougher than Goldman. I bet you have some horror stories."

Oh boy, did I. How could I even narrow them down?

Like how just a few months ago when my group went to dinner with an older male client who talked about the Red Sox for over an hour. He noticed me picking at my steak and said, "Look at me prattling on and on about this. She wouldn't know about team sports like baseball or football." When I fired back with "I follow women's pro soccer and my apartment roommate is a former NCAA volleyball athlete," he laughed and said, "Well, we all know neither of those are real team sports," and squeezed my hand. My mouth opened, ready to raise hell, but my managing director grabbed my *other* hand and muttered under his breath so only I could hear, "Gravitas."

Gravitas. An ancient Roman virtue that denoted seriousness, restraint, and dignity. It had come up more than once in my performance reviews and was something I'd tried to research in my dozens of self-help business books and couldn't quite wrap my head around it. Gravitas seemed to be a bullshit quality that men had at Hamilton Cooper, but not women. Banker bros with authority and presence, who could command the boardroom but also whoop up laughs with male clients. Others took notice of who had gravitas. They got promoted faster. They got bigger bonuses. When people with gravitas spoke, others shut up and listened. But we all knew that they weren't always the smartest or the most diligent or most honest.

Screw *gravitas*.

I closed my eyes and tried to push those old work memories from my mind. I was here to start a new career, not to rehash past events. This was an opportunity to put my previous life behind me and start all over again with a new group of people. Except for Daniel, who was a visible reminder that I couldn't fully reinvent myself. Each time I saw Daniel, he reminded me of past self-consciousness and failures.

I gritted my teeth into a semblance of a smile. "Hamilton Cooper was a grind. And honestly, I'm glad I left. But I'd love to tell you about my business idea, maybe you have some thoughts or suggestions on my approach." Fear had kept my percolating ideas close to my chest, but I needed to learn how to network with other nonbankers and maybe run things by people who might see something I missed. Maybe it was time to unveil my business pitch to someone other than my Dolly Parton photo.

I started with my elevator pitch. "Who isn't tired of eating the same old thing every week? I subscribe to the bestselling dinner prep deliveries, like Chef's Apron, Hearthbasket, and

Little Potato, and make videos with two-minute hacks on how you can take some supplementary sauces, condiments, and spices to add more variety to meals, focusing on Korean cuisine primarily."

Paul nodded along, as did the others. "Do you already have a platform?"

"Sort of, but it's from a while ago. Like the first video is nearly ten years old, but it's still relevant. During college and in my early years of banking, I made videos about quick cooking ideas for people on the go. They were dinner hacks, like packaged ramen with store-bought sliced fish cake, frozen spinach, and cracked egg. Or making lettuce wraps with plain meatballs and kimchi. I even used to show off my kitchen skills, like draining macaroni and noodles with no colander. I have some new video ideas I want to record soon. The one I'm most excited about is called 'Five-Ingredient Kimchi Chigae.' After I analyze the top cooking videos and read some books about business strategy, I'll make my video series about meal-kit hacks."

Paul nodded. "As a working professional, I would totally watch your videos. We do a lot of takeout because we get bored with the same pasta, chicken, and beef meal-kit options every week. Sadly, we even toss a lot out because we let them sit in the fridge too long."

Foodsnob added, "They're usually all super boring and uninspired too. I like heat!"

Plug-in guy laughed. "I like meal kits because they're quick and easy, and you can see all of the ingredients and modify them. The kids and I like bland and boring . . . don't shoot me. My wife would love to hack some of it so her portion at least tasted different though. I think you're on to something."

Foodsnob clapped his hands together. "You know who would be good to speak with about videos? Daniel Choi. He was just here a second ago. Have you met him?"

My stomach felt like an anvil being pushed off a cliff.

Paul periscoped his head. "Daniel's the livestreaming guru. If you want to know anything about what gear to buy, like headsets or mics or lighting, he's the best one to ask. He knows everything about Twitch, Discord, and YouTube too."

My voice cracked, like a teen boy's who was going through puberty. "He does?"

"Yeah, he's a professional streamer. StarCraft Two I think? He hurt his hand from gaming too much and it was interfering with work. Carpal tunnel's a bitch." He waved Daniel over before I could protest.

I'd had no idea about this side of Daniel. But then again, how would I have known? I wasn't a gamer and this was definitely not something my parents would have known about either. They weren't gossiping with their church friends about which kids had the most followers or subs. No, their conversations were relegated to other things they deemed important, like academics and money. But this was good to know.

Daniel took a seat across from me and I gave him a quick and exuberant rundown of my business idea. The group waited to see if he had any feedback.

He took a deep breath in and out, like a frustrated parent needing to teach a child an important lesson. "So . . . tell me . . . what's taking so long to get this business up and running?"

"I'm creating a survey to get an idea of what type of content people like. Videos, or recipe cards, or Reddit-type chats. And I have a bunch of business books left to read. Oh, and I'm still perfecting some recipes too. I'm thinking about doing some focus groups for meal-kit sauces and marinades, but that's going to take time if—"

He snorted. "You're approaching this all wrong." Five brutal words. Daniel sucker punched me in the gut.

"Well, don't sugarcoat it, Daniel," I replied flatly. "Go ahead and say what you're thinking."

"Look, if you want my advice, your business books aren't going to give you some magical plan or formula on how to get your idea off the ground. You need to learn through experience. Trial and error. Get going on those videos. Try the meal-kit supplements too, a few different ones. Try and fail, and then try some more. Failure isn't the opposite of success. You need failure and mistakes to learn and grow."

Was it really as simple as that? Recording a bunch of episodes and pressing "public" on that first one? If my cooking content was cohesive and interesting, and I posted consistently, was that really enough to get started?

Still, what he was proposing sounded messy and costly. His "throwing a bunch of spaghetti at the wall to see what sticks" seemed reckless and hard to optimize. Before I could get a word in edgewise, he said, "It might be hard, especially for you. You've been the same way since middle school. Hold on, I want to bring over someone you should definitely meet," and then walked away.

No thank you, the last time someone said that, they brought over Daniel Choi. What kind of mind games was he playing? And what did he mean *especially for me*? Why couldn't he be supportive like everyone else here?

A large man from the brick-and-mortar group came over. Daniel said, "Jeff Yee, this is Jessie Kim. She grew up here and moved back after working as a banker on Wall Street for a while."

I held out my hand and Jeff gave me a firm handshake. A brutish one, in fact. I could feel he'd worked with his hands because they were calloused, dry, and coarse. Pretty much the opposite of my hands. And probably Daniel's.

Jeff grunted. "Nice to meet you. I hate bankers."

I laughed. "I do too. What kind of business are you in?"

Daniel snorted.

Rude, Daniel.

He said, "Sorry, that just came out. Jeff is the owner of NiHao Markets. The fastest-growing Asian grocery store chain in the Southeast and Midwest. He's trying to develop some smaller Asian corner markets in college cities and towns."

"Cool." I didn't know how to respond because I didn't know what any of this had to do with me.

Daniel gave me a slightly bulgy-eyed look as he slowed down his rhetoric. "So. I was thinking. Maybe you could tell him about the meal-kit supplement idea you discussed with me. And possibly propose distributing prepackaged Asian meal-kit sauces and marinade supplements. Through his stores." Big eye bulge finale plus cocked head this time.

My whole body jolted. Daniel had thrown metaphorical spaghetti. But could it stick? Standing to meet Jeff eye-to-eye, I switched gears to banking mode and spouted off my elevator pitch again, this time mentioning that a great partnership idea was to, at Daniel's suggestion, possibly distribute prepackaged Asian meal-kit supplements such as sauces and marinades at his stores.

Then I added, "And I can promote NiHao in my video content. As my retailer. Or my sponsor? I could shop in NiHao exclusively and share videos of that too."

Daniel nodded and gave me an encouraging smile. Here was a business opportunity that had plopped into my lap, thanks to him. That had never happened to me before. But it seemed . . . too easy?

There's a saying about never looking a gift horse in the mouth. But what if that horse was suspiciously like Daniel Choi?

Jeff pursed his lips and rolled his eyes to the ceiling. His gaze focused back on me and he grunted. "Sounds good. Send me a proposal, include pricing and wholesale cost. We'd do trial distribution first at a few stores. We don't do consignment. And if you can do white label product options, that would be preferred." He pulled a business card from his pocket and handed it to me. Then, looking at Daniel, he asked, "Can I go back now?"

Daniel bounced to his feet. "Yeah, I'll walk you over there. I need to grab a cup of coffee anyway."

Paul leaned over and whispered as they walked away. "You just made a deal with the Asian godfather of the Southeast. You're on your way up."

Chapter Nine

Water droplets falling from my hair formed dark spots on my navy cardigan. I flew down the stairs with a gift bag in one hand and the car keys in the other, hoping that running in the house would make up for the ten minutes of accumulated lateness. My dad was in the garage and it was the first time I'd seen him since moving back home. Thanks to multiple technical emergencies at the factories overseas, he'd been asked to stay an extra two weeks to do damage control.

Dad was in the driver's seat, ready to take the car somewhere.

"Uh, hey Appa! I need a ride! I need to go to Celeste's house for a baby shower." I dangled my bag from my index finger, swinging it around. In addition to a giant diaper shipment already delivered to her house, I'd bought a squeaky chewy giraffe from her registry. It was nearly thirty dollars with tax and shipping. I couldn't help but wonder why squeaky dog toys were so much cheaper.

Dad motioned for me to go to the passenger side. When I sat down next to him, I smiled.

"Thanks, Appa. I forgot you came home this morning. Good to see you."

He nodded and started the ignition. "You're dripping all over." Reaching to the back seat, he handed me a small hand towel. "It's clean. From golf."

I wrapped the towel around my damp ponytail and squeezed the water out. "Where are you off to? And how was your trip?"

"Mom is taking a nap and I'm hungry. Jetlag. I don't want to make noise in kitchen, so I go buy my own lunch. Don't tell her but I am going to Popeyes for chicken sandwich." He complained that when he went overseas, he missed home cooking and Southern food. Then he confessed that every time he came home from a work trip he always went to Sonic, Arby's, or Popeyes.

"I won't tell, if you buy me a sandwich and fries for later."

Celeste's house was only fifteen minutes away, but we rode the entire time without speaking much. Dad wasn't a big talker, and I didn't want to exacerbate his jetlag fatigue by wearing him out through unnecessary chatter. We were always okay with quietness. Not like Mom, who usually liked to fill the gaps of silence by urging me to date, second-guessing my life decisions, and mentioning I should cook more instead of wasting so much money on takeout. Dad had the radio volume on low, but I could hear some country music. He tapped the steering wheel with the pads of his index fingers. "He my favorite. Garth Brook."

He'd dropped me off at Celeste's parents' place so many times that he didn't need to ask me for directions. Her parents had downsized and bought a condo in Florida, and now Celeste and her family were living at the house where she'd grown up. It was impossible to miss the exact house, seeing as how there was a colorful pastel balloon bouquet artfully wrapped around the mailbox, along with a single Mylar baby head bobbing on a string. Between two large maple trees, a large yellow WELCOME BABY III banner in crayon-y child font hung high in the air.

Cars were tandem parked three minivans deep in the driveway. Both sides of the street were lined with vehicles and there were no spots nearby. Since Dad was just dropping me off anyway, he put on his emergency blinkers so I could hop out of the car.

"What time for pickup?" he asked.

A young mom with her twin toddlers walked slowly toward the house. She had a boy tucked under each arm, and both were wailing and kicking as she lectured them on "behaving." Or more specifically, "What did I tell you two about not pulling hair and keeping your hands off each other's necks?"

I said, "An hour? Nah, make that forty-five minutes."

Dad watched the mom and her sons go into the house. "I'm going to buy sandwich and come back in thirty minute."

I added, "If they have sweet tea, can you get me one?"

He grunted and gave me a little nod. I pushed the passenger door closed and he drove away.

The walk to the door was short, but uncomfortable. Not only were the heat and humidity turned all the way up that afternoon, but there were so many gnats flying on and around the walkway. It almost looked like a photo filter where cascades of lights float around to add an ethereal effect, but in this case, the floating matter was far from romantic. It was downright disgusting.

The door creaked open with a slight push. Carrie Underwood was playing faintly in the background. I followed the swell of conversation and laughter to the kitchen, where a cluster of tidily dressed women chatted around platters of finger foods. Most of the ladies wore floral sheath dresses or summery pantsuits, making me feel incredibly underdressed in my ruffly gingham sundress and wrinkled cardigan, which was now wrapped around my waist. At work I rarely had a problem with knowing what to wear, as most female bankers like me had personal shoppers at department stores who knew the finance "uniform." The trick was finding a skirt that wasn't too short and a jacket that was fitted but not too tight. I knew how to dress as an up-and-coming executive but didn't have a clue on what to wear for a Brentwood baby shower. I guess the invitation should have tipped me off that this would require fancier attire than a simple Target sundress, with the gold embossing and the lined envelope in heavy paper stock. Real ribbon too, the hand-tied, silky, nonfraying type. This was a nice event that required a lovely, sophisticated dress or, at a minimum, what people here thought of as "church clothes," and I'd arrived in my unbecoming poly-rayon blended attire.

Too late to change now. While I briefly contemplated leaving, seeing the deviled eggs, smelling the sausage balls, and eyeing the pigs in a blanket on the table made my mouth water. I put my bag on the gift table and made my way to the all-occasion white paper plates. I'd forgotten how much I loved parties. Specifically, party food. Also, party booze. I looked around and saw wine, liquor, and sangria on the kitchen island. That would be my next stop after I filled up on calorically dense finger foods.

Two blond women stepped aside to allow me some grazing room. As I picked up a maple bacon biscuit, one of them asked, "Aren't you Jessica? Jess Kim?"

I nodded and smiled. She had short hair with blond wispy bangs. Perfect-looking tan skin, but that could also be the perfect makeup application. Who was this woman? She looked maybe five years older than me.

She laughed. "Oh gosh, it's been ages! Molly Wilson. We were in high school together, but I was in a different grade. I graduated a year after you."

Oh damn.

Molly turned to the other blonde. "I should pull out the yearbook. Jessie hasn't changed a bit."

Molly Wilson had been a cheerleader and track girl. It was coming back to me. But now who was this other woman? She really did look five years older. Maybe more.

I reached out my non-plate-holding hand. "I'm Jessie."

Molly's counterpart shook it. "I'm Molly's younger sister, Mary."

Well, shit. One thing I could rule out jobwise was one of those people who guessed age and weight at the county fair. I had no concept of age, apparently.

Molly and Mary explained they were Celeste's neighbors. They'd become close since their kids all went to the same preschool.

As if summoned, a parade of boisterous kids burst into the kitchen, wielding plastic swords, Nerf guns, and fairy wands. The moms all laughed as they marched through, grabbing chips and snack mix from the end of the table as their little-person party migrated to the living room.

Molly shook her head. "Rascals." She tilted her head and brushed the bang wisps away from her eyes with the back of her hand.

Mary turned her attention to me. "So, Jessie, are you in town for the shower or do you live here now? And do you have any kids?"

I'd just stuffed a sausage ball into my mouth, luckily buying some time before having to answer the same question I got every time I hung out with old classmates. It was totally understandable though, to be honest, especially since a large number of them met their husbands and wives in high school or college. A few of my high school classmates already had kids in elementary school.

I was nearly three decades old. In high school I thought thirty was ancient. And I thought I'd have this whole adult thing figured out by now. No way would I have ever believed that at my age, I'd be unemployed and living back home. Before, all I would have to do was utter the two words "Wall Street" and a look of instant respect from both men and women would take hold. They would assume I was putting my career first and then drop the marriage and baby talk pretty quickly. Many life decisions had been made to get me on the Hamilton Cooper track. I'd graduated high school and college in the top 10 percent of my class. I'd paid my dues with a couple of finance internships in college. I had professor and internship program reference letters. Yet, in this snapshot in time, I was a big ol' nobody. Zero source of income and I was eating my feelings away with high-calorie sausage balls.

No job, no marriage, no baby. An anti–triple threat.

I swallowed. Time to bite the bullet. "I left the golden handcuffs of Wall Street to start something new. I'm working on a new business, something I'm more passionate about." I'd rehearsed my lines so many times that I even began to believe my own words. Would they see the truth? My fear that I wasn't cut out for this?

Molly smiled as she lifted a deviled egg from her plate. "You're so brave to start your own business." She took a tiny bite. "But I suppose you have time if you're not saddled with kids. Dating anyone? I miss that so much."

Before I had a chance to formulate a response, Celeste, the pregnant guest of honor, came over and placed her hand on my shoulder, as if to tag me out of this verbal tussle. "I see you've both met my superstar friend, Jess." She gave me a hug. "My favorite Wall Street tycoon."

I smiled serenely and glanced at my watch. Only ten minutes had passed. Wow.

Apparently time didn't fly when you weren't having fun. I kept an upward tilt to my mouth and didn't let seething annoyance show as I polished off the last of my maple bacon biscuit. I'd spent so much time fake smiling for executives and clients, trained by many years in my former workplace to mask anything other than gravitas. A strong contrast to my male bosses and peers, who were given full latitude to snarl, cuss, and turn purple in the face, even at the slightest provocation. They were praised as being "passionate" and rewarded for their behavior, while women expressing the same feelings would be labeled "bitchy," "bossy," or "emotional" and asked to smile more.

Aside from fake smiling, I also knew how to make my life sound more glamorous than it actually was—another fine skill I'd learned in investment banking. One-upmanship.

I turned to Molly. "I'm going out with some friends from New York who are in town on business. We're going to that Dolly Parton rooftop bar tonight." *Keep the smile going, Jess, just nineteen minutes more.*

"Wow, I heard it's hard to get in now," Molly said. "You need connections."

Mary nodded. "I hear tourists really love it. All these out-of-towners must've seen it in some travel guides." I couldn't tell if that was a dig at me. I mean, technically I was a Nashville resident now, not a tourist, per se. She mirrored my well-rehearsed smile.

Celeste tugged my arm. "I hate to steal Jessie from you, but I need to catch up with her, it's been so long. Molly, Mary, I'll circle round later!" She blew them a kiss and escorted me to the covered back porch, which she'd converted to a second living room.

No more smiling from either of us. I let out a relieved sigh. "Thanks for the rescue mission. I didn't know how to exit that situation."

"Ugh, Mary and Molly are so nosy. I'm sorry you got caught in their verbal tractor beam. They dig all over for dirt, but they're also useful to have around because they know everyone's shit and can tell you all the town gossip. They're like *Real Housewives* meets TMZ." She hugged me again. "I was so surprised you RSVP'd, but I'm so happy you did!" She took a step back and examined me up and down. "You haven't changed much since I last saw you, though you may have dropped a few pounds." She grabbed her baby belly. "I'm the opposite. I haven't seen my feet in maybe four years."

I laughed. "That's because you keep pumping out adorable babies. And number three now, congratulations."

With a sigh, she plopped down on the couch. "I wasn't planning more than two, number three was a surprise. Our neighbor friends are thrilled to have another young one around, hence this elaborate shower. I haven't done any graphic design or art since baby number one, and honestly, I don't know if I can handle a third one without help at home. Aaron's hardly around these days. He's been working hard and traveling a lot. Kind of like your dad."

Fessing up, I told her why I was back in town.

"So you're living at home now and trying out food entrepreneurship?"

I nibbled on a praline. "Well, Wall Street is out of the question. Word travels fast and it would be tough to find another senior job there." I sighed. "It's like I'm now competing against my old life and I'm losing badly. I thought I'd try my luck doing something challenging and new, but my luck's now proven to be bad because the first person from school I ran into was Daniel Choi of all people. Although . . . he did sort of help me out by introducing me to some of his business connections."

"Daniel Choi, wasn't he that guy we called Oompa-Loompa?

Oh, nope, that was Sammy." She repinned a barrette that had come loose. "Wait, Daniel Choi was . . . PK, right?"

I'd forgotten we all called him that. PK. Pastor's kid. "Yes, that's him. He's a big deal in the Silicon Valley VC world, I hear." I showed her some articles about him on Google on my phone. He even had a Wikipedia page I hadn't seen before that talked about how he was part of a start-up incubation company and a think tank, and served as a director for many nonprofit boards. Having your own Wikipedia page meant you'd hit it big. It even mentioned his video game streaming.

"Good for him for making something out of his life," she murmured as she scrolled through his LinkedIn profile.

I shrugged. "Maybe he's changed. He gave me his number to hang out but I didn't really want to—I always feel like a loser around him."

She raised an eyebrow. "You? Stop it. You're not a loser."

I held up a sausage ball I'd wrapped in a napkin and found in my pocket. "First of all, I'm stealing sausage balls from your party. I was saving this for later. And second, I'm jobless, and third, I'm living at home again. Oh, and fourth, I got into NYU's part-time MBA program but can't go now . . . that's another thing unchecked on my life bucket list. So yeah, I make Daniel Choi look amazing in comparison."

"I know you used to compete with him in everything, but looking back, he really wasn't actually all *that* bad. He was just confident and sort of a perfectionist . . . twerp. Kind of like you, but twerpy and shorter. And with a bowl cut." Celeste clicked around till she found a recent photo of him. "Oh wow, he's hot now." She pinched the image to enlarge it. "Damn, girl."

I grabbed my phone. Okay, in that particular photo he had a stunning, self-assured smile and nice jawline, and he was wearing a perfectly fitted pale purple oxford shirt that revealed his well-proportioned strapping shoulders and chest. Determined to find a bad photo, I flipped through other images but unfortunately found a lot of the same. Daniel with a debonair grin, smartly fitted clothes, and strong evidence of an effective arm and chest exercise regimen. Ugh, he not only had gotten hotter over the years, he was also way more photogenic than anyone I knew.

"Earth to Jessica!" I looked up to see Celeste smiling at me. "I lost you there for a minute. Were you busy looking for a full-body photo of him?"

A flood of heat rushed to my cheeks. "I was uh—looking for a photo that made him look less hot."

She pursed her lips, suppressing a grin.

"Apparently there is no evidence on the internet that he is a normal human being who occasionally has bad photos." I scowled.

"Well, I personally think he deserves it. Imagine going through all of middle school with that bowl cut. Good for him, I hope he's getting a lot of action now."

I laughed. "You talk like the guys at Hamilton Cooper. They're always talking about sex. Before meetings. After meetings. In meetings."

She smiled. "I'm on my third kid. I really don't give a shit about appropriateness anymore." Her phone screen lit up and she glanced at the message. "I gotta get back to saying my hellos. It was nice catching up with you, and we should meet up soon. Maybe Daniel could come too. By the way, I don't believe in coincidences; I think you were meant to run into each other. And you were meant to move back home." Celeste looked over her shoulder and waved at someone who popped her head into the room to find her. "I should get back to my party."

My phone buzzed.

She asked, "Ooooh is it Daniel?"

"Nope, it's Dad. He's outside. And a few minutes early." *Thank God.* I gave her a hug. "I'll message you later. Have fun at your shower."

She rolled her eyes. "Honestly, I'd rather be napping. But it's nice of my neighbors to throw this party. Tell your dad I said hi."

I followed her into the house but headed straight for the front door. On the porch I messaged Daniel: *Going to a Dolly Parton bar tonight with friends in town from NYC. And maybe hanging out later this week with Celeste Sullivan, remember her? Let me know if you want to meet up soon.*

There, Celeste. See? I did my part. Let's see if you were right about coincidences.

Chapter Ten

I'd seen photos of the Dolly Parton–themed bar online, but actually seeing it with my own two eyes was a whole new, otherworldly experience. Decorated in hot and baby pinks and glitzy gold, it reminded me of my trip to Elvis's Graceland, but much more flashy and glam. Charlie snapped photos left and right as we entered, murmuring, "This is so fuckin' wild!"

The dining room was filled with bubble-gum-hued plush seating, mirrored chandeliers, and floor-to-ceiling windows. The stunning metallic wraparound bar lined with pink-and-white chairs caught my eye, begging me to sit there. But Alice wanted us to check out the famous patio by the pool, since it was one of the most Instagrammable attractions in Nashville. Like all the other tourists and locals before us, we took photos with the frilly beach umbrellas in the background and asked one of the staff to take a photo of our trio in front of the gigantic, iconic pink chicken-wire Dolly Parton head sculpture, with the city skyline as a decorative backdrop. Then the three of us sat on one of the oversize floral daybeds situated around a wading pool and waited for someone to take our order.

Alice's eyes widened as she examined the menu. "Wow, this is definitely not food you'd find in the city." She glanced up at us. "By the way, it's on me tonight." The menu was broken out into Smaller Foods, Larger Foods, Extra Foods, and Sweet Foods. A server with a nametag that read "Jolene" came by for our drink order, and it turned out her name really was Jolene. She recommended the smoked trout fritters, mussels, and white bread burgers to pair with what Alice and I ordered, the Frozen Aperol Spritz (essentially a Creamsicle slushy), and Charlie's Closed on Sundays, which was like a Manhattan. It was very Charlie of him to order that.

I marveled at the view while Alice and Charlie looked over my shoulders to check out the tourist-heavy crowd. Lots of shine and shimmer from the birthday and bachelorette groups. I counted at least five cowboy hats among the guys in the crowd. My friends were right though, my orange non–prison jumpsuit would have been totally wrong place, wrong time: everyone here was dressed to impress, which for some patrons meant going for a head-to-toe honky-tonk look fully accented with rhinestones for maximum Dolly sparkle effect.

Alice and Charlie were dead serious about being each other's wingmen: I'd thought it was a rallying cry to mobilize each other to get vacation time, but the hungry, predatory look in both of their eyes, their roaming gazes, and lack of captivating conversation suggested that they were not only hoping to meet someone at this kitschy bar but were hoping to ditch each other immediately to get some action. Alice even had on nonblack and nongray attire, having opted for a silver halter with big hoop earrings instead. I'd never seen her wear anything "fun" before, not even at my former company's holiday parties.

Charlie took a break from his visual hunting and looked at the menu again. "Did you see the desserts?"

A cute redhead in the seating area next to us called over, "Try the Millionaire's Twinkie. It's soooo good! Two sponge cakes covered in chocolate on a pool of caramel crème, sprinkled with shortbread crumbs and edible gold leaf. Perfection!"

Charlie licked his lips. But not for the Twinkie.

He didn't even look at Alice and me before he walked over to her. She was with a group of three, like us. Although now we were only a group of two.

Alice laughed. "I guess that's more food for us. Looks like Charlie's officially left." We watched as he motioned for the server to redirect his Manhattan-inspired drink over to his new table, and then bought a round of milky, pale pink shots for his new entourage. Alice and I both made cringe faces as they brought over a tray to Charlie's new table.

I asked, "What the hell is that? Alcoholic Yakult?"

She laughed. "That's something you should make in your videos."

I took a long sip. "I guess he hit the bachelorette jackpot over there." We raised our glasses to Charlie. He didn't cheers back because his arms were draped around two ladies' shoulders. Three more women had joined their table, including the bride-to-be. She put a string of purple Mardi Gras beads around Charlie's neck. A giant penis pendant the size of a pacifier dangled from it. She hopped into his lap and asked her server to take a group photo. Charlie's smile was the biggest.

Alice and I dug into our fritters and mussels as soon as they arrived. Alice told me that she and Charlie were thinking about leaving Hamilton Cooper and going over to a new hedge fund started by an ex-HC executive. Alice had worked with him for several years and he was one of the few people who had earned her trust. She perked up, shooting a look over my left shoulder and then looking down at her plate. "Okay, don't look, but there's a couple of cute guys behind you. Oh, OH! Incoming."

She took her compact out of her purse to check her makeup. When I turned my head a little, she scolded, "Uh-uh. Don't turn around, it'll be too showily obvious."

I cocked my head. "Have you taken a look around here? This place is all about showily obvious, whatever that actually means."

She whispered, "They're literally right behind you. Please. Don't. Move. Or be embarrassing." Alice burst into a fit of tinkling laughter and flipped her hair back, like I'd just said something hilarious. "Oh my God, that's SO funny. I can't believe it."

I didn't know what to do or how to react. Presumably I'd need to say something in response to her, to fill the silence, right? But she'd also just instructed me to not move or be embarrassing, so I had no clue how to respond to her fake laughter at a nonexistent story I hadn't told.

My eyes pleaded: *What do you want me to do? I don't know how to play this weird game you didn't warn me about.*

"Oh, there you are, Jessie! We looked all over inside for you. Then I realized you'd probably be outside."

I didn't need to turn my head to know that Daniel Choi was standing behind me. The hairs standing up on my forearms and the chill running down my spine were my primal Daniel detectors.

Alice did her bulgy-eye thing, which I interpreted as "You know him? You can look now, stop being so awkward." When I turned too quickly, the fast head rotation plus fast-acting alcohol made everything temporarily spin.

When the world came into focus again, I could see Daniel was with a stunningly handsome friend, a half-Asian version of Daniel but slightly taller. On a ten-point scale he was maybe a nine, or nine and a half. Damn, he was the kind of person who looked amazing, even at his worst. Just woke up from sleep? Adorable. After a long morning run, unshowered and hungover? Gross but also kind of sexy. After a drunken fist-fight, all torn up in the face? Hot.

I was *this close* to telling Daniel that he'd misinterpreted my message—I wasn't asking him to come out and join us tonight. But I looked over at Alice, who was nibbling her bottom lip while looking at Daniel's hot friend. She was interested. Her pheromones were sending up "Hot damn, let's do this!" flares. So I shut my mouth.

"May we sit down?"

Alice scooted to her left. Daniel sat next to me as his companion took a seat next to Alice.

"This is Bryan. He's a buddy of mine in town for the weekend."

Bryan said, "Daniel and I are party fouling hard by not having any drinks in hand."

Lucky for him, Alice was one of those people who would just look up and service people would run to do her bidding. She made eye contact with the nearest nametag-donning staff member, and he came trotting over. "Yes, miss, would you like to place another order?"

She looked at Daniel and Bryan. "What beers do you have on tap?"

He rattled off a bunch of imports but the two of them settled on a locally brewed IPA. After punching their order into his handheld device, he turned to me. "Ma'am, what about you?"

Ouch, I'd just gotten ma'amed. This guy was maybe twenty-four or twenty-five, not much younger than any of us. And I wasn't the only one who noticed: all three of my companions burst into a chorus of laughter.

Slightly offended, but also not wanting this guy to disappear on me without taking my drink order, I ignored my companions and asked for a frozen margarita. As he walked away, I glared at everyone while mumbling into my glass, "Screw all y'all."

Daniel chuckled. "He didn't ask for your ID? Bryan and I got carded right away."

Alice and I looked at each other. No one had asked to see our licenses. I deadpanned, "Wow, and I thought I looked pretty youthful in my sleeveless V-neck dress. Cute, in a Chico's outlet sort of way."

Daniel smirked. "Don't knock Chico's Off the Rack, my umma shops there and gets really good deals on jeggings."

One of my knuckles cracked as I punched him on the arm.

Daniel leaned back and rubbed the spot I hit on his biceps. His rock-hard biceps. Why didn't I make contact with any squishiness? Was he pure muscle? Where else was he a solid mass of muscle?

Okay, stop it, brain. Don't go there.

Bryan said, "Nice with the armor defense, PK. Or should I call you Iron Man?"

The waitperson brought the drinks fast, and we clinked glasses.

I asked, "People still call you PK?"

Daniel shrugged. "Only a few people do. Kids from Nashville, and a few high school friends too. Bryan went to high school in Texas with me and is visiting." He took a long sip. "I try to not highlight the whole pastor's kid thing. And I definitely don't mention it when hanging out with pretty ladies, so thanks a lot, *Bryan*."

Alice gave me an almost imperceptible *OMG "pretty"—I heard that—OMG did you hear that?* glance. I rolled my eyes and stated, "I have to go to the ladies' room," thinking Alice had signaled that we needed to regroup to discuss our game plan. She seemed into Bryan, and how could she not be? He was charming, funny, and a walking fitness model prototype. It would be painful, but it was my duty to help her out by keeping Mr. Arms of Steel busy and out of her way.

I heard a rustling behind me as I hurried toward the inside bar where the bathrooms were, and I assumed it was Alice scrambling out of her seat to follow my lead. Once we were out of earshot I shouted over my shoulder, "Bryan's cute. I think he's your type. I can keep Daniel occupied despite the torture."

"Daniel would love that," a baritone voice answered.

I whipped around as I held the door open. Daniel Choi was just inches away from me.

"Where's Alice?" I panicked.

He threw his thumb over his right shoulder. "Bryan's with

her." We looked at the two of them. His arm was hooked around Alice's shoulder while she put her hand on his knee.

"Well damn. He moves fast," I muttered.

"She does too." We both walked toward the bar. "I'm assuming you didn't need to go to the ladies' room?"

"I did. Errr I do. But nothing urgent." I don't know why I disclosed that last part. Bladder urgency was not something guys, or even girls, needed to hear about.

"Good, let's do a celebratory shot. It's on me."

"Free alcohol? Sure."

Daniel ordered two Lemon Drops. "I haven't had these since college. I loved them back then." Handing one to me, he said, "To me." And he bottoms-upped it.

"What the hell? Did you just toast to yourself? I thought we were celebrating something?" I shouted and scolded at the same time. The ego on this guy was incredible.

He smiled coyly. "Your turn. You can toast to me too, or to yourself."

"You're nuts," I said. But I drank the whole thing, because . . . free drink. "Now I gotta go to the bathroom for real."

I stomped to the women's restroom and mumbled, "What a clown," as I entered the stall. Daniel was so infuriatingly . . . Daniel. There really wasn't anyone else like him. Afterward, I washed my hands and checked my phone. No "Help me!" message from Alice. Given what I'd seen, the only Alice message that night would be "help me" get these clothes off, to Bryan.

With Alice and Charlie both occupied, should I head home? I stared hard at my reflection in the mirror. My body swayed a little, the Lemon Drop shot finally making its way into my bloodstream. As out-of-body as I felt at that moment, it was nice to be at a fun Dolly-themed bar. With my old work friends. And . . . fine. With Daniel. He'd bought me a drink and wasn't acting like a conceited prick. Well, except when he toasted to himself. That evening he was more tolerable than usual, probably so his buddy could hook up with Alice.

He was on his phone waiting for my return, with two more shots in front of him. These were different. They were clear. Vodka maybe?

Daniel handed me one. "They gave these to us for free. They're called Moonshine! I don't know if it's actual moonshine or they just gave it that name but—"

I threw my head back and swallowed it. The alcohol burned as it creeped down my throat. "To me!"

"To you!" He laughed and drank his, then coughed. "Oh, wow, that hurts."

"It's like paint thinner, but worse."

He smiled. "Who would have thought after eighth grade that you and I would be drinking at a bar, being cordial to each other?"

"Who would have thought that after eighth grade, you wouldn't have a bowl cut?" I teased.

He puffed his chest. "Look, my mom literally had a metal

bowl that she used for making kalbi and also as a pattern to cut my hair. I can still smell the sesame oil."

"At least your mom and dad didn't make you go to Primo Cuts, where they told the hairdresser to cut it short so it would take a year to grow back. That's how my parents saved money."

He huffed. "Whenever I got new clothes, my mom made me get a few sizes larger so I could grow into them. That's why my jeans always sagged and I had rolled-up cuffs. And that's only if I got anything brand-new, because most of what I wore were hand-me-downs from my brother, who really liked Scooby-Doo."

I always wondered why he wore Scooby-Doo shirts all the time.

"Yeah, well, my parents messed up my feet by never buying me new shoes. So I had the opposite problem, they were always too tight."

Here we were, trying to out-loser each other. Yet another way he and I competed. I was winning though.

He asked, "Is that why you always ran the slowest?"

I hit his arm of steel again, popping a different knuckle. I tried again with an elbow surprise jab, which worked a little better.

Rubbing his arm, he said, "No one likes a sore loser, Jessica."

Wow, Daniel really knew how to get under my skin. He scooted off the stool and stood next to me. "You ready to go back?"

"Not without another drink." I'd had three, maybe four? "Make that a water, actually."

The bartender offered us waters with lemon slices. "Classy," I said, guzzling mine fast. As I turned around to head back to the outdoor patio, my elbow poked the guy next to me. Unlike Daniel, this guy had a higher squish-to-muscle ratio.

"I'm sorry," I squeaked as I maneuvered around him.

"Watch where you're going," he grumbled while looking me up and down. As I walked away, he muttered, "Stuck-up bitch."

My mouth fell open, searching for words. The alcohol clouded my brain, making it hard to know how to respond.

"The only stuck-up bitch here is you," Daniel said and walked closer to the aggressor. "She said she was sorry. I believe you owe her an apology."

"I don't owe her shit. You and your girlfriend can get the fuck outta my face." He turned to his entourage and made a face that made them laugh.

Why that seemed like the best time to jump into the conversation, I don't know, but it did. "Look, you walking Dockers pants model, I said I was sorry. And you're a fucking asshole to talk to someone that way—ANY human that way—in the holiest, Dolly-est place on earth, well, second to Dollywood." I wagged my index finger in his face. "I have another apology for you. I'm sorry you took an innocent bump of an elbow into your beer pooch and tried to turn it into a personal attack. And I'm sorry to your friends for having a loser who drags down their social circle. Also, don't try to punch this guy, it'll hurt. I tried twice this evening and it was like ramming my knuckle into a brick wall. Also, we're definitely, absolutely *not* dating, and in fact, he and I have always kind of hated each other, but you don't see me being a total asshole to him, or him to me. So fuck you."

I brought the room to silence. All of the patrons had stopped mid-drink, mid-conversation, and mid–making out to see what this guy was going to do with all of that.

He turned to his friends and shook his head. "Let's go, this isn't worth it."

The loser gang walked to the elevator and I called to them, "Dolly would be offended by your manners!"

When they got in and the doors closed, Daniel clapped. "I'll be honest, I had no idea where that was going to go. That was weird and amazing to witness firsthand. I wish I'd recorded it."

"Don't make me punch you a third time." I tipped my water glass to my mouth and ate a small piece of crushed ice.

He laughed. "I wouldn't want that either. Your elbows really are pointy by the way. Very daggerlike. Like I bet you can use your elbows to smash windows to escape cars when they're fully submerged underwater. So I'm not saying I was on that dude's side, but your elbows are not to be messed with."

I attempted to elbow him and lost my balance as I took a step forward. Daniel grabbed me and pulled me into his chest to keep me from falling onto another patron on a nearby stool.

For a few seconds, time stood still. I had no desire to retaliatory punch him. My mind spun in circles of confusion because pressing against him wasn't unbearable, it was actually pleasant. Tingly all over from pricks of electricity—how long had it been since I'd been next to a guy, like this, feeling this way? A couple of years maybe? Maybe more?

A feeling of warmth and comfort passed through me as his hand moved from my shoulders down to the small of my lower back. In that instant, I was suddenly aware of Daniel.

His brawn.

His brains.

His touch.

He pulled back a little and looked down at my face. "You know, it's a shame we're absolutely not dating and you still kind of hate me."

My heart thumped hard. "A shame? Really?"

His hand made its way up my back, and then down again. "Huge shame."

He dropped his hand to his side and his face changed expressions. "Hey you two!"

I whirled around and saw Bryan and Alice coming our way. Alice asked, "What happened to you? We thought you left so we closed out the tab."

Daniel said, "You missed us taking a few shots and Jessie basically ripping a guy's balls off and handing them back to him."

The bartender wiped down the counter and added, "Yeah, that was brutal. But good for you, miss. If he didn't go on his own, I'd have made him leave. He's been rude to our guests all night."

I beamed, partly from the validation of a stranger, but mostly by being called miss instead of ma'am.

Alice cleared her throat. "So Bryan and I are going to hang out at my hotel and grab a drink." She reached out and grazed his fingertips, which in Alice's body language was like Marvin Gaye– and Sade-level of heat. "You two want to join us?"

"Sure!" Daniel said. After I elbowed him again, he whimpered, "Or maybe not." Did my elbow really hurt that badly? You'd think I'd kicked him in the nuts from the strain in his voice.

Alice walked ahead to call the elevator, and Bryan said to Daniel just loud enough for me to hear, "Don't wait up for me." He slapped Daniel on the back and trailed after Alice.

The bartender slid more shots over to us. "Those are on me. That guy you got to leave, he's always coming in here and gettin' rowdy and runnin' his damn mouth. I'm hoping you scared him off for good."

"Bottoms up?" Daniel asked.

It would be impolite to turn down a thank-you drink. "Bottoms up," I echoed. We toasted and drank. An infused citrus vodka shot.

Pleasant. Clean. Toe-tingling.

And dangerous. Tipsy Jess could go in a few directions, and it was already too late to stop the transformation.

One, there was "I don't take shit from anyone" Jess: more than a glimpse of this Jess had emerged earlier. This state usually involved a quick alcoholic hit to the bloodstream, spiking endorphins or adrenaline plus an incident to fire Jess up. If consuming alcohol much too quickly, this Jess morphed into number two, Rowdy Jess, slightly slurring words and droopy-eyed. It was best to get home quickly, within twenty minutes, as this Jess also turned into puking Jess.

And then there was Introvert Jess: observant, quiet, and sometimes philosophical, she came out more frequently than other Jesses. In a bar, Introvert Jess's energy drained as everyone partied around her and she'd usually find a way to head home early. At home, drunk Introvert Jess liked to watch serious movies or play Taylor Swift's sad songs on repeat. Pints of ice cream, sleeves of crackers, and wedges of Brie were usually demolished by the end of the night.

"Heyyyy, you're still here? Where's Alice?" Charlie and his bachelorette entourage were walking toward us. I'd forgotten about him. But it looked like he didn't need any wingman action either. "We're going barhopping. I would invite you, but you look . . . busy." The elevator dinged and the party of seven stepped in. As the door closed, Charlie double-thumbs-upped me.

"Good grief, Charlie, Daniel and I are NOT together." Oh. No. Tipsy Jess said her innermost thoughts out loud.

"Message received loud and clear," Daniel said. His face

hardened, but I couldn't read if he was mad or joking. One of the drawbacks of tipsy Jess: the inability to read microexpressions and accidentally hurting people's feelings by blurting things out without filtering them first.

My memory flicked back to a few minutes ago, when I was pressed against him. When his hand traveled up and down my back, sending electricity along its path. I wanted that feeling all over again. Longed for it, even. But I'd messed it all up, and I didn't have the courage to just grab him by the collar and climb on top of his lap. I didn't have the courage, or the dexterity.

So what's a drunken, dating novice to do in a situation like this?

Think, Jess. Use all of your remaining sober brain cells to do something.

My mouth opened and words came out. "Want to come home with me and check out my spreadsheet?"

Warmth on his face returned. "I'd love that."

Chapter Eleven

Our carshare arrived after ten minutes and Daniel and I crawled into the back seat together. I put my head against the cold window as the car pulled away. I woke up to him whispering, "We're at your house," and perked up to see him peering downward at me. My head had been resting on his shoulder . . . but for how long?

Unfazed by my shoulder drool, he nudged me gently and I scooted out of the vehicle. As we walked to my porch, Daniel said, "Wow, I haven't been here in fifteen years."

I held my index finger to my lips to shush him and then unlocked the front door. It creaked as I pushed. When we both made it inside, we took off our shoes and I whispered, "I don't know why I thought this would be a good idea."

He stifled a laugh. "We could have gone to my place, but we'd have the same problem. My mom and dad stay up late though, so it would have been worse."

"My mom and dad will kill me if they catch you in my room, even at age twenty-eight. And then you'd be next. So don't be loud."

Next challenge: the creaky stairs. Teenage Jess knew where to step to avoid triggering the moaning and groaning of the wooden planks. But adult tipsy Jess, twenty pounds heavier and far less nimble, had no clue what footing was ideal. The main problem was that over the years, the stairs had become squeakier and pliable, and of course this wasn't a high priority maintenance issue for my parents to fix. Adding in the weight of Daniel's pure muscle body density, the noise on the staircase was unavoidable.

Criiiiiick. Creeeeeeeak. Squeak!

My hand instinctively flung back, hitting Daniel square in the chest. The same quasi karate chop move Mom did in the car when hitting the brakes to avoid an accident.

He wheezed. "Damn, Jessie, I'm going to have so many bruises all over my body tonight because of you."

"Shhhhh!" I whispered. For a few seconds, all I could hear was Daniel and me breathing, heavy with both fear and anticipation. When I heard a faraway mattress creak, I knew that Dad or Mom had woken from REM sleep but was settling back in again.

We tiptoed onward to my bedroom, which luckily was the first room on the right after reaching the top of the staircase. Once we were inside, I closed the door behind us and locked it.

Pressing my back to the door, I let out a huge sigh. "I haven't snuck around like that since high school."

"Are you serious? I've been coming home late every night at midnight or later and getting an earful." He fell back onto my bed. "You're lucky, you've got a double bed. I'm sleeping on a twin."

"Would you like something to drink?" I opened a shoebox from the top shelf in my closet and showed him my attempt at a minibar set up. Earlier that week I'd gone to the liquor store and stocked up on tiny bottles of wine and spirits. I pointed at a small fridge in the corner. "I have beer in there."

He laughed, one index finger directed at my beer stash, his other one pointing at my kawaii stuffed animal collection. "It's like you're in college again, but way worse."

"You want me to elbow you again, in your face?" I threw a stuffed panda at him, which he swatted away.

"Okay, okay, I'll take a beer, and then let's check out your Excel magic. That's what lured me into your bedroom." I cracked open a Trader Joe's beer with my bottle opener and handed it to him.

"Wait, why is there a ginger ale label on this?"

"That's in case my mom looks in there."

He shook his head. "That's ridiculous. No beer for you?"

I smiled and took a cold can of Sierra Mist from my fridge. It hissed when I pulled the tab. After taking a couple of swigs,

I opened a small bottle of Grey Goose and poured its contents into the can. And then a second one. Swirling it a few times, I announced, "Vodka and soda. Voilà!"

We cheersed, gulped, and then took a look at my highly anticipated spreadsheet. I explained the organization of my worksheet tabs: business books to read, a business plan draft, some growth and risk calculations. Daniel pulled up a wooden chair and sat next to me and leaned into my shoulder to get a better look at the screen. I focused hard on the numbers in front of me, trying to ignore the heat rushing to my cheeks. "It's the alcohol," I told myself, as the lightheaded feeling came back in full force.

He asked, "May I?" and nudged my arm, sending electric currents through me.

"Sure," I squeaked, then rolled my chair over to give him better access. The wooden chair didn't scoot so well on the beige plush carpet; he had to stand, move the chair over a few inches, and then sit again. Daniel sat close, our arms barely touching, sending more tingles through me. I smiled into my soda can.

His fingers were quick. As quick as mine. For a brief moment I forgot he was trained in venture capital, an adjacent industry to banking, and we spoke the same language of numbers. He tabbed over to see other calculations based on assumptions I'd made about growth of the prepared meals market, and he took a long time staring at my competitive analysis. Nervous about his silence, I took anxious sips of my vodka soda as I waited for him to say something.

He'd nearly finished his beer, so I went to grab him another one.

"What's this?" He used the arrow keys to highlight parts of the document.

Oh no.

Oh no oh no oh no.

He was looking at my "dating requirements" worksheet.

I lunged to push his arm away from the keyboard and knocked his not-quite-empty beer bottle right onto his crotch. He leaped to his feet and the ale trickled down his pant leg onto the carpet.

"Oh shit!"

I was torn about what to do first. Slam the laptop closed or help Daniel with his spill?

Spill. I grabbed my tattered blue bath towel from the hook on the door and patted his leg with it.

Daniel took the towel and rubbed it around his upper thighs. Mesmerized by his quad muscles, I stared as he blotted them. After he was done, it was clear that nearly a third of his black slim-fit pants were wet. And the room smelled like a brewery. Unfazed by his soggy bottom half, he lifted the new beer I'd brought over and took a casual sip.

Embarrassingly, I still hadn't unpacked my belongings from New York, so I pulled a pair of sweatpants from an opened shipping box and handed them to him. "They're purple," he commented.

"Yes, purple is the main school color at NYU." I finished my vodka soda and threw the empty can in my recycling bin. The two bottles of liquor were taking their toll. I was officially tipsy again, unable to think straight.

He shot me a sly grin. "You mind turning around?" I blushed and spun the other direction. His jeans slid to the ground, his belt thunking to the floor. "Okay, I'm done."

I expected to see his jeans by his feet, but I wasn't expecting to see his boxers crumpled on the floor too. "You got me good with that spill. I almost think it was on purpose," he said with a smirk.

Damn you, Daniel.

And I hate that you look better in purple sweatpants than me.

"I'm sorry about that," I mumbled, truly regretful of my clumsiness. I stiffened when I remembered why I'd knocked the beer onto his crotch in the first place. Needing to get back to my computer, I shuffled around Daniel's side and made my way back to my desk. He reacted quicker by getting to it first.

"So where were we with your dream man?" He plopped down with a thud in my wheeled chair and pointed to the column of desired attributes. "Confidence. Humor. Brains. Career-driven. Height. Views on religion with a question mark. Smart with money. Wants kids. Why do you have such a long list? Dating isn't like looking for a job. You need spontaneity—"

I growled, "Okay, that's enough," and slammed my laptop closed. "We were here to talk about my business, not my dating life."

He leaned back in the chair. "Can't we please talk about both?"

I put both hands on my hips. "Nope." The nerve of this guy!

"Can I say one thing though?"

I raised an eyebrow. *Fine, I'm listening.*

He stood up and walked right next to me. Biting his lip, he took a deep breath and whispered in my ear, "You forgot to add 'looks hot in purple sweats.'"

With both fists, I lightly pounded his chest. *Thump, thump, thump.* My heart raced from aggravation, annoyance, and primal attraction. This infuriating guy standing a couple of inches from me was inciting so much of a physical response deep inside me I wanted to SCREAM.

He wrapped his hands around my wrists, displaying his strength and self-assurance. "It's not nice for you to maim your house guests." Daniel yanked me closer and reeled me in like a prized fish. With his face close to mine, and my body tucked into his, he murmured, "I don't know what to do with you."

I struggled to breathe. *Me either.*

He gripped my wrists a little tighter. Maybe it was the alcohol, or the tension between us that rivaled the overwrought feeling you got watching Jordan Peele's horror movies when you needed immediate release. Maybe it was Daniel's full-body press onto me. I decided to go the spontaneity route.

I pulled my wrists into my chest and stood on the balls of my feet. Lightly nipping his bottom lip, I offered a sweet kiss. He let go of my wrists and just when I thought I'd made a mistake by making a move first, he placed his hands on my lower back and kissed me, his lips firm and parted.

After that, the alcohol and attraction kicked into full gear. We fell back on the bed, kissing, stroking, and panting, fully absorbed in each other. He rolled on top and offered me light pecks from my neck down to my chest.

The sound of a toilet flushing stopped us cold. My wall clock read 3:05, and it hit me that my dad was awake, his jetlag still affecting his sleep.

Daniel's eyes looked at the door, panicked. "You think they'll go back to bed?"

I shook my head. "It's Dad. He's up for good. Still messed up from his trip to Asia. And he'll murder you if he finds you here. Or castrate you. He's small but yields a powerful knife."

He sat up and winced. "Can I hide in the closet if they try to come in?"

It seemed like a good idea. One that could work, especially since there was no way my parents would ever suspect me of having a BOY in my room.

Except.

"Shit! Your shoes."

He looked down at his feet. "I didn't track in dirt or anything."

"No. Your shoes. They're downstairs!"

We had at least a dozen pairs of shoes by the front door, but only one of them was actually nice. Daniel's Koio Capris, gleaming-white sneakers that matched the lavishness of his Mercedes.

"Oh shit." He placed his head in his hands. "I need to think straight."

"And we need to think quickly. He's going to go downstairs and put two and two together. Then kill the two of us."

He scooped up his underwear and pants from the floor. "You think you can distract him so I can make a getaway?" Daniel walked over to the window and looked down. He unlocked and slid it open, then, unexpectedly, tied his clothes into a knotted ball and tossed it down. He turned and smiled. "How's that for spontaneity?"

"Are you going to climb out?" I asked.

"Hell no, it's too steep. We need to go back to the plan of you distracting him and me sneaking out."

The faucet shut off and the sound of Dad's humming drifted down the hall.

"Go! Be the smart, crafty, genius Jessie you are!" He opened the door and scooted me out with a two-handed push.

I walked to the hall bathroom and knocked on the door. "Dad? Uh, it's me."

"One more second, I'm coming out."

"No! Wait! Uh, are my glasses in there? I took out my contacts and I can't see anything, can you check? They're on the sink or on the edge of the tub."

"Okay, I'm looking."

Daniel's face popped out of my bedroom, and I waved my hand in a fast shooing motion. *Run! Like a gazelle!*

My door creaked open even more and he shimmied out. Daniel ran down the stairs so loudly I had to fake a coughing fit to cover up the thunderous pounding.

The front door closed just as the bathroom door opened. Appa handed me my tortoise-shell librarian glasses. "They were on the bathtub."

I put them on, rendering me temporarily blind by having both my contacts and glasses in use at the same time. "Thanks, Dad."

He patted my back. "Go to sleep. You look like you have jetlag too. You need to wear pajama, your clothes not looking comfortable."

"Okay, I will." Back in my bedroom, my phone bleeped with a message from Alice.

Two things I love most: Nashville and Bryan's abs

Then one from Daniel.

Keeping your purple sweatpants

I fell back on my bed with a smile on my face.

Spontaneity wasn't so bad after all.

Chapter Twelve

What a mess! My garage looked like I'd hosted a Black Friday sale with ninety-nine-cent merchandise. I had ordered shipping supplies the week Alice and Charlie visited, and nearly three weeks later, everything arrived all at once. Stacks of boxes, shipping tape, jars of marinades and sauces, spice containers, cardboard separators, bonus recipe cards, and glossy product labels littered every square inch of the ground.

It took me an hour to put together ten Korean meal supplement kits. Granted, the first few were hard to figure out, but I got incrementally faster once I'd made a few. But I had 490 to go and the deliveries needed to be made within three days.

Celeste came over to help me, despite my protests. She insisted, saying she had a couple of hours while the kids were in school. Plus, she wanted to hang out and help me with makeup and wardrobe for my cooking videos I was shooting that day, and I would be foolish not to accept help in those two areas.

"How'd you get all these little bottles and jars of products?"

Using the back of my right hand, I wiped a fast-moving drip of sweat near my temple. "I got really lucky for once. I joined a local Asian American entrepreneurs group. There are a few guys in the restaurant and commercial kitchen business who knew some suppliers and packagers. The sauces and mixes were a little tougher, and I had to find a partner with the right bottling facilities. There's a Thai restaurant here who has their own line of salad dressing and marinades they sell at their location and they referred me to the same small batch bottler they use who knows health laws and has the facilities to process food for resale. I gave them my recipes and they suggested some tweaks to make the products more stable, then they made and bottled the products. They gave me a lower minimum because of the Thai restaurant connection. Securing all the proper licensing and insurance has been a nightmare, but I finally figured it out."

Celeste smiled. "Of course you did." While putting labels on some jars of spicy red pepper paste, she asked, "We're running a little behind schedule. You think Daniel could come over to help?"

"Nah." I shook my head.

She lifted her eyebrow. "Nah, meaning you don't think he could come over, or nah, I don't want him here?"

"I've already bothered him a lot." I conveniently left out the fact that we'd made out on my bed and almost got caught by my dad a few weeks ago. I also didn't tell her that I'd been working longer-than-usual hours to avoid Daniel's *hey let's grab dinner* text requests. "He just picked up a consulting gig in Atlanta so he's out of town a lot." Now that he was working, Daniel was texting me much less, not that I was keeping track of that. "Oh! By the way, did you know he has a bunch of streaming experience from being a gamer? I might need to bother him a lot later, ask him for advice."

She studied my face before picking up the next flattened box on the palette. "You should ask him to help, anyway. No one gives a shit about what we were like in middle school and high school anymore and we're all over it. Remember Lizzie? The real mean one in junior high who made fun of all the girls' clothes? She's running for city council! Ironically, she's a parent now and has started a local anti-bullying campaign at all the elementary schools here. Good for her. And that guy Quintin who smoked pot before and after school in the parking lot—he's at the State Department I hear. They changed. People can change. Forget about the past and just ask Daniel for help."

She hummed as she put a set of four jars inside a box. "So I know this guy, Matt. He's single. Thirty-one. He's prematurely gray, just so you know. And not the Wall Street type."

"That's a good thing," I said. "The non–Wall Street part. Not the prematurely gray part. Not that there's anything wrong with that. At all. I'll shut up now."

She shook her head and laughed at me. "He's cute and sweet."

"What's he do—" I cut myself off, remembering Daniel's words, that I shouldn't go off my spreadsheet criteria and ask about his job or his school. Right. Spontaneity.

I course-corrected. "What's he do . . . to his hair? Does he, like, keep it natural or dye it?" Smooth, Jess. Real smooth. "And is he into available women who have no job and are living rent-free in their childhood bedrooms?"

"He's a financial planner. And he frequently advises people our age. He says if parents are willing to take their adult kids in, that the 'boomerang effect' of moving back home rent-free to pay off debt isn't necessarily a bad thing. Paying off a car, clearing credit card debt, and making a dent in student loans are key to financial stability. It can also benefit older parents having kids at home, with companionship and spending more quality time as a family."

I sealed a box with clear tape. "You sound like a spokesperson for this guy. I'll admit, I'm intrigued."

"I'm pro-Jess and pro-Matt." She laughed as she stacked her package on top of the completed pile.

"That's true, you did talk me up at your shower. I'll think about it."

She smiled. "Good. You could use some spontaneity."

"Why is that the theme of my life? Did everyone get the 'preach to Jess about being more spontaneous every chance you get' memo?"

Her brow furrowed. "Huh? Who is everyone?"

I shrugged. "Daniel. He said the exact same thing the other night." *That night. In my bedroom.*

Celeste pursed her lips to suppress a smile.

I put down the roll of labels. "What?"

"Nothing." She put together a new box and flipped it over so she could tape the bottom. "I just think it's funny that two very smart people have given you the exact same advice." *Zipppppp.* "Also, since when have you been hanging out with Daniel? At the baby shower you looked like you might projectile vomit if I just mentioned his name."

Celeste knew about all of my most regretful indiscretions, like when I made out with a guy in high school who shaved his body for swim team and was super slippery all over when he sweated. And drunk grinding on the dance floor at Celeste's bachelorette party with a sexy dancer at a gay club who turned out to be into girls, I found out four drinks and a dark corridor later. She didn't know about my night with Daniel, but she'd be the person to confide in about it. But honestly, she didn't need to know about him. It was just a few desperate drunk kisses and now we were fine. We'd texted a little because I needed him to recommend some equipment to make my livestreams more professional-looking and— Oh shit!

I looked at my phone. "I have my recording in half an hour!" I'd planned to do one live program a week, plus upload daily scheduled content, to keep my subscriber base growing, and I was already running behind schedule.

Celeste put her hands on her hips and looked around at the garage. "Wow, what a mess. But we can come back to clean it up or wake up early tomorrow. Let's go get your makeup and clothes figured out."

She followed me through the house and up to my bedroom, where I'd laid out a few outfits on my bed. After picking up a plaid shirt and then a floral blouse, she held up a plain navy blue cap-sleeve shirt under my chin and nodded. "This one is perfect, because I brought something for you that'll go well with it." Digging around in her giant diaper bag turned purse, she pulled out rolled-up red fabric tied with a bow. "I took your Seoul Sistas company name and made this. Behold it's splendor."

I pulled on the ribbon and unraveled it. It was an apron with the words "I'm a Seoul Sista" embroidered on the front. The "O" had the red and blue circle from the Korean flag.

"I love this so much, thank you!" Arms outstretched, I came in for a hug and she said, "My belly is an obstacle now." I pulled her in for a sideways hug instead.

She smiled. "I learned a lot while I worked on this present! That red and blue circle is a yin and yang. All things in the universe have two complementary aspects—and they can't exist without each other. Like the yin is dark and cold, and yang is hot."

I said, "So are you calling me dark and cold, or hot? Trick question. Everyone knows I'm hot."

She laughed. "Welllll, if the blue section stands for negative cosmic forces, and the red section stands for positive ones—and both in a constant state of opposition and balance, you're both. So my answer is dark and cold. But also hot."

"Thanks, Professor, for the history lesson."

She grinned. "But if you want to keep things high-level here, the red and blue circle and the lettering are super cute, right? The design really seemed to fit you. I hope you can see them on camera."

"Me too." I put on the shirt and tied the apron in the back. My alarm buzzed. Fifteen minutes left.

Celeste took a step back. "You look great. Now on to hair and makeup!"

She went over to my dresser and grabbed foundation, concealer, powder, eyeliner, and a brush. "You don't have any mascara?"

I barked out a laugh. "My eyes haven't changed since high school. My eyelashes are still stick straight and basically invisible with how my eyelids fold."

"Hmmmm." She peered up close. "Gotcha. Okay, we'll focus on other eye enhancements. Close your eyes." She applied concealer, foundation, and powder as she chatted away about her kids and all the classmates she'd kept in touch with since high school.

With the eyeliner pencil, she stroked my lids a few times,

paused a few seconds, stroked some more, and then turned my head side to side.

"Okay, you can open your eyes."

I walked over to the mirror on my dresser. Staring back at me was a vibrant Jess Kim I hadn't seen since college graduation. Since before Hamilton Cooper.

"Wow, you're a miracle worker!" I tilted my chin up, feeling a little more dignified now with the makeover.

She stood behind me. "You're the same person. I just brought you out more. I'm like a human highlighter who happens to be good at getting rid of dark under eye circles from many years of sleep deprivation."

The phone alarm dinged and echoed in the room. Five minutes.

Celeste said, "You look great. I'll head out now and let you do your show. Let me know if you need me to help you finish up with those packages."

We both went down the stairs, but she went out the front door while I headed to the kitchen to turn on the lighting, microphones, and computer. Earlier that morning I'd put out all of the meal prep materials on the kitchen island and made sure all of the electronics were charged. With three minutes left, I turned on the mic, pulled a few items from the fridge, and then flipped on the lights. I tried to make time for some deep breathing before getting the show started, but the blinding

LEDs made it hard to relax. Worried my eye makeup would run from my watery eyes, I dabbed them with a paper towel just before my final alarm beeped.

Showtime.

My thumb hovered over the button on the clicker. I pressed it firmly, like I'd done so many times that morning during the dry run. A three-second delay, blink, blink, blink.

NOW RECORDING LIVE.

Big smile, Jess.

"Good afternoon everyone, from Nashville, Tennessee, or good morning, or good evening, depending on where you're joining me from."

Thirty people viewing. Not bad.

A few comments scrolled through. "Hi, Anne from Florida! Lee Ann and Shay from Ohio, Sherry from Georgia, and Michelle from LA. Thanks for joining!"

Deep breath in and out. Smile! "Thanks for tuning into the Seoul Sistas channel today! This is the first live episode in my cooking series *Hanguk Hacks*. This series will highlight ways to add a little Korean flair to the most popular meal-kit deliveries by hacking the recipes so you don't have to eat the same ol' boring thing. For any food authenticity die-hards, I'm sad to say this show is *not* for you. I'm here to take a boring meal kit"—I held up a recipe card for SKILLET STEAK IN BROWN BUTTER

SAUCE—"and give you the tools to make Asian-inspired dishes while keeping your life simple."

Viewers sent streams of clap and heart emojis.

A few more people joined.

Things were going well!

"First up, we have this week's BOXFRESH delivery. It comes with locally sourced, organic fruit and vegetables, which is what makes this kit different from some of the mainstream ones I'll be using in future episodes." I opened the box with a box cutter. I'd learned the hard way, two stitches later, that using a pair of opened scissors to unseal a package was not the safest solution. X-Acto knives were the way to go.

Once the flaps were pulled back, I lifted out a bunch of carrots, a potato, and a small head of cabbage. "Oooh, maybe I can do a beef stew later. Or off-season corned beef."

More comments appeared.

I love corned beef!

Omg I'm hungry now

Kiss me, I'm Irish, lol

With the produce on the table, I reached down into the box to grab a bag of prewashed Bibb lettuce for salad and a vacuum-sealed package of presliced flank steak. "Aha! Here we go." I held the beef up to the camera. "Time to make some marinade!"

A bowl on the counter already had premixed ingredients, just in case I messed up on camera. *See, Daniel, sometimes being a planner is better than always being spontaneous!*

As if I'd summoned the devil himself, Daniel wrote a comment: *Nice apron. Are you wearing replacement purple sweatpants from the waist down?*

I clamped my mouth closed, trying to keep from giggling. I needed to stay focused here. Ignore Daniel. Make meat. End show. Easy peasy.

"Recipes will be in the comments after the show, so don't worry about writing all of this down." One by one, I held up all of the marinade ingredients. "Onion. Garlic. Soy sauce. Sesame oil. Sugar. Green onion. Black pepper and sesame seeds optional. Pear puree or kiwi preferred. It helps tenderize and sweeten the meat."

A viewer asked, *Kiwi??? Do you keep the seeds in?*

I smiled and repeated the question. "I use the blender so I don't usually taste any crunchiness from the seeds. I swear, it works great. But I prefer pear puree from a jar because I hate cleaning blenders." Back in NYC, I'd made a similar dish every year for a college friend's annual New Year's Eve potluck. It was always a hit and there were never any leftovers.

I'd had the foresight to preportion out the ingredients and mixed everything on camera in one of Mom's big metal bowls.

As I stirred the marinade, I heard the pantry door open and close, and then the unmistakable hiss of a carbonated beverage being opened echoed in the kitchen.

To my right, while the livestream was going, my mom handed me an opened can of Coke.

I smiled at the camera and thanked her for the soda. "I'm not thirsty right now, but thanks Mom." She bowed and took a step back.

I continued mixing and looked for the kitchen shears to open the package of meat. Mom reappeared and handed me a pair, off camera. "I always carry in my pocket," she said, just loud enough for the mic to pick it up.

"Thanks Mom, I'll be okay."

More comments.

Omg, your momma!

She's so badass, keeping shears on her 24/7. Does she go to bed with them too

Hi Seoul Sista's Mom!

I took the shears and cut open the package, lifting the meat and placing it in the bowl, then covered all of the slices in the dark brown marinade using the spoon.

"No, no, no," Mom muttered from the sideline.

I flashed a smile at the camera and tried to keep cool, even though my umma was heckling me from the front row.

I shot her a "simmer down there" look and continued to speak over her tongue-clucking. "Because the slices of meat are thin, you don't need to marinate it a long time—"

Without warning, Mom walked on the set, standing alongside me, and poured a few ounces of Coke into the bowl. She squinted at the bright lights and held her hand over her eyes like a visor. "Ji-Hyun-ah! Coke makes meat juicier. More soft, not like beef jerky. Umma to the rescue!"

Rescue? This was an on-air destruction mission led by my very own mother.

She wiped her index finger on the rim of the bowl and put it in her mouth. I turned to the camera and, with a panicked tone, explained, "Um, she's trying some of the marinade that wasn't mixed with the meat." The last thing I needed was a string of comments about her getting salmonella.

"Something wrong," she said definitively.

Yes, what's wrong is you did a walk-on cameo on my show without clearing it with me first!

Umma eyed the ingredients and picked up the soy sauce bottle. The generic store-brand that was on sale. "You need Korean brand soy sauce." She opened the cabinet under the kitchen island and pulled out two bottles. "If you want soy sauce for jjigae or namul, this one is good kind." She held up a bottle of Sempio Chosun Ganjang next to her beaming face, like she was being paid for a product endorsement from the Sempio company. She picked up the other bottle. "For meat, like bulgogi or kalbi, I buy this one. One Hundred Percent Yangjo Ganjang!" Again, she posed with the bottle, like an Instagram influencer being paid for a #ad.

As if being dragged by my own mother about poor soy sauce selection on a livestream wasn't horrifying enough, she then added, "You forgot ginger," pointing at the metal bowl.

And she was right. I had a mangled ginger root next to the sink, but it wasn't washed or shredded. I'd forgotten to do it in my morning prep. While I prepared the ginger, my mom continued her intervention.

She took the metal spoon and tossed it in the sink, then washed her hands. "I don't like metal spoon to mix in metal bowl. Makes too much banging noise," she said, and turned toward the camera. "I use my hand to mix, sometimes I use a kitchen glove. Not today!" Kneading the meat like Play-Doh with her bare hands, she said, "This smells good, when you add the ginger, this will be a Jessica masterpiece." Then she winked at me. I'd never seen her wink before. Who was this woman?

My fake smiles fought hard against my angry frowns, to the point of looking like I was glitching on camera. I sprinkled slivers of ginger into the mixing bowl. I had to say something—it was my show. "Mom's rubbing the ingredients into the beef and, as you can see, after half a minute, most of the marinade has been . . . uh . . . sucked into the meat." My face flushed with embarrassment, and I was certain my cheeks matched my fiery red apron. *Oh GOD. Sucked into the meat? This was a cooking show, not a Dyson vacuum demonstration.*

I dropped a spoon, and the clang startled both of us. She shook her head and pointed at the screen with her meaty hand. "Lots of people talking."

Sure enough, comments were scrolling so fast it was hard to focus on what they were saying. I caught a few tidbits.

> *Subscribed to this show now, I love it*
>
> *Mom and daughter, so cute!*
>
> *Umma to the rescue! Umma FTW!*

As I set the oven and prepped the pans for broiling, I knew this needed to end harmoniously. I chatted about how Mom, Dad, and I all loved the taste of grilled meat the best, but that the point of the show was to make cooking easy, so the meat would go into the oven instead. Mom didn't argue, but she did add a little of her own soy sauce plus a few more splashes of Coke before adding the raw meat to the pan.

She washed her hands, then set aside some of the smaller

bits of meat and lined them up in a row on the pan so they'd be positioned near the oven door. In a matter-of-fact tone, she said, "These little one cook faster. We can try soon!"

Soon couldn't come fast enough. After Mom lifted my inferior soy sauce to better see the color in the light and compared it to her Korean brand, I opened the oven and took out the smaller meat pieces. She was right; they cooked in half the time. The beef sizzled on the metal pan as the fragrant smell of umami and sesame oil filled the kitchen. My mouth watered as I transferred the cooked pieces to a plate and reinserted the pan into the oven.

Mom announced, "Let your appa try." Off-screen, waiting in the wings, was my dad. More timid than my mom, he stood on the sidelines and gave a small wave, but didn't speak. Mom scooped up day-old rice from the pressure cooker and put it into a bowl. She added the meat on top and held it out. "Come try."

Dad was away so often he probably had no clue what the heck was going on with all the blazing lights and the big kitchen mess. But he loved homemade food, so he walked into the kitchen and took the bowl from my mom. She twirled her finger. "Ca-ma-ra-rul boh say yo." *Look at the camera, please.*

Dad's eyes widened as he turned to the webcam. He took the bowl from her hands and sniffed. After a pause, he announced, "Smell good!"

"Try!" Mom grabbed some chopsticks from the dish rack and bounced on the balls of her feet in anticipation.

I looked at the comments flying up the screen.

Try it!

Try!

Tryyyyyy!

Dozens, then hundreds of people begging Dad to try our bulgogi-inspired flank steak. He grabbed the pair of chopsticks from my mom's hands and poked them into the meat and rice. Dad scooped and put an entire heap of food into his mouth.

His chewing took an eternity. You know those scenes in horror movies when the music is cued and you're bracing yourself for a jump scare? That's what was going through my head. Dad was going to make a sour face and I'd be ruined. Or he'd spit out the food and food bits would spray all over the nonreturnable equipment. Or he would simply do the Korean thing where he'd find a little thing to critique, say that the food was okay but "a little salty" or "too dry" and while any Asian Americans watching the show might get that nuanced praise, the predominantly White audience would not.

A drip of sweat trickled down my left temple. None of this was in my control. I had no idea what he would say.

I couldn't shoot my parents a look and instantly communicate with them like I did with my friends. We didn't have that level of commonality or understanding. We could barely communicate in words. Expressive facial contortions were not a language they understood, nor would they ever care to. So I had to wait for Dad's verdict.

While tapping her fingers in a 1-2-3-4 pattern on the light gray granite countertop, Mom finally barked, "Well? Do you like or not?"

He pursed his lips. Then held up the bowl once more. "MASHITDA!"

The grin on his face made my heart burst. I let out a sigh of relief and the strong urge to clap took over, but then I remembered to take the rest of the meat out of the oven. Heart-eye emojis flooded the screen as my dad happily scarfed down the rest of the food sample.

My mom ripped open the bag of Bibb lettuce from the meal kit and pulled out one of the larger leaves. Taking some of the rice and meat and placing it on the lettuce, she rolled it like a taco and offered it to me. "It's ssam, that mean *wrapped* in Korean. Then you eat healthy too."

I took a gratuitous bite in the direction of the camera. "Maybe this would be good with gochujang sauce? Oh, maybe ssamjang?" Without thinking, I'd posed this as a question, which opened it up to me giving away authority and looking to my mom as the expert.

You're not a leader, Jessie.

Dad stopped chewing so he could hear what Mom had to say, while I squeezed my eyes shut and tried to push the negative self-talk out of my head.

She cleared her throat, triggering me to sharply inhale. "You know Appa and I don't like spicy. Maybe taste good. Maybe taste better. I don't know."

I don't think she was trying to make me look good. Or even not look bad. Mom was answering honestly. She and Dad hated spicy food; it upset their stomachs and they marveled at my love for heat when I'd try foods with Hatch chiles or serrano peppers. My favorite dish was tteokbokki—the spicier the rice cakes, the better.

When Mom ended her commentary about spicy foods, I let out a long breath I'd been holding far too long. All things considered, the show up to this point had gone well, but I wanted to end quickly before any other surprises surfaced.

"Thank you to all the viewers who stopped by to watch the first episode in this new series! Next week I'll continue with another meal-kit show, where we'll hack a chicken or pork dish, so please tune in. I'll also unveil my line of Seoul Sistas marinades, sold exclusively through NiHao Markets. Oh! Links to donate are in the show description. These meal subscriptions aren't cheap, so any help would make a huge difference!"

My parents held hands and bowed to the camera. "Ahnyung!" Mom and Dad never held hands. Not when praying.

Not when Dad was in the hospital for a mild concussion. Never had I ever seen any display of . . . whatever this was.

A quick bout of light-headedness hit me hard as I unsteadily pressed the button on the clicker. The "go live" light turned off and the gleaming lights went dark. We were offline. Time to relax.

"All finish?" Dad asked.

I nodded. "Yep, all done."

He pointed at the pan. "That meat is good! A little too sweet."

Mom and Dad bickered in Korean while I scrolled through the comments. There were hundreds of them, including ones from food bloggers and popular #cookingfromhome Instagrammers. This business idea was getting traction, and my social media notifications exploded with comments, links, tweets, and new followers. Thrilled at first, I mindlessly retweeted and reposted everything I could, striking while the iron was hot. My show had grabbed people's attention and made a few waves in the home cooking community. But reading the comments pouring in, I began to see a common thread.

Cooking Umma for President!

Haha her mom reminds me of my mom. I can never do right by her!

What a cute lil chef family, especially the mom!

With all the planning that had gone into my meal hacking business plan, I'd never imagined that my videos would have taken off with the help of my mom. Could I risk doing the rest of the shows without her? And just as scary, could I risk doing the rest of the shows *with* her? The last time we "worked together" was when I was sixteen and learning how to drive. She was supposed to be my instructor because my parents didn't want to pay for driver's school, but I didn't even make it out of the driveway. We got so wound up and stressed out from each other's yelling that a neighbor called the police.

Just when I thought things couldn't get more stressful, they did.

Daniel sent a message: *Hey, how'd the show go? I had to cut out early for some business meetings. NiHao Markets' COO called and wants to confirm delivery by Friday afternoon at the Distribution Center in Murfreesboro. Need help?*

All of the boxes would be ready for shipment in the morning, but I'd have to pull an all-nighter. Lucky for me, my days in banking had prepped me for this. I had a student movers and courier (bonded and licensed) service lined up for the delivery. Everything was going as planned. Well, except for the cooking show that'd just aired.

Celeste messaged too: *I have no words. That was the highlight of my existence. I can die happy now. You almost made me go into labor early from laughing so hard. Who knew your mom (and dad???) would be total hams?*

Now that Celeste had put it into words, it was clear. Mom had come on-screen, critiqued my cooking in front of an audience, and *stolen my show.* The sinking feeling in my stomach was a strong sign that I wasn't okay with it. As comments poured in, and subscribers shared the video, I couldn't believe it. My fledgling cooking channel I'd started so many years ago had finally taken off. People dreamed about this kind of thing happening. But I couldn't help but wonder in the back of my mind . . . had I taken another huge step back in independence? Did my success now depend on doing business with my mom? I couldn't think of anything more terrifying.

Chapter Thirteen

No Wi-Fi and no printer on NiHao Markets warehouse delivery day.

What else could possibly go wrong?

The boxes of marinades and sauces had been loaded onto the student truck, and the driver was on his lunch break. I thought that printing the invoice and itemized packing slips for Jeff Yee of NiHao Markets to accompany the shipment would be easy, but I'd failed to check the ink levels in my parents' printer. It was the same one that I'd used in high school and they'd kept in the living room but never replaced. It was more than ten years old! Did they even sell ink cartridges for that model anymore? I'd enclosed the required paperwork, some practice pages I'd printed early that morning, but they were severely faded and unprofessional. I needed to replace them with legible ones.

It was *not* the best time to play IT director for the Kim

household. I scooped up my laptop and headed to Flora's coffee shop, which was only a few blocks away. I messaged her to make sure she was working there that day and had a printer available. Flora's nickname at the café was Mayor: she was a networker, a problem-solver, and seemed to know everyone in the neighborhood. She ended our message thread with *I have good news! Come by ASAP!*

The bell on the door jingled as the front door closed behind me. In the few times I'd come here, it was never at full capacity, but all of the tables were occupied that morning. Flora was behind the counter and must've read my face. "We're so busy now. Schools are back in session. Lots of students come here to study and do group projects."

The average age was maybe twenty, but over in the corner was a group of elderly women with cards on the table, letting out an occasional hoot and holler.

"What's going on there?"

She laughed as she wiped the counter with a tattered rag that smelled like vinegar. "They call themselves the Gamblin' Grannies. It's like Bingo night, but they come here to play poker or blackjack with, like, twenty bucks to buy in and someone usually leaves with, like, five hundies." The way they got all fired up about the game, called one another out, and genuinely enjoyed their time together made me want that life when I got older. In fifty years, I wanted to be exactly like these Gamblin' Grannies.

I scrunched my nose, hoping to get the vinegar smell out. It was a sharp contrast to the otherwise pleasant notes of caramelized and nutty coffee aroma surrounding me.

I asked, "So what's the going price of a few invoice printouts? Extra iced latte and a few baked goods?" Today's special under the glass dome: cinnamon buns with pumpkin spice icing. "Oh wow, is it already pumpkin season?"

Flora nodded. "For me, it's always pumpkin season. I love it. But yeah, didn't you notice? They already had Halloween shit in stores in July."

I put in my order for a large iced pumpkin spice latte and a cinnamon roll. Then I pulled out my laptop. "Didn't you have good news for me?"

She shouted over the hiss of the steam wand. "Yes! But first, can we talk about how your cooking video hit my circle of econ geek friends this morning? Congratulations!"

That morning, my *Hanguk Hacks* episode had been picked up by BuzzFeed, *The Korea Times*, and even *Bon Appétit* of all places. Last I'd checked, the video had ten thousand comments and had almost surpassed a million views. Celeste had an Etsy shop and she messaged me that she'd gotten special request orders for show-themed embroidered aprons, both domestic and international orders. Neither of us could believe it. She and I had a meeting planned later in the week to discuss merchandising opportunities.

Flora squealed, "I knew you before you hit it big!"

I laughed. "Yeah, yeah. Enough about me though, what's your big news? Spill it!"

Her follow-up loud squealing made some of the grannies shoot us funny looks. "I finished my dissertation. I'm graduating soon! Finally."

"Oh my gosh, I'm so happy for you!" I hadn't heard good news since I'd been home; it was so nice to hear something positive. "Doctor Flora Barrios. I like the sound of that!"

She beamed. "Me too." Pouring the latte into the cup first and then adding ice, she slid the drink to me and then lifted the dome to pick out an iced roll. "I'll walk you to your seat."

Two college-aged students with heavy backpacks smiled at me as they stood from their seats and cleared their small square table. It was the far corner and close to the speaker, but it was better than nothing. Putting down my drink, I asked, "For my invoices, what's best—that I email you a file and you print it in the back, or I connect to the printer directly?"

"How about you send it to me, I honestly have no idea how to give you access to the printer wirelessly."

"Don't you have a PhD? Shouldn't you be able to figure it out?"

"Yeah, in econ but not in wireless technology! And my Chromebook is, like, five years old."

Flora waited as I logged on to the Wi-Fi and emailed the

attached file. I smiled at her. "Thanks for your help, you're a lifesaver! I sent you an invoice and ten packing slips. So eleven pages in all."

Flora wiped her hands on her apron. "I'll only be a few minutes, it takes a while for the printer to turn on and warm up. And then for whatever reason, it prints out like ten test pages." She walked away and called out over her shoulder, "You'll need to watch the place while I'm in the back."

"What do you mean, watch the place?"

Flora entered the back room before answering my question.

I grabbed my laptop and drink and brought it to the counter, then stood there awkwardly, praying no one would enter the café and ask me any questions about flavor, aroma, body, and acidity.

One of the older ladies at the gambling table tottered over to me. "Do you have change for a hundred?"

I looked in my zip wallet for cash. Honestly, I hadn't used actual dollar bills in so long I had no idea what I'd find, but I was nearly 100 percent certain it wasn't enough. In fact, I was certain I'd come up way short. There was a dollar in the bill slot, but she needed ninety-nine more of those.

She pointed to the counter and asked, "Can you look in the register for me? I bet you have enough in there."

The lady was probably right. The obvious problem, unbeknownst to her, was that I had no idea how to open the register. Nor did I know if I had the authority to do so, seeing as how

I was not even legally supposed to be posing as an employee. "Would you mind coming back here in about five minutes? My manager will be here then and she can handle this request." I smiled radiantly, in the most customer-service-oriented way I could.

She nodded. "Okay. I'm trying to buy into the game and I need exact change. Buncha old ninnies won't make an exception. I'm a founding member!" She harrumphed and padded away.

A loud jingle behind me scared me stiff. My heart pounded because this meant one of two things. A customer leaving, or . . . a new customer.

C'mon, Flora! Hurry up!

"Aren't you supposed to be delivering a shipment to Jeff's warehouse right now?" Daniel's voice sent a shiver down my spine. I hadn't seen him in person since his sweatpants thievery.

I whirled around and expected to see regular ol' Daniel, possibly still wearing my purple pants, but what stood before me was definitely not that. He was in a suit and tie, having donned what I'd call full banker attire. Hair coiffed, freshly shaven, and a charcoal gray suit that fit him like a glove. His bold choice of pink shirt paired with a striped gray tie drew my gaze to his chest. All I could think about was how, all those nights ago, my hands had been under his shirt and we'd been interrupted before I'd completed my full Daniel expedition.

The elderly woman came back. "You look like the kind of

man who might have change for a hundred." She waved her bill like it was a treat for a small dog.

He shot her a million-dollar smile. "I always carry cash. You never know when these high-tech machines will fail you."

She nodded so enthusiastically I thought her neck might be sore the next day. "A man of my own principles. I love it!" He handed her five twenties and she gave him his hundred-dollar bill.

"Thank you, young man!" As she made her way back to the gamblers, she turned her head and gave him little wavy fingers over her shoulder. My God, was she flirting with him?

Ugh. Everyone loved Daniel, even eighty-year-olds.

I put my hands on my hips. "I'm not late, I have a little time. I needed Flora's help to print out an invoice and packing slips. She's a barista here. My printer at home is *no bueno*. I'm guessing you're not working at home today either?" I gestured from his shoulders down to his knees.

He pursed his lips and nodded. "Yeah, I have an interview here with someone from out of town in a few minutes. Coffee meetings are popular in our industry." My stomach went sour and my shoulders sagged. Was I envious? Of a corporate job where you had to wear uncomfortable suits all day? Okay, maybe just a little.

Or was it disappointment? That he always seemed to have something lined up? That he was always in demand? Or that he might be leaving Nashville for greener pastures?

His eyebrows drew together. "But seriously, you should leave soon. Jeff Yee doesn't mess around."

"I have a little buffer. Who's the interview with?"

Daniel's story all over the Korean community was that he was on sabbatical from the top VC firm in the Bay Area. But didn't that mean he was supposed to go back? Why was he interviewing?

His face flushed to the color of his shirt. "It's nothing. Just a few job leads that probably won't go anywhere. I . . . my . . . sabbatical officially ended. I'm exploring other options now."

"You didn't want to go back?"

He offered me a wary smile. "I didn't. It's . . . a long story." He glanced at his watch. "And you don't have the time. But maybe instead of you dodging the questions about us meeting up soon by sending me an overwhelming number of animated gifs and emojis, you can pick a place and time for dinner."

Flora burst through the back door, waving several sheets of paper. "You would not believe how hard this was. The paper jammed. The toner was low and needed replacing. But it's done!"

I hugged her. "Thanks, I owe you big!" My time buffer had vanished and I was actually running a tiny bit late. "I'll message you later, I gotta run."

"Message me too! I want to hear all about your plans for video content, now that you and your mom are the newest internet sensation," Daniel said with an upturned mouth. "I better go find a seat though, my guy will be here soon. How do I look?"

My gaze traveled from his head to his toes. His practical but still sexy haircut suited him. Daniel exuded confidence and charm with his killer smile and strong jawline. His broad shoulders and chest, those muscular arms and thighs under the perfectly fitted suit . . .

"So?" he asked.

How did he look? Hot. That's how he looked. Screw the interview and my warehouse appointment, let's-get-into-the-back-seat-of-your-Mercedes-level hot. If the job interview was solely based on attractiveness, he'd be a shoo-in. Words formed and fumbled in my mouth, and Daniel needed me to say something positive, but what was running through my mind wasn't appropriate.

Flora leaned into the counter. "You look dashing. Isn't that right, Jess?"

Heat rushed to my cheeks. "Yes." I gulped. "Dashing."

"Thank you. I hope it goes well today." Daniel grinned sheepishly and pointed toward the tables, indicating he was exiting the conversation to find a seat for his coffee interview. He whistled a tune as he made his way to a table in the back. It wasn't until he was out of earshot that I figured out he was whistling "Dashing through the snow" from "Jingle Bells."

While I searched for my keys, a notification that the truck driver had departed my home and was en route to the warehouse left me nervous and giddy. Once the inventory was unloaded at the warehouse and the invoice was handed over to the

NiHao accounts payable department, this Seoul Sista will have made her first big sale. Smiling wide, I waved to Flora and left the café, laptop in hand and invoice and packing slip printouts tucked under my arm. Crisis averted.

In Mom's Camry, I took one last look at the invoice to skim for errors before I sealed the envelope. Addresses, check. Spelling, check. Quantity, check. And payment terms: Net 60. I'd get paid within sixty days of the invoice date. I'd wanted Net 30, but I'd read that retailers might be more willing to work with me if I gave them some time to secure funds.

One thing caught my eye, something I hadn't noticed when I was inputting the numbers into the billing software. The invoice was listed as "Invoice #1." It was my first official document for my only customer, Jeff Yee, but would the staff at NiHao find this unprofessional? That this was my very first retailer invoice and I had no others? Maybe it was a small thing, and something only someone like me would notice or care about, but I couldn't quell the negative voice in my head. *Amateur. You're NOT a leader, and you have no attention to detail.* Just moments before I'd been giddy from the excitement of this new venture. I'd gone from hero to zero in less than a minute.

This *was* my first rodeo. I knew I would eventually overlook things and make mistakes—it was inevitable as I ramped up on learning a brand-new business. It sucked that it actually happened though, for something as important as this.

Deep breath.

I pressed the Camry's ignition button. Nothing happened. At first, I thought I'd forgotten my keys, but no, they were here in my purse. I'd just replaced the battery, so that wasn't the problem. Checking the maintenance stickers from the dealership, it looked like the last time the car had been serviced was three years ago. And since then, Nashville had experienced record cold and heat. My hands gripped the steering wheel so hard my knuckles turned white. My heart pounded harder as I tried the button again and again. With my foot on the brake and my finger pressing the ignition, the car was silent and the only noise was my heavy, panicked breathing.

I screamed, "GOD FUCKING DAMN IT!" and hopped out of the car. I didn't have time for this shit. An Uber to the warehouse location would be $40 each way, at least.

Flora was chatting with a customer when I burst into the coffee shop, this time in a state of disarray. "Do you have a car? I'm in trouble. It's an emergency."

Her eyes widened. "Are you okay? My friend dropped me off. No car, I'm sorry. But there's someone who drove here who might not be leaving anytime soon—" She glanced over at Daniel, who was in an intense conversation with a man twice his age. Laughter erupted from the table, and Daniel's interviewer stood up to look at the assortment of baked goods at the counter. I used the opportunity to run over to Daniel to ask for help.

"Hey, how's it going?" I asked.

He looked over at the counter. "Good, so far. What's going on? Why do you look so intensely scary right now? Just a few minutes ago you looked less . . . postapocalyptic."

I couldn't help but laugh. It was a good release from all that pent-up anxiety. "Any chance I can borrow your car? I'll fill it with gas and wash it when I'm done. Mom's car died in the parking lot, and I need to get to Jeff's warehouse, warp speed."

He cocked his head. "Hmmm. Sally's a sporty model and can definitely do warp speed. But do I trust you with her?"

"Sally?" I snorted. "Do I trust a guy who names his car Sally?" Maybe this was a bad idea. The more I thought about it, it was definitely a bad idea. "Never mind, I'll take an Uber."

"No, no, it's fine." Daniel dug into his pocket. "Here're the keys. Don't run into any shopping carts, sweetie."

Just when I was ready to fire back a comment, his table companion approached. "Well, well, Daniel. You're already making friends at the café. I'm not surprised."

There was truth to this: Daniel made networking look effortless. For me, it was a huge effort just to talk to new people and shake their hands. Not for Dashing Daniel. He was the leader type. Knowing all the right people. Knowing the right thing to say.

Daniel turned on his megawatt smile. "This is Jessie Kim. She's a former banker turned entrepreneur."

The older gentleman shook my hand. "I'm Rhett Williams at Paragon Agency, we specialize in headhunting for banks, hedge funds, and VC firms." He put a cream cheese danish down on the table and pulled out a business card from his pocket. "If you ever need a job, call me. We do full-time placements, consultancy, and contract jobs too."

Daniel added, "Rhett was in town for a conference. He helped place me at my last consulting gig in Atlanta and said he wanted to tell me about some shiny new opportunities."

"Nice to meet you, Rhett. I'll let you two get back to your discussion." I held up the business card. "Always good to meet new people like you."

He smiled. "Likewise. Be in touch!"

Relief washed over me as I exited the coffee shop, as if chatting with Daniel and Rhett helped lower my blood pressure and relieved my sense of unease.

His car was easy to spot, being the only Mercedes parked on the street. Up close, it became clear to me that his car was not in fact an E-class, but an S-class, which had a much heftier price tag than an E. In fact, the S-class was twice as expensive as the already lavish E-class. Which meant Daniel was possibly leaning more into douchebag territory than I thought. A D-class. But then again, he did lend me his hundred-grand car, which made him maybe a lowercase d-class.

I was accountable for driving Sally, who was worth more than my company's value, to a warehouse where I'd be dropping off my "#1" invoice and unloading boxes of sauces and condiments. God, could this day get any weirder?

In fact, it could.

Daniel's car had no handles.

His car had handle-shaped silver things, but they were flush to the car door. I slid my hand across the driver's-side door, hoping my touch would make them pop out or something. My face flushed with anger and embarrassment as I rubbed the door in circles, as if it were a genie's bottle.

A guy in a Titans cap walking a Jack Russell terrier walked up to the car and whistled. "What a beauty! I sat in one of these at the last car show that came into town."

"Her name is Sally," I said.

"She's gorgeous." He walked around it, with his little dog trotting behind him.

Placing my hands together like I was praying, I said, "I have a humiliating confession. I need to drive this car to a meeting, and I have no idea how to open it." He looked at the car, then at me. Then back at the car. "She's not yours?"

Now he was suspicious, which he had every right to be. I was clearly not the owner of this car. But I also didn't have time for longwinded explanations.

I laughed nervously. "It's a funny story. My Camry won't start so I needed to ask Daniel"—I swallowed hard—"my boyfriend, for his keys. He's inside." I lifted the key ring and let it swing like a hypnotist would. *You will not ask any questions. You will help me.*

He pulled down the rim of his trucker cap. "Well, this is my lucky day. May I?" He held out his hand, and I gave him the keys to a hundred-thousand-dollar car. As I said, I didn't have time for long-winded anything right now.

He pressed the unlock button, and when that didn't do what we both thought it would, he pushed the button and tapped the driver's-side handle-shaped thing at the same time. A little motor sound whirred and the handle popped out.

Handing the keys back, he said, "That was, like, orgasmic. Thank you."

He whistled and jerked his head. "Okay, Mini, let's go. We gotta get back before your mama gets home." He tapped his hat brim. "Thanks again for making my day."

I smiled. "Thank you for saving me!"

Motors whirred inside as soon as I opened the door: the seats in the front and back of the car shifted and adjusted to preprogrammed settings. Glowing purple ambient lighting brightened the interior, greeting me with a visual experience akin to being on a Virgin Atlantic flight. K-pop band BLACKPINK blasted over the speakers in the back, and I leaned between the two front seats to troubleshoot the blaring music problem. On the screen affixed to the back of the passenger's seat, I tapped the glass to power it on and pressed the home icon. It took a few quick pats and screen exits, but I managed to pause the song. Trying to get back to the home screen, I hit the application for user profiles and noticed that Daniel had four of them, with thumbnail photos: his own, one for his umma, another for his appa, and another for Annie.

Yes, I was running late for the warehouse delivery. And yes, snooping around a car that was probably recording my every move would make me even more delayed. Curiosity got the best of me; I couldn't resist. My heartbeat thumped hard as I tapped on "Annie" to find out more about her. Without the speakers blaring in the back, it was easier to concentrate.

Annie's profile photo filled the screen. She was stunning, with long black hair and angular facial features like a fashion model's, with sculpted eyebrows to match. Was last logged in six months ago in San Mateo, California. She liked operas and serious musicals like *Cabaret* and *South Pacific* and probably would not be a fan of my *Grease 1* and *2* plus *Sound of Music* playlist. Or of Daniel's fondness for BLACKPINK.

The driver's-side door opened. "What the hell, Jess. You haven't left yet?"

I tapped back to the home screen and flopped back into the appropriate seat. Heat spread from my face to my neck as I tried to come up with an explanation. "I . . . uh . . . loud BLACKPINK."

He stared at the back seat. "Oh. Right. I prefer the music to come from the back speakers, so if I get a call and it can't connect to Bluetooth, it's easier to hear."

I nodded. "Makes sense I guess."

What I really wanted to know was *Who is Annie? Does she live in San Mateo? Did you break up with her six months ago? Was she as boring as her music choices?*

"Want me to drive? I'm done with my meeting. I can probably get you there quickly."

I opened the door and leaped out of the driver's seat. "Yes! I couldn't figure out how to turn it on, to be honest." I ran over to the passenger side and buckled up while he took Sally's captain's seat.

Daniel tossed his suit jacket on the back seat and turned back around. "That." He pointed to the gigantic ENGINE START/STOP button next to the steering wheel. "Press it to turn the car on. This car's a beast, but it's actually pretty simple in all the ways that are important."

As the rearview mirrors auto-adjusted to his gaze, I asked, "Why do you need all these screens?"

"The one in the middle is the media and system control panel. This one is the digital dashboard. And the one up there is an augmented reality heads-up display."

I scratched my temple. "And why isn't regular ol' reality enough when driving?"

He laughed. "It's more like an enhancement for car geeks. It displays glowing lights under the car in front of me to help maintain a safe distance, which can help at night. The system projects red lines on the edges of corners and curbs. It shows computer-generated images to help safely navigate a roundabout and when you get to your final destination, a location symbol appears that gets larger as you approach your stop. It's kind of helpful to avoid missing it and having to round the corner again."

"So these enhancements, it's like a video game, but not actually fun and not for points?"

"Something like that," he muttered while punching in the address of the warehouse into the navigation system. I tried to see if I could sneak another glimpse at any more signs of mysterious Annie on the center console but had no luck.

Twenty-five minutes between the Red Wagon coffee shop and the warehouse. Fifty minutes round trip. I fired off questions once he was on the interstate.

"So, why did you get an S-class and not a normal person car?" *Oops, that came out wrong.*

He laughed anyway. "I know you love your Camry, but I'm fond of ol' Sally. She's been there for me in tough times."

I lifted the handle on the glove compartment and the door glided open. "Well, that's straightforward and boring. I was expecting it to have its own custom laser lights show, but it's like any ol' glove box. At a minimum, there should be free Mercedes-branded fancy leather gloves included."

"You are clearly not a fan of Sally. Are you opposed to the model of car or the brand?"

I asked, "You mean, do I *hate* the S-class? Or *hate* Mercedes?"

A cheery female voice surrounded us. "What can I do for you?"

“What the—?” I yelped.

Daniel laughed so hard he nearly choked. After he took some deep breaths, he said, “*Hey*, Mercedes!”

“What can I do for you?”

He twisted his lips in contemplation. “Please turn the AC higher.”

The cool wind picked up.

I shrugged, unimpressed. Eh.

He nodded and tried again. “Hey, Mercedes!”

“What can I do for you?”

“Do you . . . love me?”

She responded, “Well, you have a very lovely voice!”

I barked a laugh. Okay, that was funny. The Camry was definitely not a self-esteem booster like the S-class ass kisser. Even so, this ridiculous voice control flattery was hardly worth the premium price tag.

I fiddled with the seat controls so I could lie back. “I’m not a car person, but I know this set you back a hundred Gs at least. So maybe I don’t hate the car, I hate the driver?”

He examined me and smirked. “You don’t hate me, Jessie.”

My body flushed warm. “Eyes on the road, buddy. Hey, Mercedes, isn’t that right?”

“What can I do for you?”

“You can tell your friend here with the lovely voice to keep his eyes on the road, Mercedes,” I responded.

The voice declined to comment. Sally was smarter than I thought.

He cleared his throat. "Sally was a rage purchase."

I repeated his words. "A rage purchase." Then I erupted into laughter. "How do you make a hundred-grand-car rage purchase? I haven't bought a car in a while, and I'm no Mercedes car geek as you know, but doesn't it take a long-ass time to negotiate and get financing approved?"

His lips twitched a little, but otherwise his face was so forcefully stoic that I couldn't tell if I'd offended him or not. I quickly backpedaled. "I guess it's better than rage buying cocaine or hookers. Or Hogwarts house paraphernalia."

Daniel's hands gripped the steering wheel tighter. I thought he was mad, but his lips finally curled into a smile. Not that I was staring at his lips. "I can't believe you just said cocaine and hookers to a pastor's son."

I settled back in my seat. "But you were okay with the Hogwarts insult? Shameful."

He straightened his shoulders and unclenched his hands, smoothly sliding them from the top of the steering wheel to both sides of it. "I had a tough time a year ago. Work was really getting to me. Some of the tech businesses I helped deploy large amounts of capital to were unethical. And there were these deals I had to oversee where the companies doing the buyouts were running minority mom-and-pop shops out of business and scooping up their properties later. A lot of these places were Black- or Asian-owned, I discovered, and that made me hate the job more, and really question my purpose in life. I was working long hours, losing sleep, and losing my mind. I couldn't stomach it anymore." Daniel bit his bottom lip. "The emotional tax was too high. I'd come home and my fiancée"—his voice hitched but he continued—"ex-fiancée, we weren't in a good place either. Annie was always nagging me about getting a better job, one that paid more, but not for my mental health. It was to support her opulent lifestyle. I went on sabbatical, bought this car in haste, and all she did was rave about how much she loved the lavishness of the car and then harangued me about how I needed to immediately upgrade everything else in my life. Maybe the car purchase was actually a test. Anyway, I broke up with her a few days later. I don't regret any of my decisions, but I'm still trying to figure out my purpose—that is still something I'm working through, even today."

This entire time, Daniel had been Mr. Perfect in my eyes. Both confident and influential. My North Star of ultimate achievement, yet only a mirage of success. For all these years, I'd been competing against someone who looked very successful on the outside but was silently imploding. I fumbled for the right words to share with Daniel and couldn't find them. I could definitely relate to what he'd gone through, questioning how I ended up on Wall Street for so many years, but it was quite possible that he'd actually experienced much worse, and chiming in now would seem like I was bringing the conversation back to me. And did I really want that? He was openly and honestly sharing his past—was I willing and able to do the same?

I stayed quiet as he went on. "This was my dream car." He chuckled. "Technically, I could afford it. You know me, I'm not fancy, I grew up here with modest means. But my fiancée hung out only with other girls who came from money. An elite group who went to Ivy League feeders or boarding schools and then went to prestigious colleges. They ate at nice places all the time. They shopped together and bought expensive things. All of this added up, and my salary wasn't enough, she said."

"Did she work?" I hated that I had to ask that question, especially about another woman, but it sounded to me like she was trying to out-Jones everyone by putting Daniel at risk, both financially and mentally. And if that was true, good riddance.

"She had a job in fashion but was let go when her company went bankrupt and never bothered to look for a job after that. The expectation was that I'd take care of her, or she'd find someone else who would. You know, a few days before we finally broke up, I found a charge on my credit card for a pair of shoes that cost over five hundred dollars. I asked her to return them, and she said they were on final sale so she had to keep them. I found the receipt in the bag: not only had she lied—they weren't on sale at all and absolutely returnable—she'd eaten lunch at the restaurant at the store too, on my account mind you, and it was over a hundred dollars. *For lunch.* I can't even imagine—" His voice hitched as he shook his head.

I asked, "You can't even imagine how much cocaine and how many hookers you could have bought with that?" Elbowing Daniel lightly in the arm, I got a tiny smile out of him.

"Exactly." We got off the freeway and followed signs to Murfreesboro. "Anyway, as my life went into a shit spiral, I decided to treat myself to ol' Sally here, something nice and impractical. You know what I drove before this?"

"A beige Camry?"

He mustered a laugh. "Close. A RAV4. Annie hated it. She kept insisting I get a new car for so long, but I loved it because it was the first car I bought on my own without my parents' help. I purchased it with one of my first paychecks after law school. But yeah, I went way overboard when I bought this car." He sighed. "I might sell it soon though. Doesn't make any sense to have a luxury car even though I paid for everything in cash. Who knows how long I'll be sporadically unemployed."

I pulled the manual from the glove compartment and flipped through it. "It's not practical, but it's pretty awesome. I mean, let's be honest. Who doesn't need ten different massage patterns in their heated seats? And did you know the headrests were heated too? I can't tell you how many times I've thought, Wow, I wish my head was warmer. Specifically, the back of it."

We looked at each other and burst into a fit of laughter. It was nice to see this vulnerable new side of Daniel, even if it was him lamenting over a $100K car that he'd already paid off.

But, of course, this intimate setting and his being open with me left the door wedged open for revelations about my own past. It was only a matter of time before he asked about it during this intimate car ride where I was trapped with no means of escape. My stomach clenched in anticipation as the silence grew.

He got off the freeway and proceeded down surface streets. "Enough about me. I want to hear why Jessie Kim left the world-renowned Hamilton Cooper. I have so many friends who'd die to work there."

Oof. There it was.

How much of the truth was I willing to bare? Did I keep it simple and honest? Every time I thought about what had happened to me at HC, my heartbeat quickened, my breath shortened, and my anxiety level was similar to when I had a fit of nightmares in the middle of the night. Nightmares weren't real though. But my layoff was.

Heat flared on my cheeks and neck. "Well, it's a long story." While he put his blinker on and turned into the warehouse parking lot, I had a few seconds to compose my thoughts. "According to the Hamilton Cooper management team, the firm was downsizing and restructuring. And since I wasn't promotable, according to the powers that be, leaving was my only option." I bit my lip and looked at Daniel, not sure what to say next.

He parked the car and turned his face toward me so we had each other's full attention. "I can't believe them. That's the dumbest thing I've ever heard! And let me guess, they worked you like a dog all those years. Everywhere I've worked, they give the best people the most work. And instead of firing people who deserve it, they pass them to other groups. I can't even tell you how many losers I got stuck with because they were lazy yet heavily connected. The institutional culture is fucked up—the places we've worked are full of white men with privilege, many of them with trust funds or safety nets, who won't change the fucking system."

He worked in a related field so probably dealt with the exact same shit I did in some cases, but not all. Daniel was a man, after all, and a good-looking one at that. There was no way around it, in the banking field, I had it worse. Way worse. Because I not only had to prove myself as an Asian American with no high-level connections and a "bamboo ceiling" just above my head—I also had to prove myself as a woman in a male-dominated field, so I had the second layer of a glass ceiling too.

Daniel's expressive dark brown eyes filled me with comfort. "Ready to go in?"

I cracked open the door and paused. "How about we go grab a bite to eat later? To celebrate my first delivery and your meeting with the headhunter?"

He eased into a smile. "I'd love that. And I know the perfect place to take you."

Chapter Fourteen

King's Hot Chicken Shack didn't exactly scream "romantic," not that I was looking for that. Clearly Daniel wasn't. The shack conveyed something entirely different, with its HOT! HOT! HOT! neon sign and posters of cartoony squawking chickens taped to the window.

Nearly all of the items offered on the menu were similar to other hot chicken places I loved, like Prince's and Hattie B's, and most were foods you picked up with your hands, a second clue that Daniel was definitely not inclined to romantic thoughts. Hot chicken nuggets, tenders, wings, quarters, and halves. Waffle fries. Curly fries. Buttered corn on the cob. All of it sounded delicious . . . and very platonic.

Like Flora's coffee shop, this place had an extensive menu, plus way too many heat levels for the average fried chicken consumer: plain, mild, medium, medium hot, hot, X hot, XX hot, XXX hot, and the ultimate heat: "hot like motherclucking hell!!!"

Daniel stopped staring at the menu and laughed in my direction. "You look so intense, like you're studying it for a quiz later."

A smile broke from my lips. "I know, menus with too many options overwhelm me. You should see me at Cheesecake Factory. The number of dessert options alone is paralyzing."

He chuckled. "For you maybe, but I see it as endless possibilities!"

Of course, he would.

I stepped up to the counter. "Okay, I think I want the wings, medium hot. Fries, coleslaw, and sweet tea, please." The cashier put in the order, and Daniel ordered the exact same thing.

"Hey, you didn't even really order, you just copied me."

He offered a lopsided smirk. "I figured if you studied the menu so hard and had come to a sound, final decision, then I should trust your judgment."

"That's basically cheating." I swatted his arm.

He raised an eyebrow. "It's called efficiency." Daniel said to the cashier, "You witnessed her hitting me unprovoked, right? She needs to apologize, don't you think?"

The cashier lifted an eyebrow. "That'll be nineteen dollars and sixty-four cents."

We raced to hand him our credit cards, and Daniel beat me by a nanosecond. He grinned at me as the cashier swiped his card and not mine.

"Thank you, sir. Here's your card and could I please get a

signature on the screen? Also, for what it's worth, I think you provoked her, sir."

Pulling out five dollars from my purse, I dropped it into the tip jar. "Thank you!"

"You're welcome, miss."

I didn't know what made me happier, that this guy agreed with me, or that he called me miss right after calling Daniel sir twice.

Daniel made a harrumph sound. The joyous sound of petty defeat.

It was past lunchtime, but no seating was available inside the restaurant. There was no way we were going to eat hot chicken outside in the baking heat either. Daniel and I exchanged looks as another party of two waiting for a table muttered, "We've been standing ten minutes. Let's get this to-go and bail." Their trays looked heavy, with nearly double the food we'd ordered, plus supersize drinks.

I made up our minds for us. "Let's get ours to-go too. Everyone just sat down with their food, no one's finishing up."

Daniel agreed. "We can eat at my house—errr my parents' house I mean—or at the church."

I asked the cashier to please change the order while Daniel grabbed a ton of napkins and ketchup packets. Our food came out quickly in two large brown bags. Daniel carried one and I took the other with the drinks inside it. Holding the top of the bag with my right hand and using my left hand on the bottom of the bag for support, I had no way to open the car door without assistance. "Can you get my door please?"

He nudged me aside and pulled on my handle when it popped out. "Here you go, m'lady! May I assist you with anything else, m'lady?"

I narrowed my eyes at him. "NOOOOOO, that's all I needed, thank you very much!"

Daniel bowed as I got into the car. "Anything else, just let me know, m'lady."

My lips pressed to a thin slash, trying to suppress a laugh. "As you were, squire." He gently closed my door.

My jaws twitched from forcefully combating my grin, so I relaxed my face muscles and relented, allowing a moment of glee to push through. I beamed as Daniel walked around the car to the other side, but then worked quickly to erase all signs of my goofy smirk when he opened his door.

He sat down in the car and once again, BLACKPINK blared from the back speakers.

I jolted upright. "That same thing happened to me! I love BLACKPINK, but not under duress. Can you turn it off, or at least turn it down?"

"It must be playing on my phone. It's connecting to the Bluetooth. At least, I think it is. I'm not very techy, even though I worked in tech for a long time."

He pulled his phone from his pocket. "Oh, I missed a call."

He turned off the music and switched his phone off Bluetooth so only he could listen to his voicemail.

I took my drink from the bag and popped the top with a plastic straw. Drawing a long sip, I tried to get my mind off the perky woman's voice on the recording. Was it someone he was dating? His ex? Whoever it was, she made his face wash over with contentment the longer she spoke.

I downed more tea when he tapped the message again to hear it a second time. Whoever this mystery woman was, she was priority number one, making me priority two.

He whispered to me, "Could I get my drink too? Pretty please?"

Scratch that. Mystery woman was priority one. Priority number two? Sweet tea. And that made me a rank lower than King's Hot Chicken Shack sweet tea. Go me.

Daniel's eyes flashed with excitement. "That was one of the recruiters from the headhunting company I interviewed with today. Apparently the guy I met for coffee already put things in motion. I have two interviews later this week. One's a consulting gig and the other is a full-time job but it's a contract-to-hire situation. If they like me, after a few months they could hire me full-time." He tapped his fingers on the steering wheel. "I have to finish up a few projects I'm helping people with though."

He chattered so fast it was hard to keep up with him, and my brain swirled with questions. What was he working on now? Would he be moving? I'd taken comfort in his life being in a similar state of uncertainty. Misery loves company and all that. Was this squeezing sensation in my chest and heart . . . jealousy? Or sadness? Was this our competitiveness kicking in, or something else? Maybe all of the above?

I sat back in my seat and tried to tell myself that he was still figuring stuff out, like me, and that this wasn't a race and there was no prize. But all I could focus on was how happy he looked right now. It was the happiest I'd ever seen adult Daniel, with his boyishly attractive face spreading into a grin a mile wide. His chest thrust out as he closed his eyes and reclined a little in his seat. The least I could do was offer him, as a dignified competitor would, a hearty congratulations, a friendly smile, and a little false cheer.

I fiddled with my straw and cleared my throat. "I know you'll do great. Good luck with everything."

"Thanks!" His beaming smile fell quickly. "You okay?"

Show strength, Jessie. Appear strong when you are weak. Channel your inner Sun Tzu.

"Yeah, I'm just hungry."

His gorgeous grin resurfaced. "Let's go to my house then. It's close."

My stomach rumbled, adding its own vote to eat soon. I tried to cough to cover up the wailing sound and failed. At least it validated that my hunger excuse was real. "What about your mom and dad? Will they be home?"

"They're painting the bathrooms at the church, so we can eat our chicken in peace."

He parked in the driveway instead of in the garage. "My parents are storing a bunch of church stuff in there."

I grabbed the drinks, and he took the food. After standing up, my stomach offered another growly soliloquy, demanding it be fed, but even louder this time. Daniel laughed and unlocked the door. "Almost feeding time," he joked.

That afternoon, Daniel's house smelled like they'd lived there for many years even though they'd settled in only a few months ago, with a familiar aromatic blend of kimchi fried rice, clean laundry, and firewood. We'd introduce the scent of spicy Nashville hot wings, curly fries, and coleslaw soon.

As soon as I found a spot at the kitchen table, I dug into my meal. I went for the fries first, because I loved fries more than anything. The wings were coated in a deep red, fiery sauce and my nose tickled from the vinegar aroma. "*Bon appétit!*" We both bit into the chicken at the same time.

The wing was so spicy that it buzzed and numbed my tongue, then surprised me by delaying a second before setting my mouth on fire. The ice in the sweet tea helped extinguish the flames only a little bit, and the coleslaw and fries didn't help much. I could usually take some heat in my food, even my parents marveled at my ability to tolerate spiciness, but this was a few degrees too many.

Daniel clamped his mouth shut, trying to hold in his

laughter. His chicken was lighter in color and not bathed in sauce like mine. Some of the crispy golden skin was visible, so I grabbed one of his wings and took a bite. Much more delicious and milder than my serving. As I chewed and swallowed, I looked at the markings on his paper box and compared it to mine. His was medium, easy sauce, extra crispy. Mine was XX hot with extra sauce!

I swapped containers with him.

"Hey," he protested.

"They got the order wrong, or you sneaked in a change to the order to punish me."

He shook his head. "Wimp." He took an emphatic bite from the fire wings and downed his tea, then finished off mine. "Oh my God. I think I burned off some taste buds."

With a stuffed mouth, I mumbled, "I trrrd to wrrrn you!" I waved a wing at him. "I lvvve thsss. A lttt."

He grabbed the wing from my hand. "That's the tax for the chauffeur services today. Plus, I paid for the whole meal, so yeah."

I ate a fry instead. "That's fair. You can have it. But only one and you owe me a drink plus ice, because you stole my tea."

He went to the kitchen. The fridge door opened and he yelled out names of drinks. "Coke? Diet Coke? La Croix? Uh, I have some Korean drinks here too. Mom and Dad buy a lot of everything in case someone in the congregation stops by."

On the kitchen table, I noticed some papers by his laptop.

His résumé, a cover letter, and a retail business financial statement. From what I could see, Daniel was doing some kind of analysis—maybe it was a case study for an interview? I wiped my saucy hands on my napkin and nudged a Post-it notepad over to the right so I could get a better look.

These documents were for NiHao Markets, Jeff Yee's company.

"How about barley tea? Homemade sikhye? Although, I should warn you, Mom makes it really sweet and she loves making it like fifty percent rice, so it's more like a pudding than a drink. I could just get you water, that's also an option."

I sat upright and called to him, "Water's good!"

Daniel entered the room with two glasses of water with ice. His sleeves were rolled up to his elbows and he'd unbuttoned the top of his dress shirt enough to reveal a deep gray V-neck underneath. I'd never seen water presented in such a sexy way before. Biting my parched lips, I had never been so thirsty.

I took my drink and croaked, "Water for you too? Copying me again?" I took a slow sip at first, enjoying the refreshingly cold drink after the recent tongue torching.

He chugged his water fast, leaving only ice cube remnants.

With a mischievous grin, he caught me off guard by asking, "Well, now that you're here, wanna take your pants away?"

My brain could not process his words. I responded, "Wuh? Uhhhh—" My body heat skyrocketed despite the ice water relief.

“So . . . no pants?” He rubbed the back of his neck. “Oh God, this is coming out completely wrong. I—I was talking about your purple sweatpants I borrowed. They’re washed and I can give them back. Right now. I’ll just stop talking and go get your sweats.” He pointed toward the staircase and scurried away, leaving me alone to slow down my rapid breathing.

My God, Jess. Did you think he’d be so forward to ask so directly if he could get into your pants in a pastor’s home?

So flustered—over a simple misunderstanding. If it was nothing though, why did I feel a pang near my heart as his grinning face barreled down the stairs, fanning my purple pants at me once he came near? And why, for a brief moment, did I want those purple pants back on him? And then off him?

I took in his rakish smirk, acutely aware of his muscular physique right next to me as he handed over the clothes, swallowing hard as I noticed his wardrobe change. He’d taken off his dress shirt, leaving only the tight gray V-neck that snugly outlined his broad shoulders and chest.

I inhaled the clothes like a spring bouquet. The fragrant fabric reminded me of him, a mix of freshly washed linens with a hint of citrus.

He laughed. “Don’t worry. I washed them myself. My mom tends to accidentally bleach things or dye them. This shirt used to be white, but it was loaded with a non-prewashed black shirt. And she shrunk it a little.” My eyes were back on his shirt again, which heavily emphasized his rippling muscles underneath. My pulse sped up and I took a quick sip of water. I forced myself to feign interest in something other than his body, so I glanced over at his television in the adjacent room.

"What's with all the electronics?" Every gaming console in existence was in the living room. There were piles of headsets, controllers, and handheld devices, as well as a pull-down green screen and several light stands, including those fancy ones with the umbrellas.

"It's my gaming stuff, and that's where I play and stream live occasionally. I don't do much of it these days. Want to take a look? Or borrow?" He motioned for me to follow him into the room. All I had in my possession was a ring light stand and one tabletop microphone. Daniel, on the other hand, had thousands of dollars of high-tech gear, like what professional photographers and videographers used. The problem with borrowing any of it was that all the equipment looked very complicated, and the last thing I needed right now in my life was more complication.

I asked, "Does any of it really make that much difference?"

His mouth hung open. "Are you kidding me? Yes!" To my surprise, Daniel guided me to the couch by putting his hand on the small of my back. Electricity pooled where his fingers lingered, sending heat up my spine. "Take a seat and I'll shoot some before and after photos."

"Um, okay?" I was hardly the spontaneous photoshoot type but wanted to see proof that this would be a worthwhile investment of both time and money. If he could prove there was a significant difference in quality, I'd definitely try to learn how to use everything. Otherwise I'd just continue with what I was doing and slowly add in new tech and tools when I could afford it with sponsorships and ads. But that would be far down the road.

With the couch situated low and the cushion placement so deep, I nearly sank to the ground. So far down that my feet flew up and I was unable to get them planted on the carpet again.

Glancing down at my outfit, I remembered erring on the side of being comfortable in case I needed to chip in and unload boxes off the truck. Never in a million years would I have expected to ride in Daniel's fancy car and end up at his house with lunch that he bought me, finishing off the day together doing a photography session, wearing a pair of denim overalls from high school I found in a drawer that I hoped were retro-cool.

I tried to rock to my feet and failed. "Nah, I'm good. I'll borrow the gear from you later."

He lifted one of the light stands and placed it a few feet away, then shined it on my face. "I'll be quick, I promise."

Time to go, Jess. One more attempt to pull myself up resulted in another failure caused by a combination of poor physics leverage and my embarrassingly weak core. I was a prisoner in this couch, trapped by my butt like a fly in a glue trap.

He added another standing light and brought over a few of those umbrellas and positioned them in various areas in the room. For the final touch, he put his camera on a tripod a few feet from the couch. "Say cheese, Jess!"

"Wait, are we—"

CLICK.

He looked in the preview screen. "Wow, you're so shiny and photogenic."

I didn't know whether to thank him or strangle him. I couldn't do the latter, with the physical restriction of my butt being under house arrest in the couch.

He flicked off all the added lights. "Okay, let's do your 'before' photos."

"Can I get a tissue, please? I want to see if I can minimize my shine." Daniel shrugged and twisted his mouth as he handed me a Kleenex box from the side table, as if to say, *Yeah, good luck with that, tissue waster.*

I had to try. After thoroughly blotting my forehead, cheeks, nose, and chin, not once but twice, I signaled to him we could resume taking photos.

I tipped my chin up and smiled toward the camera, trying my best to minimize the double chin effect that the sunken couch was built for, as he snapped a series of photographs from the tripod.

He flicked the lights on, one by one. "Okay, same pose please."

More shutter clicks. "Okay. Done! Prepare to be amazed."

He excitedly launched himself onto the couch, intending to sit on the cushion next to me, but instead toppled toward my body, pressing his thigh and arm into mine. It was like quicksand: the more we struggled to separate, the worse the situation became, with physics and poor cushion design pulling us into each other with gravitational force. At the same time, we both stopped squirming and let our bodies be. It was futile to resist. He looked at me, his eyes roving down my body, and my heart lurched. There was no denying this unmistakable magnetism building between us.

He leaned his shoulder into mine and showed me the screen on his SLR camera. "See? This is you without any lighting." He scrolled to the last image he'd taken. "And there you are. See how good you look?"

The photo wasn't of me looking at the camera. It was me gazing at Daniel, with a flicker of delight in my eyes.

He zoomed in on the image. A sweaty wisp of hair stuck on the middle of my forehead made an appearance in every picture, like I was being photobombed by my own unruly hair.

I instinctively swiped my forehead, trying to get my bangs in a more photo-ready position.

"Here, let me." He scooted closer, and thanks to cushion angles and gravity, I could feel his breath directly on my cheek as he brushed his fingers on my face.

Daniel's touch was gentle and tender, sending tiny shivers down my shoulders and back as he swept my wayward lock of hair to the side. "There," he said, gazing intently into my eyes.

I leaned forward, tilting my face toward his. He put the camera down to his side, and with both hands, he cupped my face and touched his lips to mine, slowly and carefully intoxicating me with two light, delicious kisses.

His lips continued to explore down my neck, sending small pulses of shockwaves through my body. My hands slid across his chest and down the length of his front until I hit his belt. I tugged at the edge of his shirt, signaling I wanted more.

He paused. "Want to go upstairs?"

I breathed hard. "Yes. We might get sucked into these cushions. I don't want to traumatize your parents if they discover us trapped in here."

Daniel let out a booming laugh and with his feet planted on the ground and both hands gripping the edge of the couch, he thrust himself forward. He barely made it out. The only thing missing from this awkward sequence of events was an un-suctioning sound.

Once he was standing steadily, Daniel held out his hand. A firm upward yank, and I was free. Our fingers locked together as he led me up the stairs. While climbing, he muttered, "What a day for you to be wearing overalls."

I mimicked his tone. "What a day for you to be wearing your dollar sign brass belt buckle."

We passed the first door on the right. I whispered, "Wait, isn't that your room?"

He shook his head. "Uh, I'm in the one in the back now."

It didn't fully click inside my head until we were standing in the doorway of his relocated bedroom what this actually meant. "Wait, is this—"

He flipped the light switch, revealing that we had entered the nursery.

Nothing had changed except the main furniture had been swapped, so now this room had Daniel's bed, dresser, bookshelf, and exercise equipment. "Okay, these overalls weren't a good idea, but this room is . . . literally anti-sexy. I don't know if I can do this." I backed into the hallway but he grabbed my arm.

"Don't worry, I won't turn on the mobile," he said with a half smirk.

I was definitely going to address the mobile next. It was high above us and stationary, but still distracting with all of the contrasting colors and patterns.

I shook my head in disbelief. There was nowhere for us to go. Not his house. Not mine. We were two adults, both in our upper twenties, with no place to fool around. Unbelievable.

He grabbed my waist. "Hey. I know it's not ideal, and I promise I'll redo this room, but do you think you can squeeze your eyes shut and pretend you're in the Waldorf Astoria penthouse suite or something? I did just upgrade to luxurious bedsheets this morning." He sat on his bed and smoothed out a place for me to sit next to him and patted it. "I also have a memory foam mattress topper."

Damn you, Daniel, with your mischievous, devastating grin.

I sat on the bed and closed my eyes, trying to imagine us elsewhere, somewhere other than in a nursery in his parents' house. I pictured us at a fancy hotel, together, on a carefree vacation. It also helped that both the sheets and room smelled Daniel-like. Daniel was next to me, and all around me.

"Should we pick up where we left off?" he whispered. He lifted his hand and, once again, brushed his fingers on my forehead, then gently stroked my cheek, warming them with his light touch. With my eyes still closed, I breathed him in deeply. The walls, ceiling, and floor of the room completely fell away. It was just Daniel and me.

Like waking up from a good dream, I opened my eyes and smiled at him. Unable to suppress the anticipation any longer, I placed my hand above his belt. "I think we left off . . . here?"

Interest gleamed in his eyes as his gaze slid down to my shoulders. With swift hand movements, he loosened my denim straps and pulled my overalls to the floor. At the same time, I tugged at his belt buckle, unclasping it.

His hands found the bottom of my shirt and eased underneath it. Daniel kissed me again, this time with more urgency and hunger, setting my whole body on fire with yearning.

I eased back onto the bed, pulling him down with me, our heartbeats throbbing against each other.

Pausing to kiss me again, he buried his face in my neck and whispered, "Your phone just buzzed a bunch of times in a row."

"What?" I murmured.

His lips grazed my earlobe. "Your cell phone is in your pocket on the floor and my foot is sort of stepping on your clothes. Maybe you should take a look."

My thoughts spun as I sat upright. Blood pounded through my body from both desire and worry. I tried to calm my uneven breathing as I reached down to take a look at my screen.

Flora: *Everything OK? You still with that Mercedes Boy??? Your busted car is still out front and we're closing*

Flora: *Want me to call AAA?*

Flora: *You can't park on the street overnight btw*

Flora: *Off shift. I'm driving by your house now*

Flora: *You better get home soon because I may have made your parents worried?*

"Oh SHIT." I threw the phone on the bed and struggled to put on my overalls.

His eyes widened. "What happened?"

"I need to get the car and call Triple A! My parents are looking for me. It's just a matter of time before—"

My phone rang. It was Mom.

Daniel's phone rang. He pulled the phone out of his pocket. "It's my dad."

We exchanged looks. I pointed to him, then the door. He nodded and left the room, taking his phone with him while I put Mom on speakerphone so I could hook the buttons on my overall straps. Daniel closed the door with a thud.

"Ji-Hyun-ah? Are you coming home soon? Your friend stop at home and say the car is broken. Flora is looking for you."

I cleared my throat. "Yup! I just heard from Flora. I was able to get access to a car today to get to a meeting but I'm calling Triple A now!" Whoa, I sounded way too chipper for someone whose car had broken down. "Speaking of which, I think they're calling on the other line. I have to run. I'll be home soon. Sorry I worried you."

I texted Flora back, letting her know I was okay, and also called AAA's twenty-four-hour service line. They dispatched a repair assistant who would arrive in the next forty-five minutes. Now all I needed was Mercedes Boy's help again with a trip to the coffee shop.

The door creaked as I pushed it open and I tiptoed out. After taking a few steps down the staircase, I could see Daniel wearing his earbuds, wildly flailing his one free hand while gripping the phone with the other. "I'll bring the paint *there*, you don't need to come here!"

A pause.

"They're flying me out in a few days." Pause. "Just some meetings and interviews. I'll crash with some friends in Brooklyn. I'll be back home by next Saturday and finish up any painting and help you build the Sunday school furniture and hang up the wooden cross in the chapel, don't worry."

In-person meetings and interviews? Daniel had failed to mention them to me. In the car when he was being so open and vulnerable, and I was too, I didn't know he'd already set his job search in full motion. What else was he keeping from me? Was his plan all along to have a fling with me and leave town?

I dropped my overalls for this guy.

My stomach clenched tightly as I descended the remaining stairs. The loud creaking alerted Daniel that I was nearby, causing him to pause mid-sentence before saying goodbye to his appa.

He glanced my way and shot me one of his signature charming grins, one that maybe ten seconds ago would have melted my heart and made me think I was special. But at this moment, his upturned, gorgeous, kissable mouth made my heart constrict, like someone was wringing all of the happiness out of it like a wet towel.

"Slight emergency. Dad is only a few blocks away so if you stick around I need to make it look like I'm loaning you some of the lighting and sound equipment." He ran into the living room and grabbed a light stand and a round mic that looked like an eight ball with three stubby legs.

I shrugged my shoulders, then let them droop. "I need to head out anyway. Can you drop me off at the coffee shop now? Triple A is on their way."

His brows pulled together. "Uh, okay. I was thinking maybe we could go to dinner later, but yeah, I can do that. Let's hurry up and leave before Dad comes."

He loaded the equipment into his trunk and let the power-closing lid seal itself shut. Daniel glanced at me to get my reaction to this high-tech feature, but I ignored him and sat down in the passenger seat.

"Are you mad at me?" His dark brown eyes softened.

I wanted to say, *You could have told me about your trip to New York. You hid those details! And then made out with me! Was your plan to leave here and forget about us?* But I didn't want him to see how much I cared. Or how hurt I was. Instead, I snapped, "You said hurry, so this is me hurrying."

His hand glided across his chin stubble. "Ah, okay. My dad drives slow so we're not in mortal danger." Daniel's attempt at breaking the tension with humor. Admirable, but I wasn't in the mood.

The car announced, "New text message. Would you like me to read it?" just as we were leaving his home. Daniel blushed and pulled over to take a look, fueling my belief that he was hiding things from me. But honestly, we'd never discussed anything. We were just friends. Barely friends, actually. So he could do whatever he wanted with his life, with no expectation of disclosure. And I'd do the same.

A wide grin spread across his face, dampening the nervous, awkward energy between us. "That's Jeff. He said they processed your warehouse order and the display is being set up by one of the floor managers in the flagship store on Nolensville Pike near Harding Place. Congratulations." Daniel showed me his phone. Jeff had sent a photo of my meal-kit supplements in an end-cap display, along with a hand-lettered chalkboard sign that said, "*Level up on home cooking!*" The minimalist, eco-friendly packaging was white-labeled with NiHao Market's branding per Jeff's request, but the aesthetic was all Celeste's idea. It conveyed "stress-free" and "simple" with the font choices and her line-drawn illustrations of Korean dishes and cuisine in the background.

Eyes wide in disbelief, I stared at the photo for nearly half a minute, maybe more. It was officially . . . official. I had sellable products that were being distributed in real stores.

My heartbeat raced as my brain tried to process this information. Jessie Kim. Entrepreneur. Founder and CEO of Seoul Sistas LLC. Now had products available in supermarkets.

I was forging my own path into uncharted territory, which was both terrifying and exhilarating. Everything was new, challenging, unfamiliar—I was completely out of my comfort zone. Yet I couldn't wait to see what was waiting for me around the corner.

Chapter Fifteen

Lunch with Daniel inspired the theme of the next *Hanguk Hacks* episode: "Nashville Hot Chicken vs. Korean Fried Chicken."

My plan was straightforward: I would make a hot chicken inspired sandwich while my mom made Korean fried chicken. And if Dad was around, we'd let him taste both. Viewers around the world went crazy over my mom's last cameo, so I felt obligated to offer more of the same.

While I wanted to keep things authentic with my mom, I also thought she could use a wardrobe upgrade. She vehemently disagreed.

"My shirt is okay. This one too stiff! Cheap." She threw the collared polo on her bed, not softening her words or tone even though I was wearing an identical plum-colored top. Mom had on a lime-green-and-white-striped tee she'd bought on sale at Macy's back when I was in high school. Everything I'd read online about livestream wardrobe choices said that you should avoid horizontal stripes. Most people avoided them altogether, but she welcomed them with open arms. The brighter and wider, the better! The more, the merrier!

We also debated about whether she needed special hair or makeup, but since we were getting nowhere with the discussion, I just let her be. It wasn't worth all the fighting. Frankly, entrepreneurship was taking up all of my waking hours, with all the vendor calls, manufacturing logistics, and keeping up with my inbox seven days a week. I also had a potential booth opportunity at a local farmers' market that sprang up, and a popular local food festival I'd applied for wanted more information. Most of my time was spent on operations and maybe 5 percent on the "fun" part of owning a food-related business—like coming up with new products and recipes, cooking and experimenting, and even some of the publicity. Workdays often stretched into the late evenings and weekends, just like they did at Hamilton Cooper. Still, even with the uncertainty and hard work that came with enterpreneurship, I was enjoying starting something new of my very own.

We didn't have much time before we would go live, so I needed to allocate a few minutes for rounding up ingredients, tech setup, and memorization of the recipes. Mom was a wizard in the kitchen and didn't need the same level of prep work. She could think of ingredient replacements and volume changes without any hesitation. On the contrary, I loved food science, detailed recipe cards, and using Alexa to help me with exact measurement conversions. Mom was the natural cook, and I was the book-smart one.

What I secretly hoped was that in front of the camera, Mom might pander to the viewers and divulge culinary tricks and secrets she'd withheld from me all these years. Her way of cooking drove me batty sometimes, with her pinching of salt or pepper and her pours and dashes of sauces and oil. I doubt she was trying to be elusive when it came to cooking her favorite dishes, but it made me wonder how important it was for her to pass any instruction on to me if she didn't take any time to slow down to my learning speed or share meal-prep steps with the goal of comprehension. It also made me question whether all of this risk with her being so involved in the show was even worth the trouble.

"I need to get ready, Umma. Now, remember, today can't be like last week's show where you pop in the show and um . . . argue. You promised you'd explain how to make the Korean fried chicken, okay? I'll be making Nashville hot chicken alongside you."

"No problem, no problem!" She walked out of her bedroom waving one hand in the air, indicating she was done speaking with me. Did I trust her words? Not especially. I probably should have done a quick dry run with her first, but it was too late to worry about that now.

I glanced at my watch. T minus fifteen minutes.

My throat constricted and my mouth went dry; both of these conditions begged for a tidal wave of water consumption, but no way was that happening. A small sip or two was fine but the last thing I needed now was the uncomfortable sensation of having to pee during a live video stream.

Celeste had put together a camera-ready DIY makeup kit for me, with easy instructions for concealer, foundation, blush, and eyeliner. I texted her a photo of my finished look. She sent me a thumbs-up emoji and a message in return: *Knock 'em dead, girl!*

All of the premeasured ingredients for the show were laid out on the faux marble countertop in white porcelain bowls: Mom's were to the left of the camera, and mine to the right. I set up Daniel's borrowed lighting and mic, which made the room brighter and the sound focused and crisp.

Mom came to the kitchen a couple of minutes before air-time. "Your appa is taking a nap." The implication of this of course was that he might not join us for the episode's ending, like he did on the previous show, which was a shame because he really did add comic relief when the tension built to the point of me almost losing my shit on-air. I'd have to think of another way to end the cooking demonstration if he didn't join us. More preshow stress, just what I needed.

"You ready, Umma? So I'll do an introduction, like we discussed, and then I'll let you go first by explaining how to make your own special Korean fried chicken. Got it?"

Her shoulders tightened. "Ji-Hyun-ah, no problem." With her fists balled tightly and elbows pressed to the sides of her body, her words didn't match her body language.

"Okay, we're going live in three, two, one." I clicked the button in my hand and the laptop flashed with a "RECORDING" header at the top of the screen. My voice cracked as I gave my introduction. "Welcome back to *Hanguk Hacks*! I'm your host, Jessie Kim, and I'm thrilled to bring my mom back on the show."

I paused so she could say something or ham it up for the camera like she had last time, but all she did was bow politely and offer a tight smile.

Mom never showed outward signs of distress. When tornadoes ripped through our neighborhood over twenty years ago, she barked orders for Dad and me to hunker down in the basement under a table. A few years after that, when the basement flooded, she was the first one to throw on her rainboots to carry boxes and plastic tubs up the stairs and curse up a storm in Korean. To see her like this, speechless and diminutive on camera, made alarm bells ring instantly in my head. We'd changed the show's format too much and it wasn't going to work.

I fidgeted with an apron string. "Today we have a special treat. I recently had the pleasure to eat out at one of Nashville's best hot chicken places and after some trial and error, I think I've reverse-engineered the recipe. Many meal-kit bundles come with popular recipes like chicken parm or Madeira, but after making this same old meal for a few weeks or months, maybe you might want to try something new. Maybe something a little . . . spicy? While I make Nashville hot chicken, my mom here will demonstrate how to make Korean fried chicken. What you'll notice is some of the basic ingredients of the two recipes are the same."

Comments streamed in.

I LOVE KFC (Korean Fried Chicken so bomb)

My favorite is Prince's Chicken. Sad the original location closed

I'm hungry and this is making my mouth water. I NEED CHICKEN

So sick of eating baked and pan-fried chicken ugh. Thank you I'm going to try this tonight. I hope Korean Chicken isn't too spicy> I can't handle spice

Mom stood like a flower that hadn't been watered for a few days. If I didn't take action, this show was going to be a disaster. To get her talking, I did what needed to be done to get her mojo back. I baited her.

"Before we start, we're going to try something new for this

show. Let's get some hot takes about hot chicken. Mom, can you tell everyone which one you think is better, Nashville hot chicken or Korean fried chicken?"

A fire lit in her eyes. "Korean fried chicken is best! I don't know where Nashville hot chicken come from. When I move to Tennessee many years ago, even when you were in high school, we never seen this chicken before." She raised both of her hands slightly above shoulder height. "Where it come from?"

LOL she's right. Nashville hot chicken came out of nowhere!!!

I used to eat hot chicken way before it was cool cuz Hattie Bs is near my house. But yeah it became a huge trend haha I love it. Never tried the Korean kind

Koreans know how to do fried chicken right. Your mom is the new Colonel Sanders!

To truly maximize her Korean momness, we needed to get going with the cooking so she could share her opinions on my unorthodox recipes and cooking techniques.

"I've taken out the chicken from one of my meal kits that was delivered yesterday. Usually these kits come with white meat chicken breast, so we'll be cooking with those today. I also added some wing pieces, since those are easy to get at any grocery store."

Mom added, "Dark meat is better than white meat. More flavor. Less dry."

For that comment, Mom got lots of emoji heart responses. Apparently we had dark meat chicken fans viewing the show.

"Both the hot chicken and Korean fried chicken have ingredients in common. The chicken of course, but also flour, salt, pepper, and garlic. Also, you'll need oil for frying both versions. For the hot chicken batter, you'll need eggs, milk, and hot sauce too. And you should also make sure you have cayenne pepper, sugar, and paprika handy for the later steps." I held up the premeasured cupfuls and spoonfuls and began prepping the chicken.

"Mom, why don't you go over how you're preparing the Korean version."

"I finished already while you are talking." She pointed to two bowls: a metal one with white milky batter plus a wooden spoon, and a clear one a quarter full with white powder.

She lifted the spoon, letting the batter drip. "Flour. Salt. Cornstarch. Water. No lump."

My heartbeat sped up. "Okay, would you mind mentioning how much of each you used?"

At first she looked confused, but her face brightened as she stirred. "One handful of flour. One handful of cornstarch.

Two pinch of salt. And half of this cup for water." Mom lifted a "Happy Birthday!" mug I'd painted in third grade . . . for my dad.

The comments flooded with birthday messages for my mom.

Hope your day is full of blessings. Happy lovely birthday!

Happy cake celebration day!

You're cooking on your birthday??? Tell your daughter to make you dinner lol

Like with the previous video, viewership climbed to an all-time high. On my phone, I got a message from Celeste in the comments. *OMG did you see? The Food Network, Roy Choi, and Momofuku guy all wished your mom a happy birthday!*

We continued battering the chicken pieces and dropping them into the bubbling oil. Mom said, "I like to deep fry twice. You fry, let sit on paper towel, then fry again. Makes the outside very crispy." Aha! She'd revealed something I'd suspected but she'd never confirmed. I'd thought her crispy coating came from the cornstarch. But now I knew the double-frying had a big part in that.

I joked, "I love twice-baked potatoes. Maybe more people should experiment with cooking more things twice."

While her chicken cooked, she made a sauce with gochujang, honey, soy sauce, rice wine, and garlic. Once again, she didn't give precise measurements, but gave estimates in units of fists, sprinkles, and pinches. No one in the comments seemed to mind. In fact, many viewers mentioned that their moms and grandmothers cooked the same way.

I said to the camera, "You can use the same spicy chicken marinade my mom is making for pork too. So if you have meal kits with tired old pork chop recipes, you can try this sauce instead."

The chicken hissed and sizzled in our woks. The occasional pop of oil hit my shirt in various places, making me rue the day I forgot to put my apron in the dryer. It was hard to tell with Mom's busy shirt pattern if she also had the same oil-splatter problem, but maybe she'd been right the whole time: her wardrobe choice hid stains well, much better than my clothing choice.

She whisper-hissed just loud enough for the new microphone to pick up, "Your oil pop because it too high. You need to make low so you don't get oil attack."

We both set aside our first batch of fried chicken on plates with paper towels, letting the oil escape the crunchy, crispy, and golden-brown skin. While the chicken was still hot, we brushed the pieces with our respective thick, red sauces, basting most of the pieces with the mixtures.

Mom said, "If someone think the sauce is too spicy, they don't need too much. Or they can eat chicken plain and dip in sauce." She lifted one of the cooled down, unbasted chicken pieces with her hand and dunked it into the marinade. She took an eager bite and mumbled with her mouth full, "Not too spicy this way."

Please don't double-dip on camera.

Luckily, Mom took a paper towel and wiped her hands, signaling she was done with the taste test. "Your turn," she said.

"I'll try both kinds. I know you won't try the hot chicken because of the spice level, so the people watching the show will have to take my word for it." First, I tried hers. As expected, her chicken was crispy and flavorful. The skin yielded to expose the juicy chicken meat underneath. The sweet and spicy sauce tickled and tingled my tongue with a small amount of heat. I smiled at the camera and said, "Umma, this is amazing."

My hot chicken wasn't as crunchy as Mom's, but the pieces still maintained crispiness despite being moistened by the marinade. Hot, tangy, and less sticky, my breasts and wings were tasty and had a kick to them thanks to the cayenne pepper. "Oh wow. This is super tasty too! This spicy coating doesn't work as a dipping sauce though, so you're stuck with the heat level."

Mom pointed to the living room. Dad had woken up from

his nap and looked to be ready to snack. He took a hesitant step forward, like the set was booby-trapped. "Jessie, Appa is here to taste the food!"

As we put the finished products on a fresh plate for my dad to try, I announced, "We'll have both the Korean fried chicken marinades and hot chicken rubs available for purchase soon from NiHao Markets. We'll also be selling them at farmers' markets in the Nashville metro area, if you're local." Jeff at NiHao had been happy with their first week of sales and was asking about adding more product lines and increasing their purchase order amounts.

I held up a bottle and lifted it closer to the camera. With Celeste's help, the labels were branded with an illustrated drawing of my mom with the stamped words "UMMA APPROVED!" on the front.

More heart emojis.

More happy birthday messages for Mom.

UMMA APPROVED LOL

Your dad is so cute OMGGGG

This show is making me hungry

Can we buy these products online? I'm in California but love spicy chicken!

Dad sniffed both types of wings and took a bite of mine first, then chewed and gulped. “Waaaa, very spicy! Good. MASHITDA!” Dad gave me a double thumbs-up and once again, the audience responded enthusiastically.

He sank his teeth into Mom’s chicken next, chewing and nodding at the same time. “This is good.” After wiping his hands on a towel, he pointed out that his fingers were still a little saucy. “Sticky.” Mom pursed her lips, trying to suppress her desire to scream at him on a live feed.

“How is taste?” she asked curtly. She lifted her shoulders and pulled them close to her neck.

“Very good taste!” He put the plate down and gave two thumbs-up at the camera. “Jeongmal MASHITDA!”

Mom’s shoulders eased. “My chicken is little sticky but Jessie chicken has red fingers problem. Too red.” She was referring to the fact that my spicy chicken left a red residue on the fingertips, not too different from when you ate Flamin’ Hot Cheetos. But it irked me that when Dad offered a little constructive feedback, she threw my chicken dish under the bus, on a *livestream* in front of thousands of viewers no less.

Mom was a loose cannon and Dad wasn’t helping by nitpicking on-air. I needed to end the show immediately before they ended up bickering.

“Y’all, thank you so much for watching! And don’t forget to like and comment on the post.”

More comments poured in, along with clapping emojis.

This was fun! Going to try the recipes when I get my meal kit this week!

Happy birthday!

Will there be another show next week? I love this family cooking together!

Would there be another episode? Mom being a bit of a prima donna on both episode one and two did not bode well for future shows. And her need to be the authority in cooking and the center of attention was becoming unmanageable and uncontrollable. She was like the Korean Mom Lindsay Lohan.

I waved goodbye to the camera as my mom and dad held hands and bowed.

CLICK.

I let out a huge sigh of relief as the screen went offline and the bright lights dimmed.

Dad continued to sample the chicken, which he clearly enjoyed, oblivious that he'd lit a powder keg on the show by mentioning Mom's sticky sauce. While he ate, Mom trudged upstairs to her room.

Celeste flooded me with links to social media coverage of my show. From the contact form on my website, two new emails caught my attention. First, a small publisher wanted to speak with me about a cookbook idea. Second, a local news show had an upcoming weekend food segment and wanted to know if an on-air demonstration was something I'd like to do.

Um, YES please! Opportunities were trickling in, and I'd need time to make sure I didn't screw them up. These were all exciting ways to grow my business, and I couldn't afford any distractions, including the rather big sulky one storming off to her bedroom.

Maybe doing a cooking show with Mom wasn't workable. Frankly, she was a much better cook and had been in a kitchen maybe thirty years longer than I. On air, she was so unpredictable, so capricious, that I couldn't handle it anymore. Yes, entrepreneurship had taught me that rigidity wasn't compatible with owning your own business, but Mom was like a curious, crawling baby with a randomness algorithm built in, and relying on her for any core part of my business made me nervous.

Sad as it was, going forward, it would be best if there was no longer a live Jess and Mom show. Maybe we could do holidays or seasonal shows, but as prerecorded releases to allow for editing and eliminating any unwelcome surprises.

It was time to let her know. My parents' bedroom door was slightly ajar, and she didn't notice me standing in the doorway. In front of the full-length mirror, Mom was holding up the purple polo "Seoul Sistas" shirt she had carelessly tossed on her bed not even an hour ago. While humming, she placed the collar under her chin, trying to see if the shirt fit. I stood quietly as she said to the mirror, "My name is Kim Yong Ja, I am Jessie's mom. We are cooking for you today!" She lowered her voice and turned her body slightly to the side. "Ahnyonghaseyo! Jessie and I are cooking for you today!" She smiled and bowed in the mirror, practicing the same lines over and over.

Tears trickled down my cheeks as I stepped back into the hallway, out of sight. Had this show really meant so much to her? I hadn't even considered her perspective.

Pangs of guilt rippled in my stomach when I played back memories from the show when I nearly lost my temper. Mom wasn't one for hugs and praise, but letting me move back home, supplying me with ample food in the fridge, and allowing me to settle back in without too much fuss, even *trying* to help me on my livestream cooking, those were acts of caring.

Going even further back to my high school days, my parents had missed a lot of my music concerts due to work, even the one my senior year of high school when I had a big solo in mid-state band, but they always made up for it in other ways: a good college education, fairly unrestrictive car use, and homemade meals. Umma's feeding and cooking were her own special love language to me.

The very idea of not just working with her, but having my livelihood dependent on my mom, gave me heart palpitations. We weren't two peas in a pod. We were oil and water. Or more accurately, we were vinegar and water—plus some dish soap and food coloring, swirled vigorously in a mason jar—a mother-daughter mini-tornado.

Tears ran down my cheeks again as I flicked back to the mental image of Mom in front of that mirror. This show meant so much to her, and as much as it pained me to think about the potential downside of this decision, I resolved to keep the show going. Because love wasn't shown only with the acts of cooking and feeding. Love was also about not giving up on the other person. I wasn't going to give up on her, or on us. And when opportunities arose in which I could include my umma, I'd invite her along for the ride. This was how I would show her my love and gratitude.

Chapter Sixteen

Alice woke me up with an early A.M. text. *CALL ME!*

"What's the emergency?" I croaked, rubbing my eyes from a good night's sleep. She'd woken me up from a dream about being on the Netflix show *Nailed It!* and winning the $10K grand prize. This Alice update needed to be better than that.

She switched me to video. Her dewy face appeared, bobbing up and down. Pounding noises took over the audio. "Sorry. I'm finishing. Up. Mytreadmillrun."

"Should I call you back?"

Her head bobbing slowed and then stopped. Alice inhaled and exhaled loudly. "Nah, I just finished."

My precaffeinated brain filled with confusion. "You wanted me to see you finish your workout? What's happening here?"

She tittered with laughter. Over Alice's shoulder, I could see an ogling guy one treadmill over. She grabbed her water bottle and phone and we went for a walk.

"Charlie and I are defecting. We're going to a new hedge fund called Hightower Capital. One of the old Hamilton Cooper guys loves it there and poached us. We're giving notice today. They're hiring and wanted to know if we knew any finance people who'd want to work there. Charlie and I put in a good word for you."

"You what?" All the tiredness expunged from my body, like an exorcism.

"The recruiter will be calling you soon to set up the initial phone screen." She took a swig of water. "I mean, when we saw you a couple months ago, you were ramping up and weren't exactly jumping for joy about starting a business, so I'm giving you an easy way out in case you're still waffling. They're opening up an office in Atlanta next year, if you want to be closish to home."

My breathing quickened. I'd made so much progress on building my business in just a few weeks. For the first time since I'd come home, I hadn't even considered looking for a job in finance. But now she'd advertently planted that seed in my head again.

"Oh! Charlie wanted me to tell you that with so many people leaving Hamilton Cooper, the executive team is freaking out because they're losing staff *and* clients. People saw that recent drastic restructuring as a signal that the company wasn't doing well. Even lifers like Wyatt and one of the Goldsteins have threatened to jump ship. Hamilton Cooper's fallen fast from Top Five status. Plunged, really."

"Well, clearly they're suffering because they let me go," I joked.

At least she laughed. "Yes. Definitely. And now look at all of your possibilities. Anyway, I need to hit the leg machines now." With one smooth move, Alice swept her hand from the crown of her head down to the tip of her ponytail. "When the recruiter calls, just know it's mainly a formality. Charlie and I already talked you up, so really all you need to do is answer her easy screener, go through the motions of interviews, and say yes. Gotta go. Talk later!"

A hesitant "Uh, thank you?" was on the tip of my tongue but Alice abruptly ended the call.

I sat cross-legged on my bed with my arms folded over my clenched stomach. A job had been handed to me, for the first time in my life. That's not to say I didn't work my ass off to get to the point in my career where things got a little easier, but wow. Was this what Sun Tzu meant when he said, *"In the midst of chaos, there is also opportunity"*?

Because I was certainly in the midst of chaos. But was this opportunity? Did Sun Tzu clarify how to discern what was *good* opportunity? Maybe I needed to re–check out that book from the library.

Damn it, Sun Tzu, I needed clarity.

I also needed coffee. Neither Mom nor Dad were in the house, so I had the opportunity to make breakfast in the kitchen in peace, but the nagging feeling that I hadn't seen

Flora at the coffee shop in a while made me rethink my morning plans. The last time I'd been there was a week ago, but it was for the evening regular monthly entrepreneurs meet-up, so it wasn't the same thing as being there during the day. I showered, put on a fresh change of clothes, and headed to the Red Wagon to work.

The smell of fresh ground coffee greeted me when I pushed the front door open, lifting my mood immediately. Flora was there and came around the counter to greet me with a hug and a shriek.

"Ahh! Hey stranger! Long time no see!"

"I know, I know. Been busy."

She grinned. "I noticed, I follow you on all things social. You've been making videos, launching a website, doing some blog interviews, and offering giveaways, all while trying to get more products and recipes made, like the boss you are."

I beamed and examined the baked goods selection. "Did I tell you that Jeff wants double the meal-kit supplements order? He sold out in two weeks. It's a strain on my cash flow, but with his volume increases it'll be worth it if he keeps distributing my products. Oh! And I'm publishing a cookbook with a local press here that'll be sold in local gift shops and bookstores next year."

She smoothed out her apron. "Wow! That's all fantastic! Are you enjoying yourself? Learning something new each day?"

I hadn't thought about my new career that way. At my old

job, I was always doing the same old thing, busting my ass, turning the money crank. But with this business, I had no idea what I was doing. Every time my inbox dinged with good news, even small things, I squealed with joy. The last time I squealed with joy in my days at Hamilton Cooper was when we were allowed to work from home Christmas Eve.

I grinned. "Yeah, definitely."

She said, "Good! And how's your Mercedes chauffeur?"

My smile fell instantly. "I don't know. I'm sure he's doing just fine." She responded by offering a quick consolation hug. He'd messaged me a few times saying he was in New York and wanted to know if I had any restaurant suggestions, to which I responded with a Google Doc with all of my recommendations. There was one place on the list that was a must-see, must-eat dive near my old office, McGuinness Tavern. The best shepherd's pie, they were open till one A.M., and always had a Celtic band playing on their side stage. There was also Pour, a new wine bar that Alice's friend had opened near Rockefeller Center, overlooking the skating rink. It was not only highlighted and written in all caps in the document but also on the very top of the list. Everyone raved about it around the office, and food critics loved it too. I'd always wanted to go, thinking, "One day when I have free time I'll splurge," but I never made it out there.

To reciprocate, Daniel sent a few links to video editing software and sound equipment on sale. The texts between us were friendly, but I wanted to keep some distance because he was trying to fly the Nashville coop. The last thing I needed was any kind of attachment to a guy who was going to leave me anyway.

A message on my phone stole my attention. It was from my friend Charlie, not Daniel. *I heard Alice told you the good news! I can't wait to see Goldstein's face when I quit. Btw can you send me your resume so I can forward to recruiter? Thx!*

I tucked the phone into the side pocket of my messenger bag. I could get back to him a little later.

"Oh, if you're looking for a job, my friends are at this new hedge fund. I'm sure they could use a PhD economist."

She smirked. "Maybe. But I've heard some stories about Wall Street. Are you hiring anytime in the future? I've always wanted to work at a company from the ground up at a female-owned business. And you're like, really ground level." She held her hand way down, like I needed that visual reminder of how low I was.

"So, first of all, I have business cards now, so while I'm ground level as you say, at least I've got those, and an email address. Soon I'll have a fully functional website. So I'm, like, up one flight of stairs."

She nodded at my logic. "So is that a yes?"

"That's a longwinded no. I'm not making enough to even pay myself a salary right now. I've got some dollars trickling in from video monetization, still figuring out direct and indirect distribution, and a small brewery is asking me to do IPA product placement, so things are moving in the right direction at least. I don't suppose you'd want to get paid in IPA cases?" I couldn't visualize how I'd incorporate beer on an episode, let alone the added complication of trying to explain to my mom that we needed to add beer to a recipe or talk about Korean dinners and ale pairings to earn partner revenue.

Flora thought about it longer than I expected. "I don't think the student loan bank guys will take beer as currency, but I might. Let me know if you need help though, sounds like you might if you have a big shipment ahead for that dude's grocery chain. I'll send you my résumé for your friends' company, thanks for the lead. I need to update it with my expected graduation date."

She went back behind the counter and made my usual heavily iced coffee. "Why do you get extra ice, by the way? I mean, I know it's still hot as fuck out there, but it's pretty cool indoors. We're not paltry with the ice either, but you always request more."

I whispered, "Your coffee is a little strong for me, so the ice waters it down. And I love the ice you have here. It's crushed, not cubed."

She straightened her collar. "Ahem. The technical term is *Sonic* ice. Sometimes called nugget or pellet ice. I love this ice too. You might even say I'm obsessed with it." She opened the glass case refrigerator, pulled out a large thermos, and shook it. "I take ice home every night and put it in my freezer."

I burst into a fit of giggles. "An employee perk! So you know what I mean. I'll take a blueberry scone too." I handed her my credit card. "Well, if you're offering help, I'm having a wild box packing and labeling party next week. My very pregnant friend Celeste is coming over. I'll have pizza. And locally brewed beer of course. Celeste is having ginger beer."

Her eyes sparkled. "Really? That actually sounds like a lot of fun."

I grinned. "I'll message you once Celeste gets back to me. She has to figure out childcare. And it's my birthday on Saturday so you have to come."

"In that case, I wouldn't miss it for the world! And this muffin and coffee are on the house since it's almost your birthday and all." She handed my card back.

I sat down at a round wooden table in the corner. One of the chairs had been borrowed by a group of five nearby, leaving only the one chair for me, which was fine. My bag could go on the ground.

With fifty inbox messages that morning, I didn't even notice the lunch crowd trickling in. As I cleared my table, an important email came through, one I'd been expecting all morning from Jeff Yee.

Jessie Kim,

Here's the purchase order for the next shipment.

Sincerely,

Jeff Yee

He wasn't a chatty guy, but I'd hoped for a little more correspondence fanfare given what was at stake for me. Then again, given the formatting, it was probably a form letter.

I clicked on the attachment and held my breath.

The usual purchase order details on top: the date, my P.O. box address, his business contact information. My eyes scanned for the important info: the product names and quantities.

NiHao Markets was ordering triple the quantity! I expected double, but triple? Triple the quantity wouldn't put my company in the black just yet, but it allowed me to validate my product was sellable and, more important, he could be a professional reference for the future if he was happy with me. I exhaled in relief. Selling thirty crates of Asian meal-kit supplements brought me as much happiness as landing a multimillion-dollar client at Hamilton Cooper. Every win was hard-earned. Every win was my own. My wide grin was impossible to contain.

Jeff had made one major error on the document though—he'd swapped some of the descriptions and pricing. Not a big deal. I replied to the email, asking for a quick revision to the P.O. and listing the small changes needed before officially accepting the order.

Another email ding startled me. Instinct led me to click it immediately because it was from WSMV News 4, which I bemoaned once I saw it was a response to my press release, beginning with the words "Ms. Kim, Regretfully . . ." *Ugh, way to burst your own bubble, Jessie.*

My eyes widened as I read on.

> Regretfully, our regular food and cooking feature host and segment producer are both out sick and we have a quick-to-fill segment this month. We will not be able to provide you with much time for preparation: we film at 7:30 A.M. on Friday morning. Could you hop on the phone today to discuss? Please review the attached document with filming and show preparation requirements and reply as soon as possible if this is something of interest to you.

Oh my God.

My fingers trembled as I responded. "I would be very interested in this opportunity, please let me know what additional information you need from me. I'm available all day and I've attached my virtual press kit as well as the link to my latest *Hanguk Hacks* show." Professional. Straightforward. Friendly.

What I actually wanted to write was "OMG I WOULD DIE FOR THIS OPPORTUNITY! LITERALLY, I WOULD BE DECEASED AND WOULD NEED TO HOLD MY

FUNERAL ON YOUR SHOW BUT ONLY AFTER I COOKED SOMETHING DELICIOUS. I PROMISE IT'LL BE AMAZING JUST PLEASE PRETTY PLEASE WRITE BACK AND PICK ME!!!"

Even if they didn't choose me for this TV segment, things were happening. There would be more opportunities down the road. And what better way to celebrate than with pizza, beer, ginger beer, plus a celebration cake, with two of my favorite friends?

Chapter Seventeen

WSMV studio's staged farmhouse kitchen was outfitted with a high-end fridge, stove, and oven. Viking appliances? My eyes widened as we walked across the set. The stage manager explained, "It's not as impressive as it looks. Last year we had a fire and had to rebuild everything. To minimize liability and hazards, we basically had to create an adult-size play kitchen. It looks mighty nice but check this out." He opened the oven, revealing that there were no heating coils. "These light switches work on batteries, but as you can see, no electricity or gas. Oh! The sink works though, so if you somehow accidentally set somethin' on fire, you do have a water source."

I placed my premade dishes on the counter. He scratched his bushy mustache and peered at them. "I'm embarrassed to say I've only had Korean food at my kids' school potlucks. Excited for the show. It smells great."

We walked off set, my mouth hanging open as I examined

the framed photos lining the back hallway. Country music greats like Loretta Lynn, Tammy Wynette, LeAnn Rimes, and of course Dolly Parton had once graced this very studio, possibly in the room where I'd be recording a segment in forty-five minutes.

He led me to the green room, where a breakfast spread larger than any hotel buffet I'd ever seen lay in front of me.

"Is this all mine?"

He laughed. "I wanna say yes, but a local band is recording an hour after you. So make sure you eat all the good stuff." He pointed to a chocolate croissant tower. "We get those from a bakery down the street, they're so flaky and buttery. I highly recommend 'em. Those maple bacon biscuits are killer too." I piled my plate with a wide assortment, including his recommendations. "If you need anything, ask for Brad."

"I hope you're Brad." I grinned. "If you need me, I'll be here eating my body weight in baked goods."

He nodded. "As you should. I'll come get you when we're ready. There's a lady who'll come by for hair and makeup. She's real talkative and it's best to let her ramble because she focuses better that way. If you chat with her too much, well, let's just say people have commented that they come out looking a little too smoky-eyed and electrocuted."

Before I could ask for any clarification, he closed the door.

I focused on my reflection in the vanity mirror. Was I really in a TV studio? With first dibs on a breakfast feast fit for a queen? Getting professional hair and makeup? Was this all really happening to me? All I wanted to think about, at least for a minute or two of quiet, was how different my life was now. When I moved back home I'd hit an all-time professional low. And soon I'd be on the local news, promoting my new business and brand. Chaos. More opportunity. *Sun Tzu, you know your shit.*

A knock at the door interrupted my moment of reflection. I thought it would be Brad, but it was a woman with a smoky-eyed look and slightly frizzy hair.

She barreled in and startled me with the sound of the door slamming behind her. "I'm Tammy and I *can't wait* till I get started on you. I read the call sheet. You're Jessie and you'll be sharing some of your favorite recipes, I can't wait."

Tammy grabbed me by the shoulders and guided me to the chair in front of the vanity. "Sit, please, dear."

Brad was right. She yammered on for twenty minutes about her divorces, her good-for-nothing father, her sweet grandma, and how much she hated her councilman. Even if I'd tried to ask questions, she wouldn't have heard me; she talked the entire time. "Voilà!" she exclaimed, swiveling me around to see.

In front of me was an image from an old Hollywood movie, but a little less glam. Perfectly curled hair, flawless application of makeup, and, most eye-catching of all, lipstick the color of Bing cherries. I'd never dared wear anything so bold in my life. My instinct was to scrub it off, or at least wipe some of it off to lessen the pigment, but Tammy pulled the tissue box away from my reach. "Sweetie, I've been doing this for twenty years. The camera is unforgiving. That purple polo shirt you've got on isn't star material, no offense. In this business, in this town especially, you'll need any sparkle you can get. Trust me, it's not going to look on camera the same way it does here under this terrible lighting. You can thank me when your sales shoot through the roof."

There was something about Tammy that I liked. That I trusted. She was genuine. Sassy. Honest. All traits I admired. So yes, Tammy, I'd keep it all on. Hollywood glam it would be.

My phone rang. I thought it might be Brad's way of letting me know it was time to record the show, the same way restaurants page you when your table is ready if there's a long waitlist. But it was Daniel, not Brad. I rolled my eyes and sent him to voicemail.

Tammy laughed. "Well, he's in the doghouse."

Daniel didn't leave a voicemail. He left a text instead. *Hey! Can you please call me back, it's important.*

A walkie-talkie blared in the hallway. "Is she ready? We're ready to roll."

Brad knocked at the door. "Miss Kim? It's time."

Tammy grabbed my hand, pulled me out of my seat, and stuffed a tissue in my pocket. "That's not for the makeup. That's a just-in-case tissue. For . . . just in case."

I wouldn't know what she meant until later.

* * *

"AAAAAAAND . . . ROLLING!"

"I'm Brittney Lynn and I'm thrilled to introduce our guest today. Welcome to our *Local Eats* show, Jessie Kim!"

Smiling wide, I responded in an equally chipper voice, "Thanks for having me!" I'd never been on an actual TV show before and didn't know how different it would be from my own recordings. Would I be able to turn up my energy on-screen so the segment was interesting to new-to-me viewers? Or would my presence be more reserved? Ack! Just thinking about this made my body heat turn up a few degrees, a strong contrast to my cold, clammy hands.

Etiquette-wise, was I supposed to shake her hand or hug her? I'd only seen a few recorded episodes of Brittney Lynn's cooking segment, all European male chefs who did the double-cheek kiss, which was pretty much the opposite of what I wanted to do. So instead, I offered a wave at the camera.

She clapped and rubbed her gel manicured hands together. "I can't wait! It's our 'Quick Eats for Fall' show, and we've invited Jessie Kim, the host of the *Hanguk Hacks* show and the CEO of Seoul Sistas to share a few of her favorite recipes." Brittney Lynn turned to me, her bright blue eyes wide with anticipation. If she was feigning excitement, she was good at it. "I saw your last episodes and let me tell ya, your mom is a HOOT!" She threw her head back in laughter. "I just love her sass. And your dad is adorable."

The edges of my mouth tugged into a smile. "Yes, having a show with my mom wasn't something I'd planned, but it's been really well received."

"I bet! I could never cook with my mom. She'd drive me batty."

You have NO idea, lady.

"So let's get cookin'. What special dish do you have for our viewers?"

"Thanks for having me," I repeated. *Get it together, Jessie Kim.* "For many people, I know the sound of Korean barbecue sounds good—it's a real crowd pleaser, and for good reason. But today I'd love to share a modernized recipe for Korean spicy pork, called dweji bulgogi, that I know you'll love too. You can find the full recipe on my website along with step-by-step instructions."

Brittney Lynn chimed in, "Jessie's website and bio are in our show notes, so definitely take a look! So I would love to know, and I bet our viewers would too, what you mean by *modernized*?"

"That's a great question. What we've seen with the popularity in photo and video sharing apps is a boom in *food* photography and videography. We're seeing food as culture, and culture as food. So I'd categorize my cooking as second-gen Korean, meaning it's the food of Korean America. And you'll see this less in the preparation of these foods and more in the application of these core foods in various dishes. It might be best to show and not tell though," I said with a wink.

Me, winking on camera!

And Brittney Lynn winked back!

"I'm making Korean spicy pork, fairly traditional, but we'll be making banh mi–inspired sandwiches. So what you'll need is pork shoulder, julienned or diced onion, green onion, and cooking oil." I put them all in a pan and took it to the non-working stovetop. I bristled when a sizzling sound effect shot out of embedded speakers above the fake oven. I swallowed hard to keep from howling with laughter.

Clearing my throat, I said, "Um, while that's cooking, I'll stir the marinade, which consists of gochujang, which is red pepper paste and which you can find in any Asian grocery, and I actually saw it in Kroger the other day. Also, sugar, black pepper, soy sauce, onion again, rice wine, garlic, and ginger. All the measurements are on my website. You'll add the marinade to the pork and either broil the meat or pan-fry it.

"In traditional bahn mi, along with the meat, you have pickled vegetables, so we'll do something like that inspired by Korean pickled cucumbers, which is a popular side dish. I've already julienned these, and you can also add carrots as I've done here. These ingredients are sugar, salt, rice vinegar, and garlic. You'll need to mix that all together and let it sit for two hours or more."

Someone turned up the sizzling sound, perhaps a hint it was time to take the fake-cooked pork off the fake stovetop behind me. "Oh right, the pork should be done!" I stirred and turned the stove "off," setting the pan aside on another burner to "cool down."

Facing the camera again, I offered the final steps to my spicy sandwich. "You'll need a baguette, cut in half. Then add the spicy pork, some pickled cucumbers and carrots, a little bit of cilantro, and, if you're daring, you can add sliced jalapeño, though the pork should pack enough heat to satisfy your need to feel the burn."

Brittney Lynn laughed. "I love that. Feel the burn with Jessie's spicy pork!"

On a white plate, I assembled a sandwich using pork I'd precooked beforehand and cut it in half. Offering part of the sandwich to Brittney Lynn and taking the other, I lifted mine and said, "With a few more cilantro sprigs for garnish . . . our meal is done. *Bon appétit!*"

As we bit into our sandwiches at the same time, the double crunch from the bread crust echoed in the room. I'd tried this recipe only once before, and this time it was better, with the heat not noticeable at first because of the sweetness of the sauce, but it was definitely there. If Brittney wasn't a fan of spice, then this whole segment would be a disaster.

Once again, my nerves took over because I couldn't read her

face—unlike me, she was still politely chewing with her hand covering her mouth.

I panicked and offered, "If this banh mi–inspired sandwich isn't your thing, you can also try this pork in a flavorful Cuban. No jalapeño."

She finished her bite and turned to the camera. "I have five words for you. Love, love, LOVE the burn!" To my surprise, she took another bite of the sandwich, which meant she wouldn't be speaking for a while, so I would fill the silence. "Many of the ingredients you might already have at home, but if you don't, and you're eager to cut out a lot of these steps, we have a special gochujang marinade that is basically everything you need to make spicy pork. Then all you need is the meat, oil, and a pan or grill."

"This sandwich is so addictive. Thank you so much for sharing your recipe. Where can our viewers buy your special sauce?"

My phone buzzed in my pocket, distracting me temporarily. "I'm sorry, could you repeat that?"

Brittney put her sandwich down and wiped her hands. "Where can fans like me buy your wonderful products?"

A lightness in my body signaled relief that this cooking segment was not only almost over but also that it had gone so much better than expected. "We'll be in farmers' markets in the metropolitan Nashville area starting next month and local eateries downtown are also carrying some of the products. We have a cookbook in the works too." There were other things in the works that were still not yet confirmed so I couldn't discuss them on-air. The Food Network was doing a roadshow featuring food truck vendors, pop-up eateries, and food festival vendors—they'd reached out to see if I'd be willing to take part in it. OF COURSE I WOULD BE WILLING TO BE ON THE FOOD NETWORK.

She said, "Wow! Your business is taking off. And it makes sense, with your promise of cooking shortcuts for busy people."

I beamed. "Our biggest distributor is NiHao Markets, which will have our newest products in all of their stores soon, including this spicy marinade. Jeff Yee, the owner, has been a wonderful supporter from the start."

Something changed in her face. An imperceptible shift that the camera, under all of her newscaster makeup, might not pick up, but I saw it because I was only a few feet away. A flick in her eyes. Her smile tightened, then quivered. An unshakable feeling that something was wrong.

She chose each word with purpose. "Well, hopefully with NiHao's acquisition announcement today to Top Quality Foods, it will mean good news for your business!"

My breath hitched. Acquisition? Top Quality Foods was the largest grocery conglomerate in the United States. They were known for buyouts and converting stores into generic groceries with only mainstream brands, mainly because they had massive deals with large food manufacturers. As shock rocked my entire body, I kept a tentative smile on my face and replied with a simple, "Yes."

Brittney Lynn, being the professional that she was, jumped into action. "Well thank you SO MUCH for being on our show. Your sandwich was delicious, and I'm delighted we were able to share some good ol' down-home Korean American cooking. If you'd like to download Jessie's recipe she shared today, you can find all the links you need on our show page."

"Aaaaand, CUT!"

While leaning on the counter, I exhaled and hung my head. Brittney placed her hands on my trembling ones. "Sweetie, are you okay? I swear I didn't mean to blindside you. The NiHao news made some waves here at the studio because a lot of our staff shops there and love the authentic grocery items they carry. I thought you would have found out before the news broke this morning since you were one of their suppliers."

"It's okay, but if you wouldn't mind, I'd like to head back to the green room to gather my things. As you can imagine, I have a number of calls to make." I offered a tired smile, which she returned with a small pat on the arm.

Tightly gripping my Pyrex container, I grabbed my personal items from the green room and ran out the main exit into the studio lot. My shaking hands searched for keys in the cavernous pocket of my messenger bag. When I finally unlocked the car door and ducked down to hide from any passersby, I let out a shrill scream in my sealed cabin.

My phone buzzed.

Daniel Choi.

I answered the call. "What do you want?" I barked. "Why didn't you tell me about NiHao?"

The phone was silent for so long I thought the call had been dropped. "I'm so sorry about that. Everything was moving so slow, and then all of a sudden everything happened at once. For the record, I did try to call you earlier today, to give you the news in case you hadn't heard it yet."

My body tensed. "For the record, I found out while recording a cooking segment for WSMV News 4. And I looked like an idiot!" My voice quivered. "You could have warned me or hinted something beforehand. When you were here."

"I couldn't do that—it would be unethical. I helped broker the deal, working with Jeff as a consultant. That'd basically be insider trading." His voice rang with annoyance.

Okay, so it may have been illegal. STILL. He could have mimed it or something. "You could have NOT had me go into business with Jeff at all. Never introduced me to him if you knew this was something that might happen. WOULD happen." I thought Daniel was doing me a favor when he made the introduction to Jeff, but he was up to something the whole time. Trying to sell Jeff's business, maybe even dangling vendor relationships like mine as a carrot for the acquiring company since my products had strong sell-through, while pretending he was a good guy.

To keep my hands steady, I balled my fists, but they still shook hard. Betrayal was a bitch.

He sighed. "There wasn't any guarantee Jeff's business would sell, and even so, we didn't know what the timing would be, he's been trying to sell for a while now. And anyway, how much could it be for a few boxes of sauce?"

My voice became steadier as I shouted louder. "It's a lot of money for someone with no cash flow who pours her heart and soul into a business! But you don't care, this was just a game to you. I was just a casualty, right? Oops, too bad?" As the news continued to tear away at my entrepreneurial soul, another thing became clear, making me even angrier. "NiHao tripled the quantity for the delivery scheduled next week. All of the supplies and materials have been paid for on my end, so I'm out thousands of dollars because they're not likely to accept the order now, right?" Come to think of it, Jeff had never sent me an amended purchase order, with the correct products and pricing. In my past experience, when businesses were acquired, unsigned and unconfirmed orders were nonbinding and required legal counsel to contest. Guess who couldn't afford legal counsel?

The last time I'd felt this powerless and small, this utterly defeated, was only a few months ago, on my last day at Hamilton Cooper. That was the day I had my core identity stripped away from me, leaving me exposed and defenseless. I had worked so hard to gain my confidence back, and now it was Daniel causing me to relive all of those horrible feelings again.

Tears threatened to fall, and I did everything in my power to not let that happen. "You probably got paid a lot to help with the acquisition. So a big win for you, a huge loss for me."

Daniel's voice softened. "That's not how it was. You want me to call Jeff right now to make sure he'll honor it? I'll help if you want."

A shallow laugh escaped me. "Help? Please, no. You've done enough."

The phone beeped, indicating that Daniel wanted to switch to a video call. No way would I want to see his infuriating smug face. Or let him see my pained one. "You can do me one favor though."

"Anything," he breathed.

"Promise me you'll leave me alone." I hung up and pulled the just-in-case tissue from my pocket and brought it to my eyes to catch my falling tears.

Chapter Eighteen

"Where do you want this box?" The brown crate in Flora's arms was filled with imported Korean soy sauces. They were the last items we needed to include before sealing the starter meal-kit supplement sets. These were some of the exclusive products that were supposed to be part of the shipment to NiHao but would now be rebranded and sold mainly on my website.

One of the guys in the local Asian American entrepreneur group recommended a web developer who knew a lot about UI design and had experience with e-commerce, so I was able to add an online shop to my existing website in only a few days with Paypal and Google, Amazon, and Apple Pay options. After the local cooking segment aired, emails and website messages from viewers all over the mid-state area had streamed in, asking whether the products could be shipped to friends and family elsewhere in the United States and abroad.

"Would you please put it over there by the red pepper

packets?" Direct distribution of my products to consumers, at least this early in the business ramp up, was not in my original business plan, but I hoped it would be potentially lucrative in the long-term since there was no wholesale discount. *Thank you, Daniel Choi, for adding all of this stress to my life.*

I imagined him driving his car with his annoyingly stylish aviators, his windows rolled down and hair ruffling in the wind, blaring BLACKPINK on his speakers while passersby laughed and smiled at his racket instead of shaking their fists and yelling at him about noise ordinances. Because that's the kind of guy Daniel was. And he was back to making obscene amounts of money and leaving us nobodies behind.

Well, good riddance.

Hundreds of boxes of supplies and finished products littered the garage. The way they were precariously stacked resembled a 3D version of Tetris, where any wrong move meant game over.

Celeste waved a slice of pizza. "Didn't you say there'd be birthday cake? You can't promise a pregnant woman cake and not deliver."

I smiled weakly. "Yeah, I'm sorry about that. I spoke too hastily when I thought I had that NiHao deal. Maybe this can be a pity party, and I can order pity cake." Truth was, I didn't have much savings to spare. So if any spending needed to be cut, it would be on expendables like pity cakes for people who'd just turned twenty-nine.

Flora scoffed as she hurled the box onto another one. "There will be no self-pitying here. We should still celebrate with cake. I worked through your finances . . . with these website preorders . . . assuming regular ordering will be constant . . . you'll break even end of next year. And that's without a ton of cost efficiencies on supplies like boxes, tape, or even postage. Your markup on your sauces is astronomical, but on the buyer's side it's still affordable. Honestly, with the holidays coming soon and the giftability of your products, I think you'll be in the black maybe even sooner, which is unheard of for a start-up like yours."

"Is 'giftability' a real word?" I asked.

Flora threw a wad of tape at me. "Yes it is. I have a PhD in econ, and I say so."

Celeste pointed to the stacks of smaller boxes near the garage door. "We've done all the manual labor of packing up and labeling the preorder shipments. All you need is one last quality check and then USPS can come get 'em."

"Thank you both." My phone vibrated in my pocket. It was an email notification from a local PR agency wanting to know if I offered custom corporate or promotional gift boxes, and if I took minimum orders as low as a hundred units.

I showed both of them my phone. "One hundred units. Maybe I'll get the celebration cake after all. Holy shit, this is amazing. Who needs Daniel Choi for their business to succeed? Not me."

Celeste and Flora exchanged glances.

I blew my bangs out of my eyes. "What?"

Celeste slurped her ginger beer and giggled while Flora went back to rearranging crates.

"What?" I repeated.

Flora shrugged. "You know, Daniel's not a bad guy, just kind of misguided when it comes to priorities. I don't think he was *trying* to destroy your business—he didn't think through the long-term. He might have thought he was helping you."

Celeste added, "From what you told me, it sounds like he's nicer and more tolerable now. And hotter too."

Chuckling, Flora said, "I was just about to say that next."

Putting both hands on my hips, I protested. "All he had on his mind was his NiHao deal. Let's not ruin the night by discussing Daniel the traitor."

"You brought him up first actually. Flora and I were only making polite conversation."

I did? Anyway, it didn't matter. "He's blocked now. On my phone and from my life. I have too much going on to deal with him. I don't need more drama."

Celeste put her drink down. "Are you going to do that thing again—where you keep yourself too busy with work to have any kind of personal life?"

I scratched my cheek. "Thing? What *thing*?"

She fixed her stare on me. "When you bury yourself in work and forget about your dear friends and family?" Celeste batted her eyes, taking the bite out of her stinging words. "I'm not saying you'll do it this time. I'm just hoping you'll see that tendency and prevent it, because I like having you around. I missed you. You do seem to enjoy your career now, which is great to see, but please try to keep a work-life balance. I worry about you, especially when things seem a bit rocky, like now."

Yes, things were rocky. My entire week had been booked with sales calls, publicity opportunities, and manufacturing discussions. Celeste had hinted she'd want to work with me, and I was aiming toward that goal. With Daniel out of my life, I'd need to rely more on consultation with my entrepreneur group at the next meeting, maybe even get some of the guys out for coffee or lunch so I could get their advice. I'd learned in the last four monthly get-togethers that a lot of them had gone through the growing pains of starting a new business and outsourced or hired someone to handle certain parts of the operations. I had finally reached that crossroads.

Flora grabbed a cold beer from the cooler. "I worry about you too. Oh! I cleaned up my résumé, would you mind sending it to your friends at the hedge fund?"

The recruiter from Alice and Charlie's company hadn't called me yet to set up a phone screen but according to Charlie's latest text update, she'd been busy filling some of the junior jobs and was working her way up to the more senior positions. *When she contacts you, just hear her out. She'll tell you about the company and the position. The salary's great and you'll be working with Alice again. And me! It's a win-win-win!*

Another added bonus, if Flora got a job at the hedge fund, I'd be working with her too—4 x win!

"No problem, I'll send it to Alice and Charlie. They love their new jobs, and I definitely trust them. Not like—" My voice carried off after a long sigh. *Daniel.*

Celeste asked, "Were you going to say Daniel again?"

I didn't appreciate the smirking. "I was going to say, not like *anyone at Hamilton Cooper." Nice recovery, Jessie, even though Celeste was actually right.*

I thought about Daniel a lot. I replayed every interaction over and over in my head, both business-wise and bedroom-wise, wondering how I'd managed to not see him for what he was. An opportunist. My stomach knotted into pretzel-like twists just thinking about how I'd trusted him to help make the best decisions for me, and he essentially led me into a damned-if-you-do deal with Jeff Yee. A high-risk deal for me it turned out, a low-risk one for NiHao, resulting in an outcome that put me in the metaphorical poorhouse. Daniel said he didn't know the deal would go through, but he was great at making and carrying out deals, so how would the deal NOT go through? There was never any shyness or humility when it came to his accomplishments. Daniel Choi was a rainmaker. A golden boy who made gold. Daniel the alchemist.

And his physical appeal probably helped seal NiHao's acquisition with one of his charming smiles. I'd seen firsthand how his strapping good looks and sex appeal helped nearly close deals in my own bedroom and his nursery. Daniel's rippling muscles under his fitted shirts, his powerful shoulders and broad chest, his handsome features, and that alluring smile. That infuriating, knowing grin drove me mad. And that devilish look in his eyes, unfathomable to me given that he was a preacher's son—alluring and torturing.

Daniel's motives were not aligned with mine and I hadn't seen the NiHao disaster coming, just like I hadn't seen my layoff coming at Hamilton Cooper. I could keep beating myself up for it, reliving all of the little moments we had together, overanalyzing everything and thinking about how naive I was. Or I could move on by pouring my soul into Seoul Sistas. Show Daniel that I was able to not just survive, but thrive, without any of his goddamned, so-called help.

I ordered a nonpity cake delivery on my grocery app. Because the way I looked at it, along with the good news that day, we were celebrating Daniel being out of my life for good.

Chapter Nineteen

If anyone had told me that I would be on WSMV News 4 not once, but twice, in a two-month span, I'd have called bullshit.

But it happened, and this time my mom accompanied me so we could promote our forthcoming cookbook to generate pre-release buzz. I spent many restless nights debating whether it was a good idea to put my mom on live TV, this time in a news studio and not in her own kitchen, but it was the best decision. Mom was just as much a part of the company's success, if not more, than me. Videos of me cooking alone performed well, but the ones with my mom nearly doubled those views and comments. And the ones with my dad swooping in at the end for his final food commentary? Maybe triple.

Brad the stage manager escorted us from the reception desk to the green room. "I'm so glad to see you again, Jessie. And it's a pleasure to meet you, Mrs. Kim. I'm a huge fan."

Mom shook Brad's hand up and down with fervor, like she

was pumping a bike tire with her arm. "I am a fan too! I watch WSMV morning news show every day!" When we reached our destination, Mom's eyes brightened as her gaze swept from the fruit to the meat and cheese plate to the platter of baked goods at the craft service table. "Waaaa. Can I try?"

Brad laughed. "Yes, Mrs. Kim. This is for Jessie and you. We also ordered extra in case your husband planned to join you."

Mom filled her plate. "My husband have a trip to Asia and come home tomorrow." She scanned the table a second time while Brad checked his notifications on his cell. "I have empty gallon Ziploc in my handbag, I can bring home extra food." Luckily, Brad was so engrossed in his messages he didn't hear her. And I didn't dare ask Mom about it either. Who knew what else was in her purse?

Brad put his phone away. "So sorry about that, it's been a doozy of a morning. My wife's pickin' up my lil' girl from preschool—she's runnin' a fever. Tammy'll be here soon to help you with hair and makeup. Y'all enjoy your breakfast! The coffee carafe with the orange handle is decaf." He closed the door gently behind him.

While I answered emails on my phone, from the corner of my eye I could see Mom holding up a different croissant in each hand, squinting at them. She sniffed. "This one has ham. The other one is chocolate." She took a large bite from each. "I save chocolate one for Appa."

A brief knock at the door drew my eyes away from my

screen. Tammy burst through the door and nearly knocked me over with an affectionate bear hug. "I'm so glad you're back on the show! Didn't I tell ya? My predictions were right!" Her infectious effervescence made me grin. She'd promised that my glammed-up look would be perfect for the show the last time. And that my career would take off. Tammy wasn't talking about how she'd stuffed a precautionary tissue in my pocket, which came in handy after my fight with Daniel. No need to dampen the mood with any negativity.

"And nice to meet you, Mrs. Kim." She turned on the lights on the vanity. "Who needs to go first?"

I explained to Mom in broken Korean that she needed to let Tammy do her job, which meant she'd get hair and makeup for the show, but we'd make sure it wasn't too much. She scowled and sat in the designated chair. "Can I eat?" She held up her heaping paper plate. While I'd been on email, she had gone for seconds. Maybe even thirds.

"No problem. You can put everything on the vanity if you'd like." Tammy held out her hand so she could help Mom put her plate on the flat surface in front of her. She raised an eyebrow and handed it over slowly, as if Tammy would take it and run. Mom grabbed a mini blueberry muffin at the hand-off and peeled the paper baking cup from the bottom half.

Using a large-barrel curling iron, Tammy styled Mom's hair, which helped calm her wild gray baby hairs and smoothed out the frizz from her old perm. With a little foundation and blush, plus mauve lipstick (per my mom's input of "not too pink" and "I hate red!") she was done in less than fifteen minutes, leaving me around twenty minutes for my Tammy beauty regimen.

Mom scrambled out of the chair and sat down in front of the muted TV. She pulled a notepad from her purse and fished out a pen. She was doing a good job occupying her time. What a relief.

Tammy flashed a bright smile in the mirror's reflection. She said, "Something in you's changed. Hmmm . . . I'm gonna style you a little differently today."

More change and uncertainty? Did I need that right now?

She squeezed my shoulders. "Don't worry, you'll look great."

Using the curling iron, Tammy styled my hair as she gave me an update on her ex-husbands, her new boyfriend, and how she was trying to make peace with her family, after she'd had an epiphany that she had enough negativity in her life from her marriages and wanted to harbor good feelings toward her kin. "I'm almost fifty. When you get older, shit that used to bother you won't anymore. I don't know if you grow out of it, or your priorities change or what. You'll see when you get to be my age."

This time there was less of everything: less concealer, less blush, less eyeliner. Like the time before, Tammy didn't reveal her makeup strategy until the very end.

"All done!" She swiveled me around so I could see myself in the vanity mirror.

Whoa.

Polished, sharp, and self-assured. A never-before-seen Jessie, at least not in recent memory.

Tammy turned the chair toward my mom. "What do you think, Mrs. Kim? Doesn't your daughter look great?"

What Tammy didn't know was that my mom didn't follow conventional southern etiquette by politely agreeing with kind statements for the sake of making pleasant conversation. Quite often, she spoke her mind and didn't shy away from offering her version of "helpful critiques" without couching them in compliments to make them more palatable. Especially when it came to her daughter.

I held my breath while my mom examined my makeup and hair. She stared a long time without saying anything at first. "She look exactly like Jessie dad. My husband." My dad had a round, tired, and solemn face. It was a far cry from a polished, sharp, and self-assured one. Regardless, coming from my mom this was a compliment, and I needed to move the conversation along before she elaborated any further.

Tammy sensed the same thing. "Well, you both look lovely. I gave y'all a similar curled hairstyle and complementary lip colors, since you're in business together. I didn't want it to be too matchy-matchy, you know? It's a mother-daughter business, but you both have distinct styles and personalities, am I right?"

Boy, did we ever.

We nodded, though Tammy calling it a mother-daughter

business prickled the hairs on my arms. It was technically a *daughter-mother* business. A small thing, I know, but it was a company I founded and developed. Mom was a figurehead.

Brad tapped on the door and popped his head through. "Are the Kims ready for showtime? We're all set up for the interview."

Mom lifted her plate off her lap and placed it on the coffee table. She stood and stretched, then shoved a piece of paper she'd ripped from the notepad into her gray trouser pocket. To my surprise, she'd taken my advice and was wearing a simple black floral top with plain bottoms, not her usual head-to-toe vibrant colors and patterns. Maybe it took being on an actual TV show for her to follow standard wardrobe dos and don'ts for on-camera talent.

Mom wasn't someone I'd ever call "standard."

Brad led us down the hall to the recording studio. Today's interview wasn't a prerecorded segment that would be tightened with editing and aired at a later date. This was live. My tremoring hands turned to ice when we reached the interview area. The setup itself wasn't intimidating: Mom and I would be sitting together on a couch and the interviewer would be across from us. No, the scary part was the interviewer. The one they were wiring with a mic wasn't Brittney. Seated on a nearby couch doing hair and makeup was a local celebrity newscaster who had been an on-air talent for WSMV at least twenty years, with shellacked hair, orangey-tanned skin, and super-white teeth: Mike Masters.

Mom hated Mike Masters.

Ten years ago, he jumped ahead of her in the Costco checkout line. When she called him out, he said it was a simple mistake and apologized, but stayed in the spot ahead of her, flexing his maleness and minor celebrity status. For that dick move, she would hate him for all eternity. And honestly, I couldn't blame her; I hated when people cut me in line. Maybe it was genetic. It was the one and only thing, the pettiest of pet peeves, that would make me fiercely tackle someone out of principle if it came down to it.

Mom hadn't forgotten or forgiven Mike Masters's transgressions. Fuming when she got home, she called him every Korean obscenity she could think of, and then never watched the evening news again. Why Mike Masters was doing a morning interview with a local entrepreneur didn't make sense at all, and worse, my mom's noisy breathing and reddening cheeks clued me in that she was at a snapping point.

Her eyes narrowed to slits as she watched Mike fuss over a glass of water. "I asked for Evian! This is NOT Evian!"

"I thought Brittney was going to interview us," I said to Brad.

He looked over his shoulder before speaking. "Mike just showed up at the studio and he has seniority here. Brittney's around though, do you prefer that she be the interviewer? As you know, Mike's been in the business a long time and may insist. Britt's great but she hasn't done many live interviews like this."

I observed Mike's absurd occupation of space on the couch, his arms and legs spread wide. So wide in fact that it was like he was saving seats for other people on both sides of him.

To know your Enemy, you must become your Enemy. Good ol' Sun Tzu. Mirroring Mike Masters's confidence, I shifted my stance and pulled my shoulders back. I stated firmly, "We'd prefer Brittney for the interview. She and I had a rapport last time and she'd be *perfect* for an interview about female entrepreneurship. Plus, she enjoys cooking." I didn't see the need to point out that Mike was probably not the Asian-food-hack type.

Brad nodded. "Yeah, I get it. Let me talk to someone." He walked away, murmuring into his headset.

A mid-thirties dude duo walked over and introduced themselves. "Hi, Jessie. I'm Seth, this is Jasper." We shook hands. "We're thrilled you're on the show again! I heard from Brad you were interested in an interviewer exchange. Would you mind letting us know what's on your mind? We're going live soon and wanted to understand your concerns."

I chose my words carefully. "The last interview I had with Brittney was a game changer for my business. Sales shot up, we got a ton of partner and distribution inquiries, and, most important, we had great chemistry. Actually, the most important thing today would be making my mom comfortable, and I know Brittney would be able to achieve that." Mom had found a seat a few feet away and was glaring at Mike from across the room, lips pressed together so hard you couldn't see the pretty mauve color any longer.

Jasper nodded. "Let's not mess with something that works. I'll have Brad go chase down Brittney. Now the hard part will be breaking the news to Mike." He lowered his voice and whispered to Seth, "Let's talk to him outside so if he has one of his shouting tirades, at least he'll be out of earshot." The duo wished me luck and escorted Mike out of the studio. A pungent cologne trail followed him out the door.

Brittney came through the side entrance and fluttered toward me, exuding warmth and gratitude. "Jessie Kim! How are you? Full confession . . . I've only done one other live interview before and it was at five A.M. But I'm ready! This is big time, baby!"

"I'm great! My mom's over there, chatting with Brad. I'm a *little* worried about her, she's never done something like this before. Not that I have a ton of experience either."

She patted my arm. "Well, this will be a little new for all of us then. But that's exciting!" Her eyes gleamed. "Let's get settled on set, we're rolling in five."

Brad took my mom and me over to the guest couch. "I had the pleasure of telling your mom that Mike was out and Britt was in. I've never seen anyone so happy in my life."

Mom's grin widened. "He is a bad man. Mike Masters is gone!"

Her childlike glee made Brad and me laugh. I took my seat

next to Umma and we were soon joined by Brittney. She took a last sip of water and asked, "Are y'all ready?"

Mom and I both nodded. We confirmed in unison, "Ready."

***

FUNNY THAT MIKE Masters actually taught me something. His physical sprawl in his cushioned chair, knees splayed and arms draping, reminded me to make myself "bigger." As Brittney introduced my business and bio on live television, I shifted myself in my seat. Back straight. Chin up. Arms farther out. Smile at Brittney and at the camera.

"Welcome to our show again, Jessie! Would you do the honor of introducing your special guest?"

"It'd be my pleasure! This is my mother, Yong Ja, or Mrs. Kim to most of my friends. She's also known on the internet in the *Umma to the Rescue* meme."

Brittney let out a heartfelt laugh. "Your mom is a meme? Tell us more."

"It's from my very first episode of *Hanguk Hacks*, when she walked onto my set and offered some, um, opinionated cooking advice." I cracked a smile to show no hard feelings.

"Mrs. Kim, how do you feel about your sudden fame?"

Mom clapped her hands together. "Everyone at church say I am famous. One teenager say I am cool."

Even I laughed at that. "She's cooler than I am, that's for sure."

Brittney smiled. "You're both cool! I mean, your business is booming now, right? You started out by reviving your old YouTube channel and now your food hacks business is taking the world by storm." She leaned forward. "I heard from the show producer that you had exciting news to announce on the show." Nodding toward the camera, she added, "A WSMV exclusive."

This was news that I hadn't even told my parents yet. I thought it'd be fun to share with Mom on live TV. I took a deep breath. "Last week I signed a deal with Target to carry an exclusive line of cookware!" Working with a Korean housewares manufacturer, I'd approached Target a while ago and they were finally ready to move forward with the procurement process after weeks of negotiations. I'd learned from getting burned by NiHao that I needed to make sure all the paperwork was official before moving forward on my end. Speed to market was an asset, but it wasn't something I could afford anymore. Luckily Target was okay with having timelines that included a reasonable delivery date.

Brittney's eyes brightened and her mouth fell open, a genuine and heartfelt reaction to news like this. Mike wouldn't have had this level of excitement, confirming the good decision to switch interviewers. "I have no words, I'm in shock. This is truly amazing news!"

One of the secondary cameras moved forward to capture Mom's reaction. Beaming with pride, she clapped for me. "Waaaa! Target! Good store."

I continued my elevator pitch for the new line of products. "I've partnered with a Korean manufacturer who makes Teflon-free, dishwasher-safe pots, pans, and easy-to-clean earthenware stone pots for cooking Korean rice dishes, and all of it falls in line with our mission to find tools and recipes to help busy people cook more at home."

Brittney added, "Okay, I'm sold! When will the products be in Target so I can buy a whole set for myself? In time for the holidays?"

I chuckled. "I wish, but we need time for production and shipment. So they'll be in stores in six months, next spring."

"Well, that's the most exciting news we've had on our show in a while. Mrs. Kim, I'd love to ask you about your cooking. I heard you're quite the chef."

Mom waved her hand, in a shooing motion. "Noooo, I can make Korean food. Some American food. No baking."

"That's better than me, I don't bake or cook often. That's why your daughter's cooking for busy lifestyles appeals to me so much." Brittney tucked her long fringy bangs behind her right ear. "What's your favorite Korean dish to prepare or eat that's in your cookbook?"

Mom clasped her hands tightly and dropped them to her lap. "I like rice cake soup. I used to make all the time when Jessie grow up."

I added, "We'll make that on our show next week. What's nice is you can add dumplings from the frozen section of a grocery store. And the broth with meat is essentially the same for kalbitang, another tasty Korean soup." I glanced over at my mom to see if she was planning to contradict me, as she'd done on the livestreams many times, but she didn't. Thank God. She was distracted by something in her pocket. I didn't want to draw attention to her, so I asked Brittney, "Have you had Korean food lately?"

She blushed. "After you were on the show, I watched some of your videos and made your meal-kit bulgogi. And I loved the episode you just released for kimchi fried rice. Your shortcuts were just so brilliant. Would you mind sharing that recipe for our viewers?"

"It's my favorite meal. The recipe calls for day-old rice, diced kimchi, onions, red pepper gochujang paste, sesame oil, soy sauce, and Trader Joe's precooked pork belly, also diced. Some people use SPAM. The full list of ingredients and directions are on the website and in the cookbook. It was our best performing video to date."

Mom had a piece of paper in her hands and was looking at the camera instead of me. She added, "I have some good news too."

My chest constricted. An announcement? Dear God, what was she planning?

"More good news? Let's hear it!" Brittney leaned in while I shifted uncomfortably in my seat, waiting for Mom to share what was on her mind.

She cleared her throat. "Someone named Rich Rivers call

our house and ask me to give Jessie very important message." Holding up the paper at eye-level, she read, "Message. Innovation Networks is expanding into diverse, ethnic food programming and we would like to discuss buying Seoul Sistas. Please call back immediately." She grinned and continued. "His phone number is two-one-two. Nine-six-four—"

Brittney cut her off. "Oh Mrs. Kim, no need for the phone number. That's quite an update."

"Yes. That's a lot to process." Innovation Networks was a competitor to Discovery, who owned the Food Network. They called me? How'd they get my home number? So many thoughts and feelings clattered around in my brain. Unable to form coherent words, I shot Brittney a quick glance. *Help me. I can't process this.*

Quick on her feet, she spouted a quick anecdote about how she'd put too much red pepper paste in her kimchi fried rice. Meanwhile, it gave me a chance to formulate my thoughts so we could end the interview on a high note.

When Brittney reached a stopping point in her story, I chimed in, "To celebrate our cookbook release early next year, we're offering a chance to win a signed, annotated early review copy plus a fifty-dollar Target gift card tomorrow. You can enter the sweepstakes on our website. Thank you so much for having us, Brittney, it was a pleasure."

Mom waved at the camera. "Everybody buy Seoul Sista cookbook!"

"Thank you both for finding time for us. Back to you, Rob."

When the red lights on the cameras turned off, Brittney said, "That was so fun! Please excuse me though, I have to run to the ladies' room. I drank too much iced tea!"

I turned my head to my mom so fast I nearly pulled a neck muscle. "When did you get the call? What time? What else did he say?"

She nodded. "He call early this morning." She handed me the paper, which contained the same information she'd recited on camera.

"That's really all he said?"

"You supposed to call back. I memorize the phone number. Two-one-two. Nine-six-four—"

"Okay, Mom. I'll call them as soon as we get home. Can we head out now? I really need to call Innovation back before end of day East Coast time."

"Yes, but first we stop at the other room."

"Yeah, to get our purses."

She pulled a Ziploc bag from her pocket. "And I take home cake and muffin."

Chapter Twenty

"Hi, Rich, this is Jessie Kim of Seoul Sistas. Is this a good time for you? I received your message from my m—um, I got your message and would love to discuss Innovation Networks' future as it relates to my company." I'd looked up Rich Rivers online before the call. A Wharton grad. Internships at Bank of America and Time Warner. Worked his way up at Innovation after college and was around my age. No red flags that I could spot in my five minutes of googling.

"Nice to hear from you, Jessie. Let me shut my door, hold on." A creak echoed over the speaker. "Do you know much about Innovation?"

I laughed. "Actually, yes. Other than me watching your Foodie Network and all your science channels. I used to be in banking. Media and Entertainment was the industry I covered so I'm definitely familiar with Innovation."

"Well, that's great, I don't need to tell you the long version of our company history. I'll just jump into the exciting part. We've expanded our portfolio this year and are looking to acquire more diverse food-related media properties. A few months ago, we purchased businesses in the Sicilian and Persian cooking space. We'd love to add Seoul Sistas too."

My heartbeat raced as he continued.

"Would you mind asking your accountant to share your financial statements with us?"

I bit my lip to refrain from laughing. I'd hired a bookkeeper to help me the last few months, but as the Target deal got more complicated and would affect my business accounting, I'd just hired an accountant. What luck.

So many thoughts ran through my head. The first one to formulate into actual words was "How did Innovation hear about my business?"

A siren blaring prevented us from hearing each other. "Sorry, there must be a fire nearby. So many police and fire trucks!" When the noise died down, he continued. "Your 'Umma Approved!' branding is what did it. One of our executives has a college-aged daughter who obsessively buys your products, and she said to her dad that your brand was quote-unquote 'so meme-able'. Your products and message appeal to that younger market who is really into life hacks, and that's the demographic we haven't quite figured out how to reach yet. Separately, your business came recommended by our investment bank we have on retainer when we brought this strategic problem to their attention. They came to us with a list of potential targets in the market they thought would be complementary, and Seoul Sistas was at the top as a prospective acquisition. Then we heard from the planning team at Target about your cookware deal."

A light, fluttery sensation in my stomach contrasted with my heart pounding hard against my chest. "It's so great to hear that Seoul Sistas is making waves." From my days in banking, I knew how this all worked. Innovation Networks was a media company looking to expand in the ethnic cooking space, and my products and brand fit their needs. Next steps would be to explore whether a deal would work for both parties, and to do that, I needed to sign a nondisclosure agreement and provide them with financial records. Deals like this fell through all the time. Still, there was a small chance Innovation might offer me a sizable sum for Seoul Sistas, even though it was just getting off the ground. But if there was one thing I'd learned from Daniel, other than DON'T TRUST HIM, it was to not put all my eggs in one basket.

I nodded, even though he couldn't see me. "I'll get the paperwork you need this week."

We exchanged pleasant goodbyes and hung up. I slumped back in my desk chair and tried to slow my racing heartbeat and my rapid breathing. So many issues and ideas swirled in my head, coming in and out of focus. One question I'd forgotten to ask him came up first. "How did you get my home number?" I had a toll-free number on my website that I'd recently added because Target needed a business phone number, but it had only recently been activated. I needed to investigate this, so I added it to my to-do list. Shortly after the Target deal was official, I'd also moved off my original spreadsheet and into a business project management system integrated with my work calendar. It legitimized my business, but also showed me how far I'd come since moving back home.

Some other things had not been upgraded yet, like my work-space. I was still doing business out of my bedroom, at my childhood desk. Most of the knickknacks from my youth had been cleared off so I could focus on work, but I'd kept my framed photo of the Queen of Country Music.

I grabbed the picture frame with both hands and yelled, "Dolly! The tide's turned! And finally, it's gonna roll my way."

Chapter Twenty-One

Wow, things moved fast with Innovation Networks.

The Monday after I sent the financials, Rich set up a few due diligence calls with his team and me. I had answers for all of their questions, of course, because those were the holes I would have looked for in my deals as a banker. They were trying to find things wrong so they could offer the lowest price for Seoul Sistas. I hadn't been in business very long, hadn't actually made much revenue yet, and all of my value was wrapped up in the near-term deals I'd set in motion. They had the upper hand: if they gave me a take-it-or-leave-it offer, I wouldn't have leverage to counter it without another buyer courting me.

Regardless, this was exciting, even if nothing came of it. And good news just kept coming: the Target deal had sparked interest from Williams-Sonoma, my sauces were showing up in buzzy holiday guides, and a few nonlocal news programs were interested in virtual cooking segments about shortcuts to feeding families over the holidays. The Food Network road-show was going to film in a few weeks and still wanted to feature me.

I was still running ragged, managing most things by myself, with occasional help from part-time contractors with the boxing and shipping. Celeste was close to delivery and wasn't available while she waited for baby number three to arrive. Flora was still chipping in when she could, though her time with me looked to be coming to an end. She'd been flying back and forth to New York for interviews and had made it to final interviews at the hedge fund Hightower Capital. I gave her some of my old suits for her trip. Luckily, they didn't need any alterations.

An important email from Rich a few weeks later caused me to clutch Dolly's photo to my chest. A letter of intent from Innovation Networks, letting me know they were ready to put forward an offer. My hands trembled as I clicked on the attachment that required my e-signature.

Innovation Networks wanted to buy everything. All of the meal-kit products, the video channel, the cookbook IP, cookware, and all of the "Umma Approved!" branding. In an up-front payment, they'd take it all, but there was one condition: I needed to enter an employment contract to remain at the company to oversee the existing businesses for a year, with the possibility of a six-month extension past that date. A pretty standard deal structure.

The total amount? Eight hundred thousand dollars.

Holy shit.

It was hard to believe that something I'd created from nothing would be worth that much money. At Hamilton Cooper, I'd seen deals come and go that were in the billions. For the size and scope of my fledgling business though, the amount was really promising. The offer came with a termination period, which meant I had only a week to decide. But seven days hardly seemed like enough: I needed more time. More data. I asked Rich for an extension, but he promptly replied that they wouldn't budge.

"Could I come to NYC later this week to discuss the deal in person? Anytime that works for your team would be fine with me." This trip would likely be on my own dime, and a last-minute trip to New York would cost thousands of dollars, but I wanted to meet the team and get a better understanding of what we'd both be gaining.

Or . . . what I'd be losing.

He replied a few hours later. "Wrangled the team. See you this Friday, at four o'clock!"

* * *

New York. Home of Ellis Island. The Statue of Liberty. Where hopes and dreams came true. Less than a year ago, my hopes and dreams had been torn into confetti pieces by Hamilton Cooper and then lit on fire. But that was then, and this was now. I came back to the city with mixed feelings of nostalgia, excitement, and disillusionment, like going back to a high school reunion and seeing an unrequited crush, with all the old feelings rushing back once again, knowing that then and now, he was never going to love you back.

Buying a last-minute ticket wasn't cheap, but to keep travel costs down, I luckily received multiple offers of places to crash. From Alice, who would possibly be out of town on business but still had the freeloading sister and hamster problem; Charlie, who lived like he was renting a room in a frat house; and Flora, who was being put up by the hedge fund in the brand-new Whitney Hotel for two days in a deluxe room with two double beds. It was a no-brainer that Flora would be my new temporary roommate.

My flight came in a few hours before the meeting, and Flora was in interviews all day. Next to the hotel was the world-famous Bagel Bin, where I bought a plain toasted bagel with scallion cream cheese, opting out of an everything bagel because, with my bad luck, the poppy seeds would be stuck in my teeth and remain there during the entire meeting. On a whim, I added a cup of carrot and celery sticks plus a fresh-baked chocolate chip cookie. I stuffed my purchases into my messenger bag and headed for the hotel lobby.

Flora had left the key at the front desk, along with a handwritten note.

Good luck today! There are complimentary snacks on the coffee table from Hightower Capital and omg the toiletries smell so good! —Flora

The keycard unclicked the door with a light tap. The heavy door gave into my full shoulder press, allowing brief passage before slamming shut behind me.

My eyes gravitated to the welcome basket first because it was brimming with food. Chocolates, pralines, kettle corn, and red licorice caught my eye first, but some of the healthier options like dry roasted nuts, granola, and fresh fruit looked good too.

I rolled my suitcase next to the empty bed. Flora had slept in the other: her nightgown was folded at the foot of the crisp white duvet.

The whole room was a mix of grays with white and yellow accents. The headboard, heather gray. Pillows? Yellow and charcoal gray. Carpet, plush and light gray. The color scheme continued to the sofa, desk, and bathroom. This was a corner room, so views to both the west and south were visible. A clear day meant bright blue skies and a flurry of pedestrian and yellow cab traffic in the streets below. On the same block, the Rockefeller Center rink was open, and quite a number of people were skating for a chilly December weekday. They had to be tourists, right? Who else would have the time? Around and around they went, little specks of black, red, green, and blue, diverting my attention from work as I took a bite of my bagel and observed them behind the glass window.

After devouring my meal and polishing off a complimentary Granny Smith apple and chocolate truffle from the basket, I took a quick shower, got partially dressed, and hopped on email to confirm the location of the meeting. My body ached from exhaustion and anticipation: no sleep the night before, and even now I was wired, not drowsy. The fear of sleeping through the meeting time also kept me from entertaining the idea of curling up under the white down comforter on my bed. After the meeting I could come back here and crash until the next morning, assuming everything went as expected.

That week I'd put in a few calls to some references Innovation had given me upon request. They had already acquired some food properties like mine, and there were former business owners who had taken lead positions at Innovation, similar to the agreement that had been carved out in my letter of intent. All had given neutral-to-kind statements about Innovation, no red flags. My phone buzzed when one of the heads of the media content groups called me back. It was a relief that she'd returned my call in the first place, and second, that she'd done so while I was in a hotel room all by myself. This timing was perfect, although I had only thirty minutes to chat with her before I jetted off to the meeting at Innovation's Midtown headquarters.

Ritu Gupta was the founder of Inventive Indian. An NYU

alum who also used to work in finance before starting her own foodie cooking company, Ritu was as close as I could get to having a twin.

We hit it off right away too. The warmth in her voice and her immediate inclination to laugh when we kept speaking at the same time made me a fan. So when I asked her how things were going with Innovation and I picked up a change in timbre and tone, it concerned me and warranted deeper probing.

"It's okay. The hours are decent. And the payout was nice. It leaves things open to starting a new business if I want." Where was the passion? It had been there when we were chitchatting about NYU and her portfolio of Indian cooking properties, which she jokingly called her little babies. She hadn't disclosed how much her offer was, but the scope of her business had been much larger, so her offer had probably been sizable.

I asked my one burning question: "Are you glad you sold it to Innovation?"

She paused before answering. "On the record, the business is booming. The cookbook they released is on its third printing and is in ten different languages. The online channel has tripled in subs. And this is all just in the last year or so."

I cleared my throat. "I sense a *but*."

She lowered her voice to almost a whisper. "But . . . they've done something I don't agree with that I think you might understand as being troublesome." She took a noisy breath in and out. "They're whitewashing the content and products. All the hosts for the online show are Caucasian and they're launching a new TV show soon, and those hosts are White too. The new recipes are more bland and they're really no more than adding a little curry here and there for a little flair. I've yet to see an Indian host on their new programming."

She continued. "The worst is the branding. It's completely out of my hands and, well, it shows. The new Inventive Indian logo rolling out next month has a snake charmer . . . and . . . brace yourself . . . he's sitting with a snake on a magic carpet."

My mouth dropped open and a rolling feeling in my stomach made me feel temporarily seasick. In this day and age, how was that even possible? Didn't they do market testing? Didn't companies like Innovation have a diverse enough employee base to prevent that from happening? "I am struggling to find words, I'm so sorry, Ritu. Thank you for letting me know. Did they hint to you at all that they'd do this to the brand?"

"Hmmm . . . they were vague when it came to expansion, all they said was that they'd try to bring the brand to a broader market, which I thought meant introducing it to, like, more college kids or semi-woke people, not watering down the product or promoting stereotypes to the point where it was almost a parody of Indian culture."

My "Umma Approved!" branding used an actual illustration of my mom. Worry set in fast, my chest tightening as I thought about Celeste's artwork. Would they change the fonts to make it more . . . offensively Asian-looking, with slanty letters? And make my mom's image a mockery too? Before, I was 95 percent certain I was going to take the offer. It seemed too good to be true. With Ritu's input I could clearly see the risks and wavered over the deal.

Just as we hung up, my phone alarm, which had been set to ensure I'd wake up in case I nodded off, blasted. A full-volume setting I now regretted, because my heart was frantically pounding from anxiety about this new information and the jump-scare from the alarm.

One hour till the meeting.

I made a point not to wear the same suit I had on the day I was laid off. Instead, I put on an outfit that I wore when we closed on some of HC's biggest, most lucrative deals. In front of the full-length mirror on the bathroom door, I stood with a straight back and tilted chin, turning my torso left and right so I could examine my jet-black Hugo Boss suit, peach silk blouse, and three-inch Louboutin heels. A few guys in the office used to tease me by calling me Halloween, or Jack-o'-lantern, when I'd wear my lucky outfit, but you know what? This suit had a perfect track record. I needed all the luck I could get today.

Smoothing my black hair, I told myself, *Jessie Kim, you'll do great.* As I put the final touches on my eye makeup, Mom texted.

Wish you luck!

I'd kept the specifics about the deal quiet; all she knew was I was meeting with a potential buyer. If I disclosed dollar amounts, or company names, she'd talk to her friends about it. And those friends would talk to other friends. By the time I got back from my trip, the passing along of information would have been like playing "telephone," so conflated and convoluted that I'd be offered congratulations from the entire Nashville Korean community for being offered a CEO position for a Fortune 100 company for a yearly salary of a billion dollars.

I didn't need that stress.

Thank you! I'll call you after the meeting, I replied back. Throwing on my full-length wool coat, I let the door slam shut behind me.

The boutique hotel was situated a few blocks from Innovation's headquarters, so I opted to walk in the brisk fifty-degree weather since there was no rain in the forecast and, most important, it wasn't too breezy. The last thing I needed was to show up at this in-person with an unsightly wind-swept look.

The building lobby layout was eerily similar to that of Hamilton Cooper's. White-and-gray marble floors, fanciful crystal chandeliers, and bronze busts of old, deceased White dudes were mounted behind the reception desk. The guard, who looked like a large boulder with thick black hair, grilled me with who-what-where-why questions and then asked for my ID. Cleared by security, they took my picture and handed me a photo-badge sticker with my eyes half-closed. Mortified, I squeaked, "Do I have to wear this?"

The boulder grunted, "Yes."

The homicidal look on his face gave me the impression that he was not open to retakes. I placed the visitor pass sticker under my suit's lapel, partially obscuring the photo. It was the best I could do given the circumstances.

The boulder pointed to the elevator bank. "Fifteenth floor."

While waiting for the doors to open, I did one last check in my bag. Laptop, financials, contract, and notepad were all accounted for, as was my favorite pen. I'd brought along some Seoul Sistas swag to hand out too.

The elevator was not just crowded on the way up, it was slow and stopped on every floor, two through fourteen. By the time it reached my designated level, I had only seven minutes to spare. Seven minutes early was still early though. The sensibly dressed woman at the front desk took my name and said, "Rich will be down shortly. You can take a seat."

Before I could actually sit on one of the fine black leather couches, Rich Rivers waltzed through the automatic glass doors next to the receptionist and walked toward me. He looked just like his LinkedIn photo: same wide smile and graying hair. He was shorter than I'd pictured him though, around five foot five. I expected his height to match his booming conference-call voice.

Firm handshake. Good hand temperature, not too warm, not too cold. "How was your flight?" He led me through the hallway maze and looked back over his shoulder to hear my answer.

"Good! I'm hoping to get an extra day or two in the city while I have the opportunity. I forgot how nice it is to be in New York this time of the year. I love all the holiday lights."

Rich brought me to a kitchenette. "Me too, they put them up earlier and earlier each year. Would you like a coffee? Tea? Or water?" I grabbed a cup and pushed the small blue lever on the water cooler. He took a can of sparkling water from the refrigerator and we continued our walk to the conference room. I avoided carbonation before meetings: I'd learned the hard way it resulted in spontaneous burps and belches.

"Everyone cleared their calendar to be at the meeting. My boss, Tommy O'Hara, will be there, the exec I told you about whose college daughter raved about your products. He got market validation from his daughter and her peers, and from the investment bank we have on retainer who vetted you. Tommy is thrilled and can't wait to meet you."

My hands trembled with excitement and trepidation. Was this genuine enthusiasm for my business, or was this a greedy buyout and exactly what had happened to Ritu on repeat? Deutsche Bank worked on all of Innovation's M&A business matters—very reputable.

The frosted interior windows of the Gramercy conference room prevented me from seeing the inside. We were here, at the conference room mentioned in the meeting invitation on my calendar. As Rich opened the door, he exclaimed, "Oh! We also have some of the guys already here from Hamilton Cooper; we just hired them and they're on retainer now. They were instrumental in short-listing some of the businesses we were looking into—"

Seated at the long wooden conference table was Wanker Wyatt and Daniel Choi, Esquire.

My stomach lurched and dropped to the floor when Daniel's eyes met mine. An urge to scream clawed up my throat. Had I died and gone to hell? Because this was exactly how I imagined hell to be. I clenched my teeth and took a deep breath.

Rich continued rambling. "We ran everything by them and they helped structure the deal." Rich was schmoozy and sales-y, but he wasn't a moron. He looked at me and then the others. "You all know one another?"

Wyatt had a better poker face. "Jess and I go way back. I used to be her boss." He winked at me. "I always loved your Halloween style." He pointed to my suit.

I mustered a smile. "I know Wyatt very well. How'd that Beauchamp deal turn out?"

I knew Hamilton Cooper had lost that opportunity after I left; it was all over the trade news. Rumor had it that Wyatt was the sole reason HC lost that deal.

Wyatt coughed into his coffee. "Damn, Jess. That was an NHL-level body check. You go in the penalty box."

I smirked. A triumphant verbal takedown.

Wyatt continued. "This is Daniel Choi, he's been our acting general counsel while Patrick Han has been on medical leave."

Daniel stood and extended his hand. "Hey. Nice to see you again, Jess." He looked the same, although his full designer suit threw me off. I'd seen him dressed up only once at the coffee shop, and that was a step up from business casual. Here he looked more sophisticated. Sharper. Unfortunately for me, much sexier. His devilish eyes and matching smile didn't help.

To remain cordial, I took his hand in mine and shook it. Even though this was a business greeting, there was no way to ignore his body connecting to mine, hand-to-hand, electric currents running between us. I tried to ignore the shiver running down my entire back.

Our eyes met again, his penetrating stare so intense it was like he had X-ray vision. I let go of his hand quickly, like we were playing hot potato. His warmth lingered on my skin as I dropped my hand to my side.

Wyatt asked, "Is Tommy going to make it?" He looked at me. "Tom and I are at the same country club. Innovation recently hired us as their bank of record. I'm a VP now." He said that last part like he actually deserved it.

My mouth hung open and it took a few seconds to form nonoffensive words. "And Daniel? Your legal counsel? How is he here?" I whispered. *Did you dig down into my worst nightmares and assemble a torture team?*

Wyatt held his finger to his ear. "What? Always so quiet, Jess, it's hard to hear you sometimes." He laughed at his own joke. "And to find out you started your own business, well, *surprised* is an understatement. But back to my boy Daniel, he's covering for a friend of his from law school who went on leave. Tommy helped Daniel get the role because they'd worked together before and Tommy *loves* him. Danny Boy's contract ends today, actually. We're hoping he accepts our full-time offer since we have a few legal positions open."

Daniel dipped his head and looked at me regretfully. "Remember that meeting with the headhunter?"

I nodded. Yes, I remembered that day. Riding in his fancy car. Going on a hot chicken date. The bed. I still relived that day sometimes in my daydreams.

And here we were again. This time with $800K on the line. This time with Daniel teamed up with Wanker Wyatt, who always managed to fail up with confidence and land better opportunities.

The door opened and a burly red-haired man with wire-framed glasses entered the room.

"Sorry I'm late. What did I miss? I'm guessing not much, since Rich and Jessie are still standing. Please, have a seat!" Exuberant, jovial, and commandeering. This had to be Tommy. He didn't even introduce himself; maybe he knew it wasn't needed.

Rich stammered, "We were just doing some rounds of introductions. Or rather, reintroductions. Turns out Jessie and the extended team have crossed paths before."

Tommy plopped down in the nearest chair and silenced his

phone. "Well, let me do my quick intro. I'm Tommy O'Hara and I've been in Innovation's Strategic Acquisitions Group for nearly five years. Before that I was at Bain, and before consulting I was at Morgan Stanley and then a few VC firms. Anyway, my daughter is, as she says, *absolutely obsessed* with *Hanguk Hacks* and Seoul Sistas. If we're able to close the deal, ideally today, I'd be her hero. And those opportunities are hard to come by."

I laughed at his joke, because it was genuinely amusing. Quite different from Wyatt's immediate personal attacks disguised as humor. The idea that his college-aged daughter was practically driving this deal interested me, and that Tommy was pursuing it was even more fascinating.

Although the offer was a large sum of money to someone like me, for a company like Innovation, it was mere peanuts—and not the fancy kind you found in a Harry & David holiday basket or the organic ones at Whole Foods. I had worked on a few deals like this at HC, ones that were brokered "for the relationship," where our bank would help a client out of goodwill with no financial gain for the bank. They were usually passion projects or deals that helped out a friend. And I certainly wasn't anyone's friend here in the room, so the reason to acquire Seoul Sistas had to be by default a project of passion.

While the early part of the meeting wasn't going at all like I pictured it, it also wasn't going badly. I'd just need to avoid all eye contact with Wanker Wyatt and Daniel and focus solely on Tommy and Rich. Ignoring Wyatt would be easy, but Daniel had taken off his suit jacket and rolled up his shirtsleeves, revealing his distractingly tan, muscular arms for my viewing pleasure.

Tommy asked Rich to get us all copies of the offer terms and financial printouts. He ran out of the room, mumbling that he'd left them on his desk. This left more time for chitchat.

"Wyatt and I are at the same club in the Hamptons, but our families go way back too. I've had the pleasure of working with Daniel before in my venture capital days. When I told him about our company's growth areas, he nearly fell all over himself to get your name and number in front of me. He must think highly of you. Luckily, my daughter had already been raving about your company, so everything lined up perfectly, with Daniel vouching for you. I asked Rich to make some introductory calls and he said your mom picked up the phone. I'm glad you called us back."

So that's how he got my home phone number. Eyebrow cocked, I shot a look at Daniel, to which he replied, "I tried your cell on numerous occasions to give you a heads-up, but the calls weren't going through."

My cell wasn't working because I blocked you, and, quick recap, I blocked you because you screwed me over on a business deal. My skin prickled, thinking about how he'd tried to "help" me but put me in more debt instead. I'd had an enormous, unplanned inventory glut and had to dig my way out of that mess. Was this another one of his special business arrangements where I got screwed and he got paid big bucks for screwing me?

Tommy said, "Well, we're glad you came today. Did you have any questions about the amount offered, or the key terms? For a company just starting out, we evaluated Seoul Sistas a little unconventionally, mainly looking at your upcoming partnerships and supply deals you've secured, your growth potential, as well as brand value. Regarding the latter, it's hard to reach the eighteen-to-twenty-four-year-old demographic with products other than apps and clothing, and you've managed to do it effortlessly. As part of the agreement, we do want you to also stay on to oversee the business for a minimum of a year. That employment contract was sent to you along with the letter of intent."

I folded my hands on the table. "Well, thanks for bringing up brand value, it might be the only topic I wanted to discuss today. I had a chance to speak with Ritu Gupta on the phone this morning."

He winced a little, like he'd just eaten a sour candy. "Yes, Ritu was part of an acquisition a year or two ago. That was another deal I had the pleasure of leading. Inventive Indian. Have you seen the new line of cookbooks we're releasing in a few months? We also have a show on Netflix running now. That brand has grown so much the last year, I'm proud of what we've accomplished."

I didn't want to throw Ritu under the bus by disclosing any

of her off-the-record comments, so I proceeded carefully. "That level of growth is very impressive. To better understand my role at the company upon acquisition, would I still be a decision maker?"

Tommy took off his glasses and polished them. "I think the way we'd see your role is as an influencer. So maybe not the final decision maker, but you'd definitely have input."

"I see. As for branding, would you see that staying the same? Or being tweaked?"

He laughed as he put his wire frames on. "It's rare to see a brand stay the same over a long period of time. But I will say this—I love your branding. Your mom in the logo is genius. And I should also mention that my daughter loves it too."

That put me more at ease at first, but then I remembered what Ritu had said about their growth plans. I asked, "Do you see Innovation trying an aggressive growth strategy with Seoul Sistas as it did with Inventive Indian?"

He nodded. "Maybe even more aggressive. We want to bring the brand to a broader market. Definitely."

The bagel, celery, carrots, and cookie I'd consumed earlier threatened to retreat from my intestines. Nauseated, the room suddenly felt smaller, bringing Wyatt and Daniel even closer to me. I asked, "Would it be okay to take a short recess? I'd love to get some air, think about what we've discussed, and maybe even take a quick bio break."

Tommy checked the clock on the wall. "Sure, how about ten

minutes? I'll stay here to make a quick call, so if you want to leave anything, it'll be safe."

Wyatt jumped out of his chair. "Can we make it fifteen? There's a smoothie place around the corner that does great CBD shakes. It's part of my self-care routine." He flung open the door without even looking back to see me trailing right behind him. It almost banged me in the face, but Daniel's lean arm shot over my head, halting the door from striking me.

"Thanks." I darted through, trying to create some distance from Daniel.

He continued to trail me as we walked down the hallway. "Can we talk for a minute?"

I slowed my step and turned. Daniel trotted toward me and pointed to an empty conference room next to us. "Let's duck in here. I have a lot to say and I'm sure you do too."

The windows were frosted on the top half only, as such we could see movement of dozens of legs and feet hurry by once we were inside. He closed the door behind us. Not long ago, the possibility of being in a closed-door room situation with Daniel would be titillating. But not now. *Jess, don't get hypnotized by that handsome face, those wide shoulders, that oxford shirt hugging his taut, muscular body.*

If we were going to talk, I was going to have my say first.

Crossing my arms, I blurted, "I can't believe you're working with Wyatt. He's a horrible human being."

"I wonder if he's having a private conversation with someone, saying the same thing about us," he teased.

"No, Daniel, you don't get to pretend we're an *us* here. You are literally on the opposing side today."

To my surprise, he nodded. "You're right. I'm sorry. A lot's happened the last few weeks. I got this short contracting gig at HC and I swear I had no idea about the bad blood between Wyatt and you. He didn't talk about his deals at HC, but it makes sense he'd keep that quiet if he lost the Beauchamp deal." He ran his hand down the side of his face, swiping to the bottom of his chin.

I balled my fists. "And my old firm happens to be the bank on retainer of the strategic company trying to acquire my business? With Wyatt at the helm of this deal? Is this the universe playing a joke on me?"

He leaned on the wall and shoved his hands into his suit pants pocket. "Actually, I gave your name to Tommy directly. He trusts my judgment. Wyatt didn't have anything to do with it—he was assigned to work with me once it was official, and he wanted to work with Tommy because they're country club buddies. Tommy'd already heard about your business from his daughter and it aligned with his growth goals, as he said. There's no money being made on the bank's end for this deal, and I'm not getting anything from it either. I wanted *you* to make money though, which is why I insisted they call you."

Is this really happening? I shook my head. "You know, giving him my home phone wasn't the best idea. In fact, it was the worst idea. Did you know my mom answered the call and told me that Innovation left a message on live TV?"

Pressing his lips, he tried to stifle a laugh. "I'm sorry about that. I wasn't certain about sharing your cell number since I wasn't able to call or text you. Thinking about it now, I'm assuming you blocked me. And the only other number I had for you was your parents' home." Daniel glanced at the door, then his gaze fell on me. "So what are you thinking about the offer? Are you going to take it? Or leave it?"

Could I trust Daniel? I'd been so burned by him last time. How could I know he was truly helping me this time? How could I trust myself to know?

The longer he stared at me, the more my face flushed with heat.

He took a step forward. "Ask me anything. I owe you from the NiHao screw-up. Let me know how I can make it up to you."

My mind clattered with all of the possibilities. The one that pushed through the haze was the branding and expansion concerns. "Can we talk off the record?"

Daniel nodded. "Yes."

Can I trust you, Daniel Choi?

"I swear, on my dad's New Revised Standard Version of the Bible. Korean translated, of course."

Well, that was convincing . . . and damn it . . . charming. I relayed everything Ritu had told me, about the complete whitewashing of Inventive Indian in the cooking shows, the recipes, and even the cookbook authors. His look of concern transitioned to horror as I explained Inventive Indian's change to their new magic carpet and snake charmer branding.

I raised my voice. "It's not even whitewashing, it's insensitive and just—" I couldn't even articulate how wrong all of it was. "Ugh."

He shook his head. "They only brought me in on parts of the deal development. But everything you shared is new to me. The dollar amount they're offering you is fair, but it doesn't factor in the risk for you giving up full control . . . the way they instructed me to write the deal with full buyout is . . . well, shit, I'm not allowed to say because of my contract, but maybe we could—"

My heart jumped to my throat when Wyatt's tilted, ogling face popped into view in the bottom half of the window. He yelled, "There you are! Time to get back—it's almost five! Quittin' time! We've been looking all over for you."

Daniel and I exchanged looks as the door flung open. Wyatt had a half-consumed green smoothie in his hand. He raised it in a toast. "To closing this deal today so we can celebrate all weekend!"

Wyatt prattled on about his CBD addiction as we reentered the Gramercy conference room. Tommy and Rich chatted about their weekend plans as we all took our seats. Daniel leaned forward and whispered, "I know how to get out of this. Can you trust me?"

Could I trust him?

My heart tugged. *I did.* I mouthed, "Yes."

Tommy rolled his chair up so his midsection touched the table. Hands folded on the smooth pressed wood, fingers intertwined, he asked, "So did you have time to think about it? Can I brag to my daughter that we have a deal?" I had to admit, he was a really good salesman. Earnest. Friendly. Persistent.

I took a deep breath. "I have concerns." I racked my brain for recent business examples to use in my explanation. "My biggest fear is taking this uniquely Korean American brand and erasing the Korean part."

He nodded. "I see. We wouldn't want that either. It's the Korean part that's the appeal. We wouldn't want to tamper with that. It's the essence of the business!"

"And what about the branding—I know it's not in the offer, but could we amend it to make sure the integrity stays intact?"

Rich spoke this time. "I don't get what that means. Can you be specific about what you're worried about?"

Still mindful of Ritu's concerns, I explained, "I wouldn't want this to turn into a generic Asian hodgepodge, for example. Or a brand where the Korean part is no longer core to the business. Or the branding is offensive. Remember when Abercrombie and Fitch had all those offensive Asian T-shirts a few years back? I wouldn't want that to happen."

Wyatt slurped his straw. "Jessie, sometimes you really overthink it all. For a company your size, the offer is more than fair. You'll have so much money, you can go invest it somewhere and retire on a secluded beach. These guys, Rich and Tommy, they have vision! They make magic happen with any business they acquire. Their Persian Eats cookbook based on their Netflix series has held the number one spot on the bestseller list for three months. The author is this fancy Culinary Institute of the Arts instructor. Dudley something; I forget his name, some English dude. Tommy, didn't you tell me he was chomping at the bit to do a splashy Seoul Sistas cookbook?"

My whole body tensed. "We already have one coming out. And did you just say a White dude would be writing a *Korean* Seoul *Sistas* cookbook?"

He backtracked in the most Wyatt-like way. "I never said that exactly. And I didn't say he was White."

"With a name like Dudley, he's not exactly a sista."

The silence in the room was palpable. Wyatt asked, "So no deal? Any *smart* business leader would jump at this opportunity."

My God. Was he serious?

"No deal." I looked at Daniel, pleading for any lifeline he could throw me to get me out of there.

He stood from his chair. "Rich, Tommy, as always, it's been a pleasure working with you these last few weeks, but my contract ends now, at five P.M. And Wyatt, I'm respectfully declining your offer of full-time employment."

Wyatt's mouth formed a perfect O. "But . . . why?"

"I have a new client to counsel. Jessie Kim. And effective immediately, we'll be declining your offer and evaluating all of our options for selling or retaining her business."

I stood and pushed the chair back with my leg. "Thank you so much for finding time to meet with me, and it was great meeting you, Rich and Tommy." Shooting a death stare at Wyatt, I continued. "As a *smart business leader* in a new and growing category, it's best for me now to consider my options and explore alternatives."

Looking only at Rich and Tommy, I added, "Best of luck at Innovation. Have a great weekend." Daniel opened the door for us, steering clear of hitting me in the face. We walked out of the room and I let out a huge sigh of relief when we were out of earshot.

"Are you really offering me your legal counsel?" I asked Daniel. "You've seen my financial statements. I don't exactly have the cash flow to hire a fancy lawyer like you."

He pressed the down button on the elevator.

DING!

Of course the elevator would come right away for Daniel Choi.

We rode to the lobby. "I still owe you big for the NiHao debacle. How about a drink? We should celebrate your business not being sold to Innovation."

"Sure. That sounds good. It's on me."

As soon as we reached the lobby, my mom texted. *How did meeting go?*

My shoulders slumped as I pictured my mom's eager, earnest face. "Hold up, I need to give my parents an update."

Daniel nodded and shoved his hands in his pockets. "Okay, I'll go walk around. Text me when you're ready."

I found a nice cushy couch in the lobby and called Mom.

"Sooooo, I have bad news, or good news, depending on how you look at it. I didn't take the deal."

In sharp staccato, Mom said, "I see. I see. Okay." After a pause, she asked, "Did they cheat you on money?"

I laughed. "Dollar-wise, it was a good offer, I just didn't want to sell Seoul Sistas short by giving it to a company that would take the heart and soul out of my brand." I sighed. "Literally, they would be taking the Seoul out of Seoul Sistas. I'm sorry, I know you're disappointed."

Disappointed that I didn't take the deal. Disappointed I don't have a regular job. Disappointed in everything about me.

Mom softened her tone. "Nothing to be sorry."

My chest tightened and the urge to cry took over instantly. *Keep it together, Jess.* "I saw you humming in front of the mirror after one of the shows. It made me want this business to be successful. I wanted to make this deal work, so you'd be proud of what we accomplished, and you'd be proud of me." My voice hitched. "I know the business means so much to you."

She let out a big breath. "No, no, no. I want *you* to be happy." She paused. "And also to have health insurance."

A laugh burst out of me.

She continued. "Ji-Hyun-ah, you work so hard. I help on the show and be part of your business because I do it for *you*. For *you*, not me. You are not disappointing me. You are my hard-working daughter. I am very proud Umma. You are *Umma Approved*."

I jumped to my feet and walked straight toward the revolving door. If Tommy, Rich, or Wyatt came down to the lobby, I didn't want them to see me with tears running down my cheeks. "Thank you for saying that. I really needed to hear those words today." I took a tissue from my bag and patted my teary face.

"So you coming home tonight?" she asked.

Daniel rounded the corner and offered me a small wave. I waved back. "Not till tomorrow or maybe the day after, I have one last thing to take care of tonight."

"Okay, okay. I hear from Pastor Choi that Daniel is working in New York now. Maybe you can call him and have nice dinner? Maybe ask if he dating anyone?"

I grinned as he approached. "I'll see what I can do, Umma."

Chapter Twenty-Two

Rockefeller Center at dusk, a wonderous sight. Daniel and I observed the bundled-up skaters teeter, clomp, and zoom around from the window of Pour, the wine bar on the top of my NYC bucket list. Even though I'd walked these same blocks many times when I lived here, and eaten at restaurants close by, I'd never had time to sit and enjoy this view. The immensity of the towering sixty-foot Christmas tree, adorned with colored LEDs, was impossible to miss. It was one thing to see it on TV during the lighting ceremony, or on someone's Instagram post, or in passing on a brisk walk to work or to a client. To experience the massive branches, multicolor lights, and the star tree-topper the size of my short-waisted torso as close as we were—it was a very New York experience. One I'd missed even when given many opportunities, one that *almost* got my mind off of the fact that Daniel Choi was here with me.

Almost.

We clinked our wineglasses. I toasted first. "To me!"

"Hey," Daniel whimpered. "That was my line."

I shrugged and took a sip of my Malbec. "So, what's next for you? Are you staying in New York?"

He folded and refolded his paper napkin. "I'm still figuring all that out. The headhunter has set up interviews all over, some even in Nashville. I wish I had my life figured out like you."

Good thing I'd already swallowed the wine, because I sputtered, "What?" right at his face.

He cocked an eyebrow. "C'mon. You think my mom and dad comparing us all the time in middle school was a fluke? You've always inspired me to work harder. You were always the one to beat. Good grades, normal social life, best oboe player." Daniel jumped back when I pretended to cock my fist.

I shook my head. "That's bullshit." We were compared all the time because he was Mr. Perfect. Minus the bowl cut.

He threw his palms in the air. "Okay. Fine, don't believe me. Ask my parents. But . . . I also had to live in my brother's shadow. You know, the doctor. The one who's marrying a doctor next year." He took a sip and grunted, "They'll have little future doctor babies, I'm sure."

"Bitter doesn't suit you. I prefer Smug Daniel, to be honest."

"You got me all wrong, Seoul Sista. I'm not bitter. Well, maybe a little. There's no measuring up to the oldest doctor son, I gave up on that long ago. Anyway, I call this confidence, not smugness. And it's only because I realized in law school that it was possible to have a life after BC."

Confusion clouded my head as I took another gulp. "Before Christ?"

He smirked. "BC. Bowl cut." In the dim light, his dark brown eyes looked even more opaque, giving him a mischievous and devilish look.

"I could use more of that confidence." I sighed. "It's why I got let go from Hamilton Cooper in the first place."

"Well, they're all clearly incompetent." He put his glass down and looked straight into my eyes and grabbed my hand. "Jess, you're amazing. Everything you do is so smart and thought through, and executed so well. I'm in awe of you. You're basically the opposite of Wyatt, who fits the Hamilton Cooper mold. You don't, and that's a good thing."

Heat flushed straight to my cheeks. "You're right." I put my empty glass down. "I need to own my shit."

He nodded. "I've seen a lot of shit in my life, and you have good shit. It's golden. Don't shortchange yourself, you are way more impressive than you think."

I smiled and grabbed my bag. "Thank you. Speaking of good shit, want to come to Flora's hotel room? There's a whole basket of free food. We can talk about Seoul Sistas' other business options. And I'll order room service dinner as my legal payment."

Daniel guzzled his last sips of wine. "Count me in."

***

FLORA HADN'T BEEN back to the room after her interviews. That probably meant things were going well for her.

On the couch, Daniel had a room-service burger in one hand, a beer in the other, and my financials spread out on the coffee table in front of him. Was this how he worked at home and in an office, both hands occupied with food and drinks? How much would his productivity increase if he had an extra set of arms—

"Jess? Did you even hear my question?"

My gaze fixed on his handsome face. Amused, Daniel stated the question once again. "Would you be open to a fifty-one, forty-nine percent acquisition deal where there's an option to buy out in the future? Or one where they structure an earn-out so if you hit the profit projections, you get paid more? We can raise capital with food VCs or go on *Shark Tank*. I know a guy."

I sat next to him on the couch and smirked. "Of course you know a guy." I popped a fry in my mouth and chewed. "I'd like to keep growing the business. Hire more people. So maybe seed capital is the way to do it, on my terms."

Our fingers collided as we both reached in the basket for the twice-cooked, thick fries at the same time. When we touched, electricity pulsed straight down my arm, sending a network of tingles all over my body. He laughed and said, "We might need to order more. We demolished them." Daniel offered me the last fry and a packaged hand wipe.

Without thinking, I said, "I love these. Lemony fresh." My face flushed as he tore open a package and sniffed.

"You're right."

He stood, stretched, and walked to the window. Pulling open the curtains, he revealed a magnificent view of lit skyscrapers around us and a sea of red and white lights from the streams of cars below. New York City at night.

"Wow." It was all I could manage to say. The view left me speechless.

He stared southward. "The top of the Empire State Building is overrated. It's freezing cold up there, and really windy." I stretched my neck to see if it was visible.

Daniel asked, "Is it really all that romantic up there? *This* is much more romantic, don't you think?"

How many times had this almost happened? But now there were no parents around. My body jolted into action, eager to accept this invitation. Reaching for his shoulders, I brought our bodies closer together as his hands wrapped around to the small of my back, locking on the base of my spine.

He whispered into my ear, "Well, here we are again." Daniel's breath was warm and sent shivers through me.

Standing on the balls of my feet, I brought my lips to his, offering a feather-light and tender exploratory peck. He took a turn, caressing me with slow and passionate kisses, on my mouth, then against my neck. My heartbeat throbbed against his chest as he moved his hands farther down.

I loosened my grip around his shoulders and tugged him over to my bed. Lying back, he eased on top of me, with one hand holding his weight, the other slowly unbuttoning my blouse, unveiling my lacy bra hidden beneath the silken fabric.

He kissed the hollow of my neck, sending my heart lurching. My hands moved down the length of his chest, unbuckling his belt, releasing his tucked shirt from captivity.

A beep from the door drowned out my hammering heart.

We froze as the door opened. "You home, Jess? The interviews went great! I'm dropping off my satchel and changing my shoes so Alice and Charlie and I can go out and they want you to—"

Flora took one look at our tangled bodies on the bed and turned on her heel, like she was doing a spin move in basketball.

Her bag fell to the floor with a thud. "Uh, forget the shoes. I'm out. Have fun!"

She flung the door open and scurried out.

"Where were we?" Daniel laughed.

I let my hands roam down from his shoulders and unbuttoned his shirt. "Here."

His body melted into mine as the door finally clicked and auto-locked.

Chapter Twenty-Three

Six months later

"Who would have thought that tailgaters would be our biggest and most profitable market?" The energetic crowd laughed. "We tested some tailgating recipes and sold custom marinades in a few key cities. Our business took a huge leap forward after that. I had no idea that would work. Korean marinades and football fans. In my mental model, this was incongruous."

I looked at the camera, then back at the audience. Especially over the last few months, I'd become well versed in public speaking in front of real-life people, a different skill altogether from recording in an intimate studio or kitchen setting. Giving a TED Talk was something I'd always dreamed of, even back in my days as a banker. I couldn't have ever imagined I'd be here, on this stage, talking to hundreds of people about leadership and finding your voice, and connecting with hundreds of thousands of people watching the talk on their computers at home or at work.

The audience nodded. "One important thing I've learned about entrepreneurship is that frequently there isn't any, or enough, information to make data-driven decisions. Sometimes you're left trusting your gut and trying out ideas that your dependable staff came up with. As someone who loves to wallow in Microsoft Excel, Google Sheets, and MySQL, you can imagine how difficult it was to change my way of thinking. But luckily I had people around me to help me grow. To help me change. One of my biggest supporters who whole-heartedly believed in my tailgating idea is in the audience today." In the front row, Daniel gave me a little wave. He'd cleared his calendar that day to free himself of any consulting responsibilities. I smiled back and returned his hello with a nod. Next to him, my mom wasn't supposed to have her phone out, but she sneaked in a photo anyway. Beside her, Dad looked serious, but I expected that from him. Earlier he'd expressed worry that a camera might pan to his face, which I told him it wouldn't, but he didn't believe me.

"My first exposure to the term 'leadership' was in my undergrad business classes at NYU, where we talked a lot about the differences between a good manager versus a good leader. Can you be one without being the other? Some of us thought no, some thought yes, some, like me, were simply confused. I got a B in that class."

More smiles and titters from the audience. "I worked for

many years in investment banking, where I saw that management and leadership take all shapes and forms. I was laid off because I was told I had no leadership potential. I worked my ass off doing my job well and trust me, I have receipts. While I was working there, I thought I'd pay my dues and learn leadership skills once I'd reached the upper levels of management. I assumed leadership was something that would come with seniority, or that could be learned. After I was let go, I freaked out, thinking it was a nature vs. nurture issue, and they were sending me a message that I didn't have what it took. I believed that because I wasn't born with it, I never would."

A ripple of gasps and then silence from the onlookers. "So I did what anyone would do when faced with an existential crisis. I moved back home and used Sun Tzu's *Art of War* for inspiration. I figured, if there's anyone who can teach me about winning in life, it was Sun Tzu."

I laughed at my own joke, and others followed.

Sun Tzu quotes appeared on the screen behind me. I read them aloud.

> *"In the midst of chaos, there is also opportunity."*
> *"To know your Enemy, you must become your Enemy."*
> *"Know yourself and you will win all battles."*

"Building my business from scratch, the *Art of War* principles ran through my head every day. And now, according to *Inc.*

magazine, Seoul Sistas is a quote-unquote 'company to watch' in the ever-changing food industry, and I just closed another round of funding last week. And it wasn't because of Sun Tzu. It was because of *me*. I didn't let my former workplace define who I was. In fact, they pretty much did me a favor by making it clear that my voice was suppressed in that environment and it wasn't a good fit. But maybe I wasn't meant to find my voice in the banking industry because I found my voice elsewhere. It took time, but I finally believed in myself. I bet on myself. I learned how to lead myself and others. For those of you still looking for your voice, I'm so proud of you. With time, I hope you not only find your voice, like I did, but also, when you do, that you'll help others find theirs too. Thank you."

Dad shot up like he'd pressed an eject button for his chair and the crowd followed suit. Soon the entire auditorium was on their feet, clapping wildly.

I walked toward the exit and turned off the mic clipped to my jacket. The last thing I wanted was for everyone to hear my huge sigh of relief as I clip-clopped off the wooden stage. The talk had gone better than any of my rehearsals and for a long moment my body floated like a hovering cloud. This was the biggest professional moment of my entire life.

The tech team helped me unwire. One of the cameramen said to me, "Great job. So relatable and inspirational. I'm going to show this video to my daughter."

Daniel and my parents met me backstage. With Mom and

Dad saying hi and then beelining to the craft service table, which was covered in platters of fruit, pastries, and sandwiches, Daniel and I had some time to talk alone.

He checked his phone. "Flora and Celeste send their congratulations. They're so proud of you." Flora had moved to New York and moved in with Alice after her sister and the hamster moved out. Turned out that Alice missed having company. Celeste had her newborn at home and was getting her part-time nanny up to speed so she could work from home for Seoul Sistas in a few weeks.

In an ice bucket, there were two craft ginger beers. Daniel cracked off the metal caps and, looking over at my parents, kissed me gently on the lips.

He handed one to me and lifted his green glass bottle. "May I propose a toast?"

I nodded and clinked his drink. "To me!"

A booming laugh escaped him and his eyes twinkled with his salute. "Most definitely, to you."

He added, "And to us."

A smile broke from my lips as I touched his hand and squeezed. "Most definitely, to us."

Acknowledgments

When drafting an entire book in quarantine, the phrase "writing in solitude" reaches a whole new level. Without coffee shops or libraries, I sat in the same chair at my kitchen table and, over the course of four months, drafted this story. But don't get me wrong, by no means was this written in complete isolation: I still have plenty of people who helped me get from "Chapter One" all the way to "The End."

Thank you to my editor, Carrie Feron, who over lunch last winter listened to me string together awkward sentences that sort of resembled a pitch for this book and still encouraged me to write it. Your support and enthusiasm along the way brought me to the finish line. Thank you so much for helping me get there.

To Asanté Simons, you've been such a joy to work with and I honestly don't know what I would do without you. Thank you for everything.

Brent Taylor, agent extraordinaire: I can't believe just two years ago we were reviewing contracts. So much has changed (for the better) and I owe it to you. SIPS AHOY!

Thank you to Lee Ann Gliha, Stella Ho, Lisa Lee, Susan Kim, and Jane Lam. Hearing how the world of banking works from your perspectives was educational and fascinating. Your input was so helpful and insightful. Thanks so much to June Lee for helping me connect to so many people in the finance world.

To the production, design, marketing, and sales teams at Avon/Morrow, thank you for your input and support. Ploy Siripant, Ashley Caswell, Joel Holland, Diahann Sturge, Evangelos Vasilakis, Laurie McGee, Emily Fisher, Julie Paulauski, Naureen Nashid, and Angela Craft, I have so much admiration for what you do!

Enormous hugs to Helen Hoang and Roselle Lim for your friendship and your helpful beta reads. I'm so lucky to have friends like you! Whitney Schneider, thank you for speed reading those CP pages. You're a wonderful friend and I am so lucky we found each other all those years ago.

Huge thank-you to my writer friend circle: Alison Hammer, Annette Christie, Judy Lin, Jenny Howe, Chelsea Resnick, Kristin Rockaway, Kathleen Barber, Nancy Johnson, Amy Poeppel, Sonali Dev, Sarah Henning, Kellye Garrett, Alexa Martin, Sarah Partipilo, Falon Ballard, Liz Lawson, Dante Medema, Mike Jung, and Stephan Kim. Thank you to my

MAPID writers group, Ken Choy, Michael Hornbuckle, and Katrina Lee, for bringing out the "Suzanne-ness" in my story. Special thanks go to Julie Kim, who helped me with my Korean phrasing and forced me to leave my house to get fresh air. Everyone needs a Julie Kim in his or her life.

The support and kindness that book bloggers, librarians, bookstagrammers, book clubs, and podcasters showed me for my *Loathe at First Sight* debut was unparalleled. A huge thank-you for keeping the enthusiasm going for *So We Meet Again*'s cover reveal and beyond. Special thanks to Joshilyn Jackson and the Decatur Festival for inviting me to their event during my debut year: it meant so much to me to have your early support. Thank you to Emily Henry for reading and championing SWMA—I apologize that the book caused hunger pangs. Humungous thank-yous to Susan Elizabeth Phillips, Madeleine Henry, and Sonali Dev for taking time to read *SWMA* and for your kind words.

To my #StandUpforAAPI family (nurse_bookie, ashareads, belcantobooks, booknerdkat, noseinabook, oomilyreads, travel ling.the.pages, AH Kim, Jen Chow, and Jayci Lee), we became fast friends and I owe you so much for inspiring me to write again.

Kathleen Carter, who jumped right into the fire and helped me keep my head on straight during the hectic months of pre- and postlaunch promo, thank you from the bottom of my stress-relieved heart.

My family has been extremely supportive throughout my publishing journey—thanks to the Parks, Fouchers, and Brimers! Trevor, as always, thank you for being so supportive, and for not asking why half of the kitchen table had Jenga-esque mounds of investment banking books and piles of loose Post-it notes littering it. To CJ, who grew up before my very eyes during this past year, thank you for spontaneously asking me about my daily word counts, keeping me on task. I know tough love when I see it. I love you. To Sarah and Melissa, you're always enthusiastically championing my books, it really means so much to me.

Many snacks and drinks were consumed during the drafting and revising process. Thank you to the companies who make the following products: Doritos Flamin' Hot Nachos, See's Candies, and Hint Water. You helped get me through the rough patches.

And last, but definitely not least, I have so much love and appreciation for you, dear reader, for picking up this book. I'm in a big puddle of tears thinking about how my writing dreams have come true. Thank you so much for your support!

About the author

About the book

Insights,
Interviews
& More . . .

Meet Suzanne Park

Joanna DeGeneres

SUZANNE PARK is a Korean American writer who was born and raised in Tennessee.

In her former life as a stand-up comedian, Suzanne was a finalist in the Oxygen network's *Girls Behaving Badly* talent search and appeared on BET's *Coming to the Stage*. She was also the winner of the Seattle Sierra Mist Comedy Competition and a semifinalist in NBC's "StandUp for Diversity" showcase in San Francisco.

Suzanne graduated from Columbia

University and received an MBA from UCLA. She currently resides in Los Angeles with her husband, female offspring, and a sneaky rat that creeps around on her back patio. In her spare time, she procrastinates.

She is the author of *The Perfect Escape* and *Sunny Song Will Never Be Famous*, two YA romantic comedies, and *Loathe at First Sight*, an adult rom-com.

A Recipe from Suzanne

Umma-Approved
Quick Kimchi Fried Rice
(Kimchi Bokkeumbap)

SERVES 2 (OR 1 IF YOU'RE REALLY HUNGRY)

This is one of my comfort food go-to meals because it's tasty and easy to make. The key ingredients are well-fermented napa cabbage kimchi (my mom refers to it as "the old and soggy one") and some day-old cooked rice. My mom and I are not the types of cooks who use measuring spoons and the like, so this recipe reflects the best approximations of "pinches" and "fistfuls."

1 teaspoon canola oil
¼ small onion, diced
½ scallion, chopped (white and green parts)
¾ cup diced kimchi
1 cup diced Trader Joe's Fully Cooked Pork Belly, SPAM, or SPAM Lite
1 tablespoon "kimchi juice" from jar

1 small splash soy sauce (I'm sorry, but it's just a splash, maybe a half teaspoon if you want to be technical.)
1 heaping teaspoon gochujang (Korean chili pepper paste)
2½ cups cooked, day-old rice
½ teaspoon sesame oil
Salt and pepper to taste
Fried egg and green onions, for garnish (optional)

1. Heat the canola oil, then add the onion and scallion. Stir-fry quickly over medium-high heat for thirty seconds. Next, add the kimchi, diced meat. Stir-fry until the kimchi turns soft and semitranslucent, around 3 minutes.

2. Reduce the heat to medium-low and add the "kimchi juice," soy sauce, gochujang, and rice. Stir until everything is well mixed (everything is basically reddish-orange) and the clumped rice is broken up, another 3 to 4 minutes.

3. Once the rice is evenly coated with the seasonings, add the sesame ▸

A Recipe from Suzanne ***(continued)***

oil, turn up the heat to medium-high, and continue to fry the rice, turning occasionally for another minute. Add salt and pepper to taste as needed. Can be served with fried egg on top and/or with green onion garnish. Serve right away.

Letter to the Reader

Dear Reader,

If you heard "two investment bankers and a writer walked into a bar," you'd probably think this was a setup for a joke, not that this was exactly how my novel *So We Meet Again* came to be. Hearing my female banker friends exchange cringeworthy tales of racism and sexism on Wall Street made me furious, and I wanted to do something about it. So I did. I interviewed women who work in banking (and boy, did they have STORIES) and wrote a book about a laid-off investment banker trying to find her path in life.

Having been born and raised in a religious Korean community in Nashville, I wanted to pay homage to my Korean Tennessean roots and drew upon my own experiences growing up (including having a competitive relationship with the pastor's son!), as well as later ones from moving back home with my parents the summer before attending grad school. If you're a fan of foodie fiction, in addition to highlighting several popular Korean dishes, the story also features a mother-daughter YouTube Korean cooking show that underlines how loving, comedic, ▸

and adversarial a parent–adult child relationship can be.

So We Meet Again is part coming-of-age, part romantic comedy, and part foodie fiction: all three together aiming to bring joy and comfort in this strange, upside-down world we're living in now. Early readers had one universal complaint about this story that I wanted to bring to your attention . . . that it made them hungry. So I apologize in advance if you also experience this discomfort.

Thank you so much for reading *So We Meet Again*! I know there are so many books to choose from and I really appreciate you giving this one a try.

Much love,
Suzanne

Reading Group Guide

1. Describe Jessie's relationship with her mother. Do you think they have a close relationship? How do they express love to each other?

2. Have you ever worked in a male-dominated work environment like Jessie has in investment banking? Have you had any similar experiences to Jessie's?

3. Do you think it was the right choice for Jessie to become an entrepreneur instead of going back to the corporate world? What would you have done if you were in her shoes?

4. When Jessie moves back home, her mother tries to set her up with Daniel. Have family members ever meddled in your dating life? Have you ever been set up?

5. Although the last time Jessie and Daniel saw each other was in middle school, he was happy to see her and she was . . . well . . . not exactly thrilled to see him. Were you surprised that she took a while to warm up to him? ▸

Reading Group Guide ***(continued)***

How would *you* react if you ran into your childhood rival?

6. If you had to start a business with a family member or friend, who would it be? Who would it *not* be?

7. Do you think Jessie had "no leadership potential," as Hamilton Cooper said?

8. Professionally, Jessie is a methodical planner whereas Daniel believes that spontaneity, trial and error, and making mistakes are important to achieving success. Are you a planner or more spontaneous?

9. Food plays an important role in how Jessie and her mother relate to each other. Are there certain foods that have special meaning to you and your loved ones?

10. Where do you see Jessie and Daniel in five years?